THE BLACK WIDOW

Faye stroked at Sam's intimate flesh. 'If you had been wearing knickers I could have gagged you with them,' she explained. 'Not that anyone will be able to hear you in here,' she added quickly, 'but just for my own peace of mind.'

Sam felt her heart beat faster. She wished that her fear and arousal had been separate emotions. If that had been the case, she knew she would have been able to cope with one of them. As it was, she could not decide if the threat of being gagged had caused terror or excitement. Her desperate need for release was no longer confined to the desire to be free from the chair. She was overwhelmed by the urgent longing to give her body the fulfilment it so desperately craved.

A NEXUS CLASSIC

THE BLACK WIDOW

Lisette Ashton

This book is a work of fiction.
In real life, make sure you practise safe, sane and consensual sex.

This Nexus Classic edition 2005

First published in 1999 by
Nexus
Thames Wharf Studios
Rainville Road
London W6 9HA

www.nexus-books.co.uk

ISBN 0 352 33973 X

Typeset by TW Typesetting, Plymouth, Devon

The Random House Group Limited supports The Forest Stewardship Council (FSC®), the leading international forest certification organisation. Our books carrying the FSC label are printed on FSC® certified paper. FSC is the only forest certification scheme endorsed by the leading environmental organisations, including Greenpeace. Our paper procurement policy can be found at www.randomhouse.co.uk/environment

MIX
Paper | Supporting responsible forestry
FSC® C018179

Printed and bound in Great Britain by Clays Ltd, St Ives PLC

One

Sky grinned encouragingly at John as he settled himself in the birthing-stool.

Phase one of her plan was virtually complete and there could be no going back. If he had not been making it so easy, she might have had second thoughts. Doubts about the legality of what she was doing had plagued her from the day she had decided to take this course of action. The only thing that had kept her going was the knowledge that she had been wronged. She had to have revenge.

John smiled back at her, unable to mask the excitement sparkling in his eyes. Eagerness was apparent in the broad grin that stretched across his face. The pulse of his erection was another telltale sign of his arousal.

Studying his pale blue eyes, Sky knew that he was oblivious of her plans. He was simply anticipating pleasure and had no way of knowing her real intentions.

'Faye Meadows asked me to get rid of this a while back,' John explained. He tapped the side of the birthing-stool before lying back in it. 'She believes it goes against the general ethos of Elysian Fields and, while I agree with her in principle, I've been longing for a chance to play with it.'

Sky nodded, barely listening to him. She had heard

the name of the owner and it was an automatic reaction to ignore the rest of the sentence. The sound of the woman's name was enough to make her anger rise and she did not want to give in to that emotion just yet. The time for that would come later.

They were in a corner room on the furthest side of the little-used west wing. Slats of golden sunlight streamed through the partially open blind behind John. The brilliant white paintwork still looked clinical and fresh. There was, however, a vaguely musty air in the room, indicating that it was seldom visited. John had already told her that the room was used only for storage, but she had not wanted to believe him. This all seemed too good to be true. They were alone and isolated.

Apart from the birthing-stool, there were a handful of boxes stacked in one corner and a haphazard pile of dining-chairs in another. On a small table, beside the door, lay Sky's briefcase.

She glanced cautiously at the whitewashed walls, wondering if they were soundproof. They were far enough away from the main area of the building to enjoy some privacy. She knew that if he started shouting, though, someone would eventually hear. Of course, she could gag him, she realised, but that would spoil part of her fun.

A cruel smile flickered across her broad, sensuous lips.

Walking slowly over to the birthing-stool, she cast a cursory glance over John's naked body. He had the sort of figure she would have anticipated seeing on the manager of a health farm. His chest was broad, rippling with a subtle lining of well-formed muscles. His biceps were large, though not so overly muscular as to appear ugly. The flat hairless stomach led down to a smooth, depilated pubic area, which accentuated

2

the length of his erection. His balls were a tight pink sac that already looked close to the point of explosion.

She noticed that he was grinning at her with blatant admiration. Smiling into his handsome face, she ran her fingers through his short blond hair.

John closed his eyes, a blissful expression etching his features.

While his attention was diverted, Sky took advantage of the moment and fastened the clasps on his wrists.

John's eyes opened suddenly. He stared at her with uncharacteristic suspicion as she secured the fasteners on his ankles. His mood seemed to have changed with the metallic click of the final clasp.

'I'm not sure about this now, Sky,' he began tentatively.

There was a nervous tremor in his voice and she could see that he was beginning to lose some of the confidence he had been exhibiting all morning. 'Bondage and restraints definitely go against our policy here and this was just meant to be –'

'Shut up,' Sky snapped. 'Shut up, or I'll gag you.' She kept her tone low but there was enough ice in her voice to show who was in control.

John fell silent.

Sky could see his panic rising. She was surprised by the ease with which she could read his thoughts from his facial expressions. He stared at her warily, his pale blue eyes flickering as he tried to equate her harsh tone with the quiet, attentive woman he had been escorting throughout the morning.

Until this moment, she had been nodding indulgently and making blithe observations as he led her through the rooms and treatment areas of Elysian Fields. Even when they walked through The Eatery, the health farm's small dining area, she had managed to feign interest in his words. Whenever he had glanced at her, she had broadened her smile and treated him to a glimpse of the most alluring come-to-bed look her hazel eyes could manage. The zip of her black tracksuit top was pulled down, revealing a tantalising glimpse of sun-kissed cleavage. The tracksuit bottoms were also black and made from the same contour-hugging lycra. The fabric clung to every curve, from her delicate ankles up to her muscular thighs. It was a stark contrast to the pastel-pink uniform that the other female staff wore and she knew that John had noticed this. Like a new face in an office, she had seemed exciting to him because she was a little bit different. It was a carefully calculated part of her plan and it had worked exactly as she had hoped. The fact that he was strapped to the birthing-stool was testament to just how well it had worked.

Sky felt a pang of sympathy for him but she quashed the emotion before it could develop.

'Poor John,' she whispered, stroking cool fingers against the burning flesh of his arousal. 'You and I have a lot in common.' She brushed her lips against the sensitive flesh of his neck. Her tongue darted quickly against the lobe of his ear. 'You see, I was an innocent victim once, so I know how bad you're feeling.'

John was trying to appear brave. 'I'm not feeling bad,' he told her. He made an unsuccessful attempt to stifle the note of panic but his voice still faltered.

Sky laughed darkly. 'Don't worry,' she assured him. 'You will.'

Taking hold of his shaft in one hand, she realised that despite his nervousness his erection was still hard. As her fingers moved up and down his length, she curled them into a tight fist and squeezed.

4

John's eyes opened wide and he stared at her with a gaping expression. 'This really does go against the principles that we teach here at Elysian Fields,' he told her through ragged breaths. 'Elysian Fields is devoted to the perfection of the human body through the delights of –'

Sky squeezed his cock harder, using a vice-like grip that cut off his words abruptly.

'Don't tell me what this place is all about,' she hissed through clenched teeth. 'I know how Elysian Fields works. I wrote the fucking blueprint for this place.' There was a wicked glimmer in her eyes that defied any challenge he might dare to make.

John exercised a sick grin.

Sky eased her punishing grip slightly and cursed herself for becoming so angry. She did not want to succumb to that emotion just yet and, when she eventually did, it was not going to be directed at John.

Part of her annoyance was caused by his constant use of the name 'Elysian Fields'. When Sky had originally envisioned the health farm she had wanted to name it either 'Paradise' or 'Nirvana'. 'Elysian Fields' was the title conjured up by a woman who had robbed her of that dream. The repeated use of the name was only adding to Sky's blackening mood.

The morning had left her full of conflicting thoughts and feelings. First and foremost was a sense of accomplishment. She had written the blueprint for Elysian Fields and the place was exactly as she had pictured it. John's patronisingly informative tour of the building had been an exciting ego trip, made tolerable by the fact she was seeing a reality that had been made from her dream.

New clients were greeted in a sumptuous foyer, then taken to a discreet counselling room. There, in a reassuring atmosphere, their tastes and predilections were carefully assessed and a detailed health plan was drawn up. As she had always envisioned, the health plan was little more than a diet of sex and low-calorie, organic food. From her own experience, she knew this was the only way of obtaining a perfect body.

After John had shown her the preliminary rooms, he had moved his tour on to the main facilities. They had glanced discreetly into the massage rooms and she had watched two professional male masseurs working on clients. It was exactly as she had pictured the health farm when the idea first occurred to her. The two women, both naked and enjoying themselves with determined passion, were furiously fucking the masseurs. One was standing against the wall, happily enduring a vigorous knee-trembler. The other had forced the blond masseur to lie down on the floor. She was straddling him in a squatting position, working the muscles of her inner thighs as she raised and lowered herself on to his long, thick cock. Her stamina was greater than anything Sky had ever seen previously, including Olympic hopefuls. But the client seemed unaware of her own efforts. Her concentration was devoted solely to enjoying the muscular Adonis on the floor. The physical exertion she employed was little more than a means to an end and, because of this, she was willing to work even harder in the urgent pursuit of her own self-indulgent satisfaction.

The aerobic room was just as orgiastic and with the same dedication to controlled physical activity. Under the supervision of a member of staff, four female clients were sweating, laughing and fucking one another rigorously. All were in pursuit of a healthier body, and, from Sky's perspective, they looked close to attaining their goals.

John had taken her to the sauna room, swimming pool and Jacuzzi. In each area, Sky had felt her excitement rising as she witnessed displays of hedonistic revelry. It had been impossible to watch the carnal enjoyment of the others without giving in to a thrill of sexual excitement. Peering voyeuristically on to each scene, Sky had felt her own arousal beginning to stir. In a moment when John had been distracted, she had dared to caress her own nipple through the tight fabric of her lycra top. The gentle pressure of her fingers against the responsive nub of her breast had been so exquisite it was almost painful. She had stifled a groan of pleasure and tried valiantly to regain her composure when John tested a curious smile on her.

The pulse between her legs had been as powerful as her sense of accomplishment. It took a gargantuan effort of willpower to restrain her own salacious appetite. That effort had been helped by the rising anger that welled inside. Elysian Fields had been her dream and, while there was a degree of satisfaction in seeing it completed and working, she still felt as though she had been cheated and robbed. Unwilling to give in to the anger, even though it was helping to maintain perspective, Sky had focused on her plans for revenge.

With these memories tumbling through her mind, Sky continued to stroke his cock. A thoughtful smile teased her ripe lips. Her hand moved up and down John's length in easy, languid strokes. She rolled the foreskin tightly back, then pushed it quickly forward. Her fingers travelled easily over the smooth, hairless length and she was beginning to enjoy the feeling of his rigid shaft in her hand.

'I suppose you're wondering what I want from you,' she said softly. Her smile was almost reassuring

7

as she glanced into his questioning expression. 'Don't worry. It's not a great deal.'

He swallowed. 'What do you want?'

'You decide,' she told him. 'I'm giving you a choice. I want control of Elysian Fields, and I can have it in two ways. You can either leave and never trouble me again, or you can stay as my submissive.' She rolled his cock between her fingers, her lips hovering enticingly over his face. 'Which are you going to choose, John?'

He blinked and shook his head. 'I can't do either of those things,' he told her. 'I have a job here and I'm not willing to –'

Sky squeezed hard on his erection. She had pulled the foreskin back as far as she could and was now stretching the skin beyond the point of pleasure. Her carefully manicured fingernails were coated with razor-sharp acrylic. The polished red tips bit hard at the base of his length, burrowing deep into the yielding flesh above his balls.

The sudden pain was enough to stop John midway through his sentence.

'You're not telling me what I want to hear,' Sky whispered. Moving her lips down his chest and over his flat, hairless stomach, she blew gently against the burning flesh of his erection. She darted her tongue out quickly and touched the wet end against the tip of his raging length. 'There is a third option but, since you're uncomfortable with your current state of bondage, I don't think you'd like it.'

Wordlessly, John glared at her.

Sky rolled her tongue over the tip of his cock for a second time, then took the head between her lips. Sucking gently, she smiled awkwardly up at him. She released her hand from his length and glanced at the spot where her fingernails had been. The flesh was

8

still creased, as though invisible fingernails still rested there, but the skin was unbroken. Judging by the ferocity of his hard-on, she guessed that his excitement remained unaffected.

Grinning at her own wickedness, she took a step towards her briefcase. As she moved, she was aware that he was watching her. His close attention made her smile broaden and she decided it would be prudent to give him something more to watch. As long as his attention was focused on her, he would be less likely to shout for help. After unfastening the clasps on the case, Sky turned to face him. Her fingers rested over her cleavage, fondling the tab of her zipper. Once she was happy with the ardent attention he was showing, she began to draw it slowly downward. The tight lycra was forced back by the swell of her large breasts, revealing an expanse of light-copper flesh. After tugging the zip free, she slipped her arms out of the top and stood before him. The lycra bottoms accentuated the slenderness of her waist and the lithe muscularity of her thighs. Underneath the top she wore nothing but a lacy black bra. The gossamer fabric contrasted starkly with the sun-bronzed hue of her flesh. She raked splayed fingers through her long blonde hair, guiding a handful of loose tresses away from the swell of her breasts.

Secured in the chair, John chewed on his lower lip as he watched her. There was a pained expression lighting his eyes as he vainly tested the clasps at his wrists.

Enjoying his nervousness, Sky reached for the waistband of her bottoms and pulled them slowly down. She kicked her feet out of her trainers then stepped out of the tight-fitting pants. Placing her hands on her hips, she allowed John to admire her figure, clad only in a snug-fitting bra and matching black G-string.

His excitement was so great that under other circumstances she would have found it comical. John's features were a writhing mass of conflicting emotions, each one struggling for a position of power on his face. His fear seemed to have dissipated, for the moment, while his arousal had increased monumentally. The nervous flicker at the back of his pale blue eyes showed he was still a little uneasy with the prospect of what she had in store, but he seemed more than prepared to overlook those qualms.

Sky could feel her confidence soaring as she watched this. Her plan was working better than she could have hoped. Turning her back on him, she bent over the briefcase, allowing him to see the rounded swell of her backside. The copper-coloured cheeks were separated by a thin strip of black fabric. The strip widened slightly as it went between her legs, the narrow gusset of the G-string barely covering the lips of her sex. Taking a short riding crop from the case, she turned to face John and walked back to the birthing-stool. Using the flat, spade-like tip of the crop, she stroked his hairless balls.

'You don't need to worry about my taking control of Elysian Fields,' she told him thoughtfully. 'I'm more than capable of running it. I've worked in gyms and health farms before.' A bitter smile twisted her lips and her mood darkened a shade. 'I've had to work in them,' she added unhappily. Trying to emphasise her distress, she pressed the tip of the riding crop firmly against his tender sac.

John shrank back in the stool, desperately trying to put some distance between himself and Sky.

She laughed softly. 'I know what you're thinking,' she assured him. She took a step closer and stroked her fingers against his rigid length. At the same time, she pressed the tip of the riding crop against the rim of his arsehole. 'You think that I might be an unsuitable sort of person to take control, and in a way I can sympathise with your fears. I used to live my life under the same hedonistic principles that Elysian Fields now works to. But things have changed since then.' A frown furrowed her brow. 'Things have changed a lot since then,' she said heavily.

John remained silent, studying her with a wary expression.

Sky was oblivious to him. She was talking more to herself than John, lost in her own world of harsh memories and bitter retribution. 'I guess it was the hard work that cured me of my ideals,' she said idly. 'Years of penury and hardship killed my dreams. It warped my principles out of all recognisable shape.' She laughed again, a harsh, mirthless sound. 'They had a nickname for me at the last health farm where I worked,' she told him. 'They called me the Black Widow.'

John swallowed nervously. His face was crumpled with helplessness and he struggled against the clasps on the birthing-stool.

'I suppose the Black Widow is a fitting name,' Sky went on. 'I am a widow, and I invariably dress in black, but I think they named me after the spider.' She turned to smile at him, an evil glint sparkling in her hazel eyes. 'You know. The big black spider that devours its partner after mating.' She grinned rapaciously. 'I'd begun to get that sort of reputation. Not that I killed or ate any of my lovers. But some of them were left wishing I had.'

With a sudden, vicious movement, she raised the riding crop high in the air, then brought it down smartly against his thigh.

Startled, John gasped for air.

'Give me a decision, John. Which is it going to be? Are you leaving? Are you staying? Answer me.' She raised the crop again and brought it down with three sharp, successive swipes. The first striped the inside of his left thigh and the second scored a red line on his right. The third blow landed squarely on his scrotum.

As John howled in a high-pitched scream, Sky reconsidered the idea of gagging him. It would not be ideal but if he was going to make this sort of noise it would only be prudent. She dropped the crop to the floor and stepped closer. With her right hand she grabbed his aching balls with talon-like fingers. Ignoring his protests and cries for release, she moved her mouth over his and kissed him. Her tongue slipped between his lips and she traced the silky wetness inside.

John's moans of protest subsided and she felt his erection stiffen against her wrist. Shaking her head ruefully, she mentally chastised him for making things too easy. She moved her mouth away. 'Did you ever wonder how this birthing-stool got here? Were you on duty when it was delivered?'

Aware of his nervousness and confusion, she shook her head and continued to answer her own question. 'I had it delivered, with no return address and strict instructions that the carrier wasn't to take it back. I figured it would end up in a storeroom like this when I sent it. And I knew the time would come when I would be here to use it.'

He was unable to mask his fear as he stared at her.

Sky kissed him softly and gave his balls a reassuring squeeze. 'I'm telling you this, so that you know how much planning I've done. Your involvement in my scheme is negligible and I've worked too long and too hard to let you be more than a minor irritation. Now, which is it to be?'

12

He rolled his head from side to side. 'I can't leave Elysian Fields,' he gasped. 'I have a job here and I've made a commitment.'

'That's a shame,' she told him with feigned sadness. 'I suppose the owner made a wise choice employing someone with your dedication. It's a pity you got caught in the middle of all this but, if things work out the way I intend, then I might consider reinstating you.'

He was staring at her with obvious panic.

Sky was surprised to discover the depth of her own malicious streak. The pleasure she was gleaning from his obvious discomfort went beyond the enjoyment she had anticipated. Watching him squirm on the birthing-stool, she could feel the pulse between her legs beating to a quickening tempo.

'Don't you just love the design of this thing?' she asked, slapping the side of the stool. Her hand moved beneath him and she teased the smooth flesh of his backside through the cut-out semicircle of the birthing-stool's seat. The tip of one finger touched the sensitive rim of his anus and John tried to shrink away from her.

With her resolve hardening, Sky pushed the finger towards the centre of his arsehole and forced it inside him.

John's eyes opened wide, a combination of excitement and horror contorting his features. Sky wondered idly if her sharp fingernail was causing him discomfort, then decided that she did not particularly care. She allowed her finger to wriggle inside him for a moment, then slowly withdrew it. His sphincter tightened spasmodically as the finger made its languid egress.

John groaned as she took her hand away.

'That's just one of the advantages of this

contraption,' Sky said. With a broad grin, she moved to the side of the birthing-stool and began to climb on to it. 'I didn't just have it delivered,' she told him as she positioned herself over him. 'I had the damned thing specially designed. The wrist and ankle cuffs were the first part I had fitted. Then I had these steps added, so that a person could climb on it, the way I'm climbing on it now.' She was poised directly over him, the front panel of her G-string brushing purposefully against his nose.

'Why are you doing this to me?' John asked quietly.

She graced him with a wicked grin. 'Don't take it personally. You just happen to be the wrong person, in the wrong place, at the wrong time.' She laughed softly. 'That sounded quite melodramatic, don't you think?'

He shrugged awkwardly. 'What are you going to do with me?'

'I can't make you leave – you told me that much – so that means you're going to have to stay and we can do things in one of two ways.'

John frowned, appearing more uneasy with each word she spoke.

'There's a nice way, and a not so nice way,' she began. 'You show me what a good boy you can be, and I'll trust you to behave that way. But if you fail to please me right now, I'll have you tucked away in a forgotten corner of this place. You'll be left bound and gagged, then fed and watered when I remember.'

He glared up at her, blatantly scared by the malice of her casual threat.

'But let's not dwell on the unpleasant things that might happen,' Sky said. 'I've told you what's at stake and I'm sure that you're bright enough to do the right thing. Right now, you're going to tongue my pussy and make me scream with excitement.'

14

Carefully, she teased the front panel of her G-string to one side and pushed herself close to his mouth. For a moment she did not think he was going to respond. He was a wilful bastard, she thought ruefully, and not the sort who enjoyed being dominated. Controlling him in the chair was taking more effort than she had allowed for. Trying to control him out of the chair would be a full-time occupation and she did not have the time for such an indulgence.

Before she could give this thought any more consideration, John had lifted his head and pushed his tongue against her flesh. The slippery wetness of his mouth stroked against the flesh of her pussy lips. Like John, Sky depilated her pubic bush and his tongue was able to travel smoothly against her exposed sex. A tingle of excitement coursed through her as she rolled her pelvis up and down against the squirming of his tongue.

Memories of the tour through the building were still fresh in her mind, guiding her thoughts into a lurid channel. She could feel the swell of her arousal returning with a furious energy. In the tight, lacy confines of her bra, her breasts ached for attention. She teased her fingers against the ultra-sensitive nubs of her nipples, shivering as tremors of euphoria swept over her. Squeezing the hardening buds tightly, Sky realised the pressure was bringing her dangerously close to orgasm. It seemed incredible to be so close to climax after only a little of John's tonguing and her own caresses. Regardless of how incredible it seemed, Sky wallowed in the pleasure of her dominant position.

The tip of his tongue caressed her labia as he sucked one lip, before moving on to the next. He moved his mouth until he had found the pulsing pearl of her clitoris. His tongue flicked quickly over the exposed ball, causing Sky to take a sharp intake of breath. As his mouth travelled lower, his bottom lip brushed against the thin line of flesh between her arsehole and her pussy. With an eagerness that Sky found exhilarating, John pushed his tongue deep into her sodden cleft. His head moved furiously back and forth as he repeatedly plunged his tongue into her.

Sky heard herself squeal. The pleasure of being tongue-fucked was a rare treat, especially from someone as capable as John. Enjoying the warm wetness of his mouth against her sex, she pushed herself on to him with renewed vigour. After giving her nipples a final squeeze, she slipped her hands from her breasts. Pushing her fingers through his short blond hair, she held his head firmly in position. Keeping tight hold, she rode herself against his face. His nose and chin were quickly covered with the lubrication of her pussy honey and she could see him trying to blink his eyes open through a viscous veil.

Feeling orgasm rushing towards her, she ignored his gasps for breath and concentrated on her own satisfaction. She had not allowed for an interlude like this one in her plans, but, now that she was enjoying it, she was determined to extract as much pleasure as possible.

The climax came in a searing blaze that felt almost triumphant as it tore through her. A dynamic explosion jetted through every straining muscle and she pulled John's head hard against her flesh.

He continued to use his tongue as her orgasm shot a golden stream of juice into his mouth. Sky sighed contentedly, her entire body undulating with a series of powerful contractions.

She released his head as the pleasure began to subside, then eased herself away. There was still a hint of fear in his eyes but she could see that it was not affecting his arousal. His length stood hard between his legs, the tip leaking a thin stream of pre-come.

'I want your cock now,' she told him, uneven breaths forcing the words to rise and fall. 'But first, I want an answer. Will you be submissive to me? Or do I have to lock you away?' She curled her fingers round his shaft, pressing her nails into the rigid flesh.

John forced himself back against the birthing-stool, writhing from side to side in the chair. He struggled vainly against the clasps at his wrists and his tortured expression was so pitiful Sky felt a genuine wave of sympathy.

She brushed the tip of his cock against the febrile flesh of her labia. The gusset of her G-string had been pushed to one side and the bulbous tip of his swollen cock was allowed to stroke her smooth skin without obstruction.

'Which is it to be, John?' she whispered. 'I need an answer quickly. The invitations have already been sent and the wheels are in motion. Do you want to spend the next fortnight locked in this chair? Or can I trust you to be an obedient little boy for me?'

He began to nod eagerly and, in that instant, Sky realised she had won.

'I'll be yours,' he assured her. 'I'll do whatever you want,' he said quickly. 'I'll –'

She pushed the tip of his cock against her wet hole and slid down on to him. He fell silent as soon as she made the move. As his cock continued to fill her, they both began to groan.

Sky's fingers went to the base of his length. She squeezed him hard, using the pads of her fingertips this time rather than the cruel edge of her nails. He bucked beneath her, his hips going forward as he struggled to slide further into the tight confines of her

17

moist interior. His jaw was set in a determined grimace, the exertion contorting his features. The straining cords of his neck muscles pulsed with pure adrenaline as he fought to contain his orgasm.

Panting happily, Sky squeezed his cock harder and stared down at him. 'Do you promise to be a good boy?'

He stared back at her with obvious admiration and nodded his assent.

She studied his eyes, searching for a hint of rebellion in the pale-blue irises. The expression she saw there was one of absolute submission. Perhaps it was just the moment, she thought, or perhaps he was a damned good actor, but she doubted it was either. Her every instinct told her that she had total control over him.

Releasing her hand from his cock, she fell heavily on to his length. The shaft jerked with a spasmodic rhythm, shooting the white-hot spray of his seed deep into her cleft. Her velvety inner walls were treated to a staccato titillation as his cock pulsed. The sensation was so fulfilling that Sky felt her own orgasm wrench its way through her body.

Easing herself away from him, she watched his still-twitching shaft as it slipped from her satisfied hole. A dollop of thick white semen sprayed at her flat stomach and fell there like whipped cream.

As his euphoria began to wane, Sky realised John was staring at the spatter of come.

'Lick it off,' she told him sharply.

For a moment, she saw a flicker of rebellion lighting his eye. The expression was only there for an instant, quickly replaced by a look of alarm. John began to shake his head and tried to tell her that he did not want to lick his own come from her bare belly. But Sky was no longer listening.

'I'll get my crop, if that will help you.' She made as if to climb from the stool.

'OK,' he told her quickly. 'I'll do it.' He sounded weak and defeated as the words were torn from his throat.

Sky did not allow him the chance to reconsider his decision. Forcing her stomach towards his mouth, she waited until she felt the warm tip of his tongue trail over her flesh. He made a muffled sound beneath her, as though he was gagging at the taste, but this simply made her smile broaden.

'I don't just want that little smear licking up,' she said, moving her stomach away from him. She eased herself higher up the stool to the position she had taken at first. Lowering her sodden lips over his face, she said, 'I want you to lick me properly clean.'

With a moan of despair, John pushed his tongue inside her and began to lap at his spent seed.

Sky laughed softly as his tongue teased the spilt fluid from her sex. She knew she was beyond the point of enjoying another orgasm but it was still a pleasing sensation to have him lick her in such a way. His obvious reluctance and painful unhappiness served only to heighten her enjoyment. Sky rubbed the lips of her sex hard against his face, continuing to press close to him long after he had licked the last droplet of his come from the depths of her cleft. When she was finally satisfied with his submission, she stepped from the birthing-stool, picked up her riding crop, and returned it to her briefcase.

'I won't help you to hurt anyone,' he said suddenly. 'I don't care what you do to me, but I won't be a part of something like that, whoever it is.'

Sky had been on the point of fastening the briefcase, but she paused. She glanced back over her shoulder towards him, her frown darkening beneath the fringe of her blonde tresses. Snatching the crop back from the case, she marched swiftly to his side and brandished it at him like a pointing stick. 'Don't think you can start telling me what to do,' she hissed menacingly. 'Because you're in no fucking position to dictate anything.'

Still secured to the stool, John struggled to back away from the woman.

Sky sliced the crop through the air twice, each time scoring the sensitive flesh of his inner thighs. His spent cock lay limp between his legs but the threat of an erection began to stir as the explosion of pain burnt into his skin.

She ignored his growing excitement. Shaking her head with frustration she struck him again with the crop. The spade-like tip brushed dangerously close to his balls and he winced as though it had hit him squarely.

Sky was panting as her anger increased. 'I'm going to have to be more like a black widow than ever before if I intend to do this properly, aren't I?'

His frightened expression looked pathetic but she felt no pang of sympathy for him this time. 'You're not going to kill me, are you?' he whispered nervously.

Smiling, she shook her head, and raised the riding crop high in the air. 'I'm not going to kill you.' But I can't trust you to go about your business and do as you're told. Like the spider, I'm going to have you wrapped for consumption later.'

As he stared nervously up at her, the Black Widow began to laugh.

Two

Jo Valentine flicked the double-headed sovereign high in the air. As it span on its upward spiral, she mounted the last step of the staircase and stared at her office door. A frown creased her forehead.

Painted in black, the words VALENTINE INVESTIGATION AGENCY had been peeling away from the opaque glass for the last few years. Beneath the arch of the letters, there was now a new addition. Someone had taped a small, cardboard sign to the glass: THIS AGENCY HAS MOVED TO NEW PREMISES: POPLAR TREES.

The tinkle of her sovereign striking the dusty wooden floorboards snatched Jo's thoughts away from the sign. 'Shit,' she growled, barely aware that she had spoken the word aloud. 'As if the day hasn't been bad enough . . .'

Jo did not bother to complete the sentence. The morning had been sufficiently depressing and she doubted things were going to improve. Reaching down for her coin, she ignored the twinge in her back and tried to decide what would be the best course of action.

The idea came to her suddenly but, when it struck, she knew it was exactly the right thing. 'I'm going to kill the bitch,' she said cheerfully. She pocketed the sovereign. The idea had a warming appeal and it was hard to suppress the grin it inspired. 'Samantha

Flowers is a dead woman,' she told the empty corridor.

Turning back to the steps, Jo started down them, heading for the address she had just read. Her resolve was so great that she paused only once en route, and would not have made that stop if she had still possessed a hip flask. She drove through the early-morning traffic with more patience than was normal, distantly realising there was a reason for this uncharacteristic display of control. Her anger now had a focus and she was determined to vent it.

She paused outside the Poplar Trees, trying not to be impressed by its welcoming exterior. She was familiar enough with the area. The office complex was a recent addition to the city's outskirts, playing host to a wide variety of professional services. A handful of Jo's clients used the solicitors who worked from the building and she had recently dealt with a software company at this address. They each seemed like respectable businesses with high-profile, go-getting images.

Jo had despised both of them for their pretensions.

Flanked by a handful of high-reaching poplars, the building was designed to look simultaneously modern and old-fashioned. Bathed in glorious morning sunlight, against a cloudless blue sky, Poplar Trees could not have looked more inviting. It had a heavily stated air of 'olde worlde' charm that Jo always found irritating. She quashed the feeling, determined to direct her anger at Sam. She had never been very good at placing architectural styles and could not say what era it was meant to imitate. The building was an amalgamation of yellow Yorkshire stone and gold-tinted glass, with ornate Roman pillars guarding the entrance. Admittedly, it was a little more prestigious than the battered doorway of her previous premises, and Jo had to concede that the address was slightly more respectable than 'above the off licence, opposite the 24-hour garage'. But she wilfully ignored its affectation of respectability.

She was surprised to see that there was a freshly painted parking spot on the forecourt. Her surname was emblazoned on the black tarmac in bright-yellow letters. It was a pleasant touch and it would have mellowed her mood if she had not seen Sam's convertible parked in the spot next to it.

The sight of the blazing-red Lotus rekindled her anger. In the shadow of Sam's brilliantly polished sportscar, her own rust-eaten Ford Fiesta looked poxier than ever. As Jo parked her car, she contemplated scratching her own vehicle against the side of Sam's. The only thing that stopped her was the fear of losing the Fiesta's precarious front wing. She consoled herself with the thought that she could do just as much damage to Sam's paintwork with the edge of her double-headed sovereign. Murderous thoughts still filled her mind and they continued to rage within her as she stormed into the building's reception area.

'Can I help you?'

Jo glanced at the pretty, blonde receptionist, trying to take in the sumptuous surroundings of the building at the same time. A gold name badge with BECKY printed on it hovered over the swell of her right breast.

'I'm here to murder Samantha Flowers,' Jo said calmly. 'Can you tell me where her office is?'

'Excuse me?' Becky started hesitantly.

'Ignore my grumpy friend,' Sam said, appearing on Jo's left. As always, she looked radiant. Long red hair flowed over the shoulders of her bottle-green jacket, framing her pretty, bespectacled face

23

and accentuating the modest swell of her pert breasts. The short skirt she wore revealed long, coltish legs and Jo glanced at them with reluctant admiration. Sam was not wearing stockings this morning and Jo found her gaze drawn to the smooth cream-coloured flesh of her partner's legs.

Sam grinned easily at Jo, then turned her attention to Becky. 'This is my partner, Jo Valentine,' she explained. 'And I suppose it would be best if you got to know her, so she can get into her new office.'

Jo glared at Sam and then flashed Becky a tight smile. 'It would be nice to stop and chat for a moment,' she said with forced sweetness. 'But Samantha here has a problem with her breathing and I'm about to sort that out.'

Becky frowned and struggled to find something appropriate to say. Before she could manage it, Jo had grabbed Sam's arm and dragged her out of the reception area.

Sam walked quickly alongside Jo, seemingly untroubled by the arm-lock she was being held in. They marched through the long, richly carpeted corridors, Sam occasionally tugging at Jo so they got to the right destination.

The corridors were lined with the occasional mirror and Jo caught sight of her own reflection as they walked. She was surprised by the way she seemed to fit into the smart decor of the building around her. Her anger was still smouldering and she had expected to see a wild-eyed lunatic staring back at her. Instead, she saw that her tailored suit was looking as good as ever, drawing attention to the inviting rise of her ample breasts. The navy trousers concealed her long, muscular legs, but, with the jacket open, the high waist accentuated her slenderness. She appraised the reflection with a flash of her dark eyes, noting that her long, brown hair had retained the loose, flamboyant style she had opted for that morning. It was almost disappointing that she did not look like a potential murderess. That was the image she had wanted to project.

'How's your morning been, darling?' Sam asked pleasantly.

Jo was trying to ignore the rising excitement that always affected her when she held Sam close. She felt perfectly entitled to harbour a degree of animosity after the annoyance of the morning, but it was difficult to hold on to the feeling. The gentle pressure of Sam's breast against her arm was an intoxicating aphrodisiac and her intimate use of the word 'darling' did not help.

'My morning has been shit,' Jo growled.

Sam gave her a sympathetic frown. 'Do I take it you're not overly pleased with my little surprise?' she asked carefully.

Jo stopped and glared at Sam. 'Do you mean this place?'

'It's the most prestigious address I could find.' Sam grinned cheerfully. 'And don't you think it's the prettiest building imaginable?'

'I think it looks like a stylised latrine. We'll discuss it more when we reach our office.' She glanced around the corridor they were in and tried to decide which way she should be heading. 'This is like a rat's maze. Do I get a piece of cheese when I find the right door?'

'This way,' Sam said, pulling them forward. 'What did Doctor McMahon have to say to you?'

Jo took a deep breath, trying to keep her thoughts focused on her anger. She suddenly wished she had told Sam just how furious she was at the unannounced change of address. Having to talk about her trip to the doctor's that morning was bound to disperse some of her exasperation.

'Doctor McMahon is a third-rate quack,' Jo snapped. 'And I'm not sure that her qualification is legitimate.'

'Did she say that you were working too hard?'

Jo stopped and studied Sam's face. The dark-green eyes behind her spectacles were difficult to read but she could sense that her partner was trying to conceal something. 'You've talked to the bitch,' she gasped, shocked by the realisation. 'Hasn't that woman heard of patient confidentiality?'

Sam shrugged. 'Perhaps they don't teach that to third-rate quacks. A fortnight's R and R is what she told me. She also said that a detoxification clinic might not be a bad idea.'

'I can't do detoxification.' Jo hated the defensive position she was being forced to adopt. 'I have difficulty saying the fucking word for a start. Besides, the only thing that keeps my body going is the steady diet of impurities.'

'You need a break and you need to get into better physical shape,' Sam said calmly. 'I can always sort something out for you. All you have to say is –'

Speaking over Sam's offer, Jo said firmly, 'I have no intention of taking a break. And unless you want to discuss it some more with your friend Doctor McMahon, the topic is well and truly closed.'

Sam shook her head and leant forward. Her lips met Jo's and suddenly the pair of them were kissing. Jo could feel her irritation being swept away as Sam's hands caressed her body. Their tongues explored one another and she could feel the rise of her passion increase as her anger waned.

'In here,' Sam said, heated urgency apparent in her voice. She pulled Jo through a doorway, kissing her again as they went into the office. Jo had a moment to read the words on the door, then it was pushed closed. They were still kissing when the words she had read finally hit home.

'Flowers and Valentine.' She broke out of Sam's embrace and opened the door to read the name again. 'You put your name first,' she screeched incredulously. 'I can't believe you've done that. I told you that it sounds like a bloody florist or a card shop.'

Sam shrugged. 'You told me we could do it that way last night.'

Jo rolled her eyes. 'I was drunk last night,' she said petulantly. She used the excuse as though it qualified her position.

Sam shrugged again and said, 'You're drunk most nights.' Her tone of voice was infuriatingly neutral and free from accusation. 'Perhaps Doctor McMahon's advice isn't as poorly diagnosed as you thought.'

Jo glared sullenly at Sam, chewing her lip with rising annoyance. 'I want my name to go first,' she said flatly.

'And Valentine and Flowers won't sound like a card shop?' Sam commented with quiet irony.

Jo continued to glare at her.

'It's a bit late now, anyway,' Sam said, sounding as though she was dismissing the topic. 'The business cards are being printed and the stationery will be delivered this afternoon.' She took a step towards Jo and reached for the buttons on the front of her blouse. 'Are you wearing that lingerie I bought for you yesterday?'

Jo considered slapping the hands away, her anger with Sam still rankling. If it had not been for the excitement inspired by the redhead's touch, she felt sure she would have done it. 'I'm wearing them,' Jo said, her tone indicating that her mood was still volatile.

She watched Sam's fingers move down her blouse and tease the buttons from their holes. The sight of her own cleavage, and Sam's fingers brushing against the warm flesh, was more exciting than she wanted to contemplate. The spreading heat of her arousal was already beginning to spark fires deep inside. Jo could feel all attempts at resistance failing.

Inwardly, she cursed. The partnership had been in operation for a fortnight and already it was beginning to work to a pattern that she was not happy with. Sam would do something to annoy her and Jo would become angry. Then Sam would become all pliant and remorseful and Jo would allow her to do whatever she had been doing in the first place. If it had not been for the pliant and remorseful stage, Jo would have stopped the partnership. As it was, the pliant and remorseful stage was invariably sexual, torrid and extremely gratifying.

Still unfastening the buttons, Sam stepped closer and kissed Jo. The intrusion of her tongue was welcome and Jo felt the last of her anger disappear.

'I'm sorry about the company name,' Sam whispered. 'If you want me to change it to Valentine and Flowers, then I shall.'

Jo shrugged, wishing Sam would do more kissing and less talking. 'Whatever,' she conceded. 'I guess we'll be doing the same work regardless of the company name.' She gave a tight grin and tried to ignore the triumphant smile that illuminated Sam's eyes.

'That looks gorgeous on you,' Sam said, pulling Jo's blouse open.

Jo glanced down at the balconette bra she was wearing and found herself agreeing with Sam's

28

verdict. The semicircles of her areolae were clearly visible above the midnight-blue satin. As she watched Sam's fingers brushing against the dusky-pink flesh, she felt her arousal increase.

'It's not too tight here, is it?' Sam asked. She eased the tip of her index finger inside the bra and nonchalantly stroked Jo's breast to indicate where she meant. There was a knowing glint to her smile and Jo felt sure Sam was aware of the arousal she inspired.

'It's getting tighter,' Jo said, excitement darkening the words. She could feel the thrust of her stiffening nipples against the satin. The subtle tickle of pleasure deepened her breathing.

'Do you want to see how mine looks?' Sam asked, reaching for the buttons of her jacket. 'I'm wearing the same style as you.'

Jo glanced nervously around. Even though the office had her name on the door, she still felt like an intruder in the place. She took in the pastel-pink walls and the modern, stylish furniture at a glance, then turned her attention back to Sam. She had removed her jacket, revealing that all she wore beneath it was a balconette bra identical to Jo's.

'I'm still pissed at you,' Jo whispered.

'You have every right to be, I guess. I should have consulted you before I moved us from Old Kent Road to Mayfair, but I wanted it to be a surprise.'

Jo frowned, unhappy with the way that Sam had shifted the focus of her anger. 'It's not just the change of address,' she said firmly.

Sam nodded as though she understood. 'I know. And it was wrong of me to be interested in your physical health and wellbeing. I apologise for that too.'

Jo opened her mouth, about to say something else, then decided not to bother. There was no arguing with Sam, she realised. Whatever she had to say, Jo knew she would be wrong. The simplest solution was to apologise first and ask questions later. It would be easier to go with the flow and let Sam lead.

Grinning, as though she had read Jo's thoughts, Sam began to slide out of her skirt. 'Our first client of the morning is scheduled at eleven.' She pushed the bottle-green skirt over her narrow hips as she glanced at her wristwatch. 'So that gives me a little time to try and make up for upsetting you.'

Jo was about to raise a word of protest, then caught sight of Sam's French knickers. The midnight-blue fabric was not the most suitable colour for her skin tone, but Jo did not think that spoilt the image too greatly. Sam stood with her hands on her hips, legs apart, treating Jo to a smile that was eager and alluring in the same moment. Circling her right leg was the black garter that Jo had bought for her exactly two weeks earlier. Even when she was not wearing stockings, Sam continued to wear the garter, as though it was an engagement ring.

'They look good on you,' Jo whispered, trying to look at the underwear and not Sam's body.

Sam took a step towards her. The difference in their heights put her face close to the exposed cleavage between Jo's breasts. As she exhaled, her breath warmed the orbs, forcing the nipples to stand harder.

'You're getting excited,' Sam observed. She unfastened the button on Jo's trousers and allowed them to fall to the floor. Smiling, Jo stepped away from the clothes with elegant grace.

'You really do have a very strong hold over me, don't you?' Hesitantly, she reached out and cupped one of Sam's small, pert breasts. The satin fabric was tight but she could feel the ardent thrust of her nipple through the material. Her fingertips pressed firmly against the yielding bud and the two women both drew excited sighs.

Sam placed her hand on Jo's hip, tracing her fingers against the flimsy fabric of her French knickers. 'These feel so luxuriant,' she whispered. 'I just had to get you a set as soon as I'd tried them.'

Jo made a noncommittal sound, stroking the bare flesh of Sam's waist and enjoying the way she trembled beneath her touch.

Sam's carefully caressing fingers had moved from her hip and were now stroking her buttocks through the silky fabric. With slow deliberation, she eased her fingers under the leg of the pants and began to stroke the intimate flesh beneath.

Jo drew a shuddering breath and tried to take a step away.

Sam followed, her cool, exploring fingers remaining where they were.

'Are we safe to do this sort of thing in here?' Jo asked suddenly.

Sam laughed, gesturing to the two adjoining doors with her free hand. 'These are our offices and we can do whatever the hell we please.' As she spoke, she moved her hand back to the heated cleft between Jo's legs. Exploring the moist line of flesh, she raised her eyebrows in mock surprise. 'But I think that I'd better act quickly,' she said, teasing the tip of her finger against Jo's pussy lips. 'You feel so hot down here you could set off the fire alarm.'

Jo smiled, gasping as Sam pushed a finger inside the warm depths of her sex. The slippery wetness of her arousal allowed Sam to penetrate her in one fluid motion. 'How are you going to cool me down?' she asked, still stroking Sam's breasts through the satin.

'Like this,' Sam replied, wriggling out of Jo's reach.

She lowered herself to a kneeling position, hooking her thumbs in the waistband of Jo's knickers as she moved down. With a gliding motion, she pulled the French knickers from Jo's waist, over her knees, and down to her ankles. Her face was on the same level as the thick swatch of Jo's pubic bush and she nuzzled the curls lovingly.

Jo felt a shiver course through her. She reached one hand down to Sam's head and grabbed a fistful of the Titian tresses. With the other hand, she raked her fingers into the wiry dark hair above her own sex. Her fingers teased deliberately through the thatch, making for the hood of her clitoris.

'Oh no you don't,' Sam said firmly, guiding Jo's fingers away. 'If you want to play with a cunny, you can play with mine in a moment. This one is for me.' Placing a hand on each thigh, she moved her face close to the warmth of Jo's arousal. Her tongue darted forward and she flicked the tip against the ambrosial wetness.

Jo groaned and pressed herself back against the wall. Her fingers gripped tightly in Sam's hair and she tugged the woman closer. Holding her head in such a fashion allowed Jo to press the woman's mouth firmly against her pussy. Sam was able to force the tip of her tongue into the most sensitive recess of Jo's wetness. The intimacy provoked an electric prickle of pleasure that snatched her breath away.

Spreading her legs, Jo allowed Sam to lick deep inside her, enjoying the delightful tremors that went spiralling through her body. She wanted to taste the woman's juices and revel in the heady sensation of licking at Sam's crotch, but she resisted the temptation, for the moment. Once again, Sam had overstepped her duties as the junior partner and, this time, Jo was determined to make her pay for it.

She gripped tighter on to the waves of red hair, extracting a small groan from the woman between her legs.

'Ouch!' Sam complained. She continued to lap at the inner folds of Jo's labia as she spoke. The words were muffled but clear enough. 'Be careful. That hurts.'

'You deserve it,' Jo growled breathlessly.

Sam traced her tongue against the pulsing heat of Jo's clitoris. She played the tip against the sensitive nub in a staccato dance, kissing the lips of Jo's sex with passionate intimacy. 'I suppose I deserve to be spanked as well.'

Jo heard herself groaning as she drew breath. She tried to ignore Sam's suggestion, made uncomfortable and excited by the image in the same moment. The sound of her cry seemed to come from miles away and, distantly, Jo realised she was caught in the throes of a sudden, stunning orgasm. The tip of Sam's tongue was fuelling a fire in her clitoris that quickly seared its way through her entire body. Every nerve was taut with a burning frenzy of euphoria. A tumultuous explosion of pleasure pulsed through her veins and she shrieked as her body achieved its climax.

Staggering with the aftermath, Jo stared down at Sam, her features etched with a mixture of gratitude and anticipation.

'You screamed,' Sam observed, a wry smile teasing her lips. 'Did I hurt you?'

Jo chuckled, leant forward, and dragged Sam from the floor. Wrapping her arms tightly round the redhead, she kissed her. With their mouths joined together, Jo could taste the remnants of her own pussy honey glazing Sam's lips. The subtle flavour of her excitement added an infuriating degree of eroticism. As they kissed, Jo ground her thighs together in a dry simulation of her body's desire. Her hands traversed Sam's scantily clad contours, cupping her small breasts and teasing the taut nubs of her nipples. Before the intense pleasure proved too much for either of them, Jo moved her hands down. After exploring Sam's narrow waist, she allowed her fingers to stroke the smooth flesh of her hips. The urge to have and possess her was so powerful she could not resist it.

Breathing heavily, Jo swept Sam from her feet and carried her to the desk in the middle of the room. Their mouths were still joined and she was able to see the redhead's eyes open wide with surprise when the carpet was pulled from beneath her. Jo pushed her on to the desk.

The hint of a warning flared in Sam's eyes and Jo sensed she was about to deliver some pious reminder about Doctor McMahon's advice. Unwilling to have the mood broken, Jo pressed her mouth harder against Sam, kissing her with a ferocious passion.

When she eventually broke the kiss, Sam stared up at her, wordless excitement shining behind her wire-rimmed spectacles.

Jo grinned down. Her hands were moving over the redhead's legs with rough, demanding caresses. She moved her fingers over Sam's inner thighs, pausing only to trace the line of her garter. Then her hands were moving to the French knickers, the tips of her fingers sliding beneath the loose fabric at the legs.

Sam gasped. 'I'm not sure we have this much time,' she whispered.

'We'll make time,' Jo assured her. Her index finger had reached Sam's warm, velvety wetness and she blindly stroked the slick flesh.

Unconsciously, Sam bucked her hips as her body responded to the touch.

Jo tugged the French knickers away from her in one graceful motion, tossing them to the corner of the room. The sight of Sam's pubic bush always excited her. There was something exquisite about the swatch of fiery red curls surrounding her labia. The vibrant colour seemed to capture the heat of the redhead's passion. Unable to resist the temptation, Jo knelt down and lowered her lips to Sam's pussy.

As her tongue trailed against the glistening flesh, Jo inhaled the musky fragrance of Sam's scent. Lapping at the sweet honey, she savoured the intimate flavour before swallowing avariciously.

With mounting excitement, Sam groaned and writhed from side to side on the desk.

Jo moved her mouth away and turned the redhead over. Sam moved easily into the position, as though she had already guessed what Jo intended. Instead of lying with her back on the desk, she was now spread over it, feet buried in the carpet, stomach and breasts pressed firmly on to the surface.

Jo pushed her nose between Sam's legs and nuzzled gently. Her tongue slipped into the velvety depths and she lapped greedily. Using her fingers to tease Sam's sex wide apart, she forced her tongue further into the warm, musky cleft. She stroked the side of her thumb over the tingling nub of the redhead's clitoris, inspiring a guttural groan.

Gently, still licking as she did it, Jo eased two fingers into the wet hole. Sam's arousal was so great they slid easily inside. Jo could feel the tingling inner walls of the woman's pussy clenching hungrily around her. Eagerly, she pushed the fingers deeper. As her tongue moved over the tip of the clitoris, Jo noticed that her thumb was brushing against the tiny

35

circle of Sam's anus. She did not even contemplate pushing her thumb inside, she simply did it.

Sam screamed at the unexpected intrusion. Every muscle in her body was furiously taut as she released the sound. As Jo pushed the thumb deep into the forbidden depths of Sam's arse, she felt the inner muscles contracting repeatedly. It was a disturbingly arousing sensation. She could feel her own fingers brushing her thumb through the thin lining of Sam's heated channels.

When the orgasm struck, Sam clenched hard against the intruding fingers.

Jo's knuckles were forced uncomfortably together and almost pushed from their tight confines by the shivering muscles.

Sam's scream began to taper off, only to be renewed when Jo slid her fingers deeper inside. She continued to work her tongue on the pulsing tip of Sam's clitoris, greedily drinking the spray that erupted from her second climax. Beads of sweat glistened on Sam's forehead and her lips were curled into an animal grimace of passion.

'Too much,' Sam whispered, easing herself away. There was a reluctant smile on her lips when she turned to face Jo. 'Far too much,' she said, leaning forward to kiss her.

Before their lips could meet, a small beeping sound from Sam's wristwatch broke the mood. 'Blast,' Sam said, glancing at her watch and turning off the alarm. 'It's almost eleven. Perhaps we can finish this later.' She reached for her discarded clothes and began to toss Jo's garments towards her. 'We have an eleven o'clock coming in two minutes.'

Stepping back into her suit, Jo watched Sam dressing. The embers of her satiated arousal glowed dully. 'I'm still pissed at you,' Jo said calmly. 'You've moved the offices and changed the company name. Do we still do investigation work, or has that changed too?'

Sam opened her mouth as though she were about to reply, then shook her head. 'I have been doing a bit of research into areas where we could diversify,' she said quickly, 'but we'll discuss those later.'

Jo rolled her eyes and squeezed her fists into tight balls. It was not the first time she had thought of punching Sam. She did not think she would have actually done it even if they had not been disturbed, but it was still an attractive idea.

'Flowers and Valentine?' the woman asked, pushing her head around the door as she knocked.

'Valentine and Flowers.' Jo scowled at Sam, who looked set to correct her, then turned her attention back to the woman. 'That's us. You must be our eleven o'clock.'

'Mrs Meadows,' Sam said, stepping forward and extending a hand. 'We spoke on the phone. I'm Samantha Flowers and this is my partner, Jo Valentine.'

Taking the hand, Mrs Meadows smiled politely. 'Call me Faye.'

Jo watched as Sam ushered the woman into a chair and then sat behind the desk on which they had just been fucking. With a frown of annoyance, she realised she was virtually redundant in what was supposed to be her own office.

'You'll have to forgive our chaotic appearance,' Sam told Mrs Meadows, gesturing at the uncluttered room around them. 'We've only just moved in this morning and we're still trying to get everything in order.'

'Will you be able to take on my case?' Mrs Meadows asked.

'Of course,' Sam enthused.

'That depends what it is,' Jo said, fixing Sam with a menacing glare. She stepped behind Sam's desk and sat casually on the surface, smiling tightly at the client.

Faye Meadows was tall and blonde. There was an expression of cool confidence on her thin face that gave her an authoritarian appearance. Yet, in spite of her smile, her ice-blue eyes were hard and uncompromising. She wore a light grey trenchcoat that had the patently unflattering look of expensive designer-wear. Her diamond engagement ring was large, and, coupled with her recent, professional manicure, it indicated that she was more than a little affluent.

After a cursory glance at Poplar Trees, Jo had already decided that she needed to increase her fees to meet the overheads. Faye Meadows looked like a woman who could help with that problem. But, as always, Jo was being cautious. 'What is it you want, Mrs Meadows?' she asked calmly.

'Faye,' the woman corrected. She reached into the pocket of her coat and produced a small, brightly coloured brochure. She placed it on Sam's desk, then reached back into her pocket and retrieved a small piece of cut plastic. It was the size and shape of a credit card.

Glancing at the brochure, Jo saw the words WELCOME TO ELYSIAN FIELDS in ornate script across the top of the front cover. Silently, she turned her questioning gaze to the client.

'I received this in my post yesterday morning,' Faye explained, holding up the credit-card-shaped piece of plastic. 'It's an invitation to spend a fortnight here.' With the tip of her elegantly manicured fingernail, she pointed at the brochure.

Jo reached for the booklet, intending to flick through it. Before she could catch hold, Sam had snatched it from the desk and was leafing idly through the pages. As though she was accepting a consolation prize, Jo picked up the invitation. It was a slim piece of bright-red plastic embossed with gold lettering. 'Elysian Fields' was printed on one side. On the other, Faye Meadows' name was written, along with the offer of a fortnight's stay at the premises. Jo glanced at the printed date and realised the break was scheduled to commence the following day.

'Was there anything else sent with this?' she asked.

Faye shook her head.

Jo shrugged. 'Well, it's a little intriguing,' she started. 'But I'm still unsure as to how we can help. If you've got a problem with junk mail then the post office is probably your best bet.'

Faye flexed a tight grin across her thin features, treating Jo to an expression of rueful disdain. 'I don't have a problem with junk mail,' she explained patiently. 'And if I were any other woman in the world, I would be delighted to receive a fortnight's free treatment at Elysian Fields. The cost of such a stay is painfully substantial.'

'Then what makes you so special?' Jo asked.

Faye looked as though she was about to say something. Before she could speak, Sam had interrupted her.

'Are you the same Mrs Meadows who owns Elysian Fields?' she asked, glancing up from the brochure.

Silently, Faye nodded.

Jo glared down at Sam.

'That doesn't make sense,' Sam said, ignoring Jo's dour expression. 'Why would someone send you an invitation to your own health farm?'

'That's what I'd like you to tell me,' Faye said simply. 'If it's a managerial cock-up, then I want to know how it happened and who's responsible. If it's someone's idea of a joke, then I want to find out who sent it, and why they think it's funny.'

Jo frowned, uncomfortable with an idea that had just occurred to her. She was about to ask a question, wanting to know why the woman did not simply telephone the health farm and find out what was happening for herself. Before she could give voice to her query, Sam broke in.

'This is a tariff of our fees,' she said, passing an A5 sheet of paper across the desk. 'Those prices don't include expenses, all of which will be confirmed in your final account.'

Faye thanked her, placed her hands on the arms of the chair and looked set to leave the office.

'Hold on a second,' Jo said suddenly. 'I'm not sure that we'll be able to throw much more light on this case than Mrs Meadows could manage herself.'

'I appreciate you doing this for me,' Faye interrupted calmly. 'I do have other businesses to attend to. I have two nightclubs in the town centre and a string of other interests. While the idea of a fortnight at Elysian Fields appeals to me, I can't afford to take the time off from my other commitments. Besides, I'm not sure that the invitation would be honoured. I've never seen one like it before.'

'You own a health farm and a couple of nightclubs?' Jo remarked, raising her eyebrows. 'Isn't that taking diversity to an extreme?'

'I'm an entrepreneur, not a specialist,' Faye replied, not meeting Jo's gaze.

Jo studied her suspiciously, positive that she was being lied to, and wishing she knew why. Her gut feeling to turn this case down was overwhelming. There was something dangerous about the whole situation and she did not trust it at all. Instinctively, Jo realised it would be wisest to let Mrs Meadows take her business elsewhere.

'We'll give you our report in seven days' time,' Sam said, standing up and offering Faye Meadows her hand. 'If we have any important progress prior to that, we'll call you and let you know what's happening.'

Jo stared at her partner, unable to believe she had just accepted the case without asking her advice. She struggled to find words that would take back what Sam had just said, but, as each moment passed, she realised the opportunity was getting further and further away. By the time she had thought of something appropriate to say, Faye Meadows had already left the office, leaving Sam and Jo alone.

'I can't believe you just accepted that case,' Jo said, shaking her head incredulously.

'I can't believe we were so lucky as to get it,' Sam countered. 'It's like a lottery win, or divine intervention or something. Here you are, in desperate need of a stay at a health farm, and what lands in your lap but an invitation to this place.' She wafted the brochure in front of Jo's nose, smiling giddily up at her.

Jo shook her head. 'There is no way that I'm going to visit that place,' she said, not disguising the note of disgust that crept into her voice. 'I didn't want to accept the case if we're being totally honest. And I'll be damned if I do a job that I didn't want to take.'

Sam grinned and stroked Jo's arm with intimate affection. 'Come on, darling,' she whispered. 'You need the break and we both know it'll do you some good.'

Jo shook her head. 'There's no way I'm going to that health farm, and nothing you can do or say will get me there.'

As soon as Sam kissed her, Jo could feel her resolve weakening.

Three

Arthur Knight stared out through the Venetian blinds, two fat fingers twisted between the slats at eye level, so he could view the car park discreetly. The shafts of sunlight that fell into his office were pale blue, and filled with the eddies of swirling smoke.

'There must be a lot of money in private-investigation work,' Arthur observed, squinting out into the morning light. 'Have you seen the fiery red sports car that the Flowers woman is driving? They cost a chuffing fortune and she's barely old enough to chuffing drive it.' There was the distant lilt of a Yorkshire accent in his voice which always became more pronounced when he was excited or in a hurry to express himself. The accent had been thickening all morning as he watched the Poplar Trees' newest tenants arriving.

In the silence that followed, Poppy knew better than to say anything. With her long, mousy-brown hair, willowy figure and unspectacular choice of clothes, she seemed to blend into the smoky shadows of the dimly lit office. She stayed silent, wondering how Arthur Knight was going to respond to the request she had made.

She wished she had been able to make the request to his brother, Derek. Derek was just as brusque and intimidating, but Poppy had seen him smiling slyly at

43

her from time to time. She suspected that Derek had a secret desire for her and she would have been happy to exploit that if it could have helped her. But Derek was not in the office this morning and she had been left with no option other than to ask Arthur.

'That Valentine woman doesn't seem to be doing as well as her boss,' Arthur noted. He pushed his face against the blinds, trying to determine the make and model of the dirty, rust-eaten car Jo had been driving. 'What is that? A Ford Shitheap or a Renault Crock?'

Poppy remained silent, studying her hands as they played nervously in her lap.

Arthur closed the Venetian blinds and turned to face her. 'I can't believe you're asking me for time off.' He dropped heavily into his seat at the head of the conference table. 'More than anyone else, you should know how busy we are around here at the moment.'

Poppy shook her head, loathing her own servility but unable to think of any other way to act. 'I suppose it is wrong of me to ask.' She risked a nervous glance at him. 'But I haven't had any leave for the past two years, and yesterday morning –'

'You haven't had any leave since you worked so bloody ineptly on the Meadows case, have you?' he broke in.

Poppy glared at the conference table, wishing he was not constantly reminding her of that one mistake. Admittedly it had been a large mistake, ruinous for their client, and potentially crippling for Knight & Knight solicitors. The threat of compensatory litigation had hung over the company like the sword of Damocles. There was still the danger of the ruined client making a successful compensation claim, but, as each day passed, the chances diminished.

'It was just before I started working on the

Meadows case when I took my last holiday,' Poppy confirmed.

Arthur Knight sat back in his chair, shaking his head thoughtfully from side to side. He placed the tips of his sausage-like fingers together and began to gently squeeze them as he spoke. 'Your cock-up on that case damned nearly ruined this company,' he reminded her.

Poppy glared unhappily at the table, knowing that he was exaggerating but not daring to point that out. Her cock-up had been an embarrassment but it had not caused ruination. 'I know,' she whispered. 'And I really am sorry,' she added, for what felt like the millionth time.

'The problem with a divorce case like that one is that we can get more money by stretching the proceedings out.'

'I know,' Poppy said miserably. Over the past two years she did not think a week had gone by when she had not had to endure this lecture. Every time she asked Arthur Knight for the smallest favour or service, he reminded her of the foolish mistake she had made on the Meadows case. If the idea of a fortnight's break had not been so tempting she would not have set herself up for this purgatory again.

Thinking back to her mistake, Poppy supposed it was the sort of error that had been bound to happen sooner or later. Knight & Knight solicitors had been dealing with the affairs of Malcolm and Sky Meadows from the day that they announced their engagement. They had continued to work with the couple throughout their marriage and, when the pair decided to divorce, it was inevitable that one of them would want to use Knight & Knight.

Perhaps, Poppy thought, things would have been different if Sky Meadows had used a different solicitor. Malcolm Meadows was always in the office, attending to other matters of business that did not concern his divorce. In those circumstances, she supposed that a mistake was inevitable.

She had been a lot younger back then and eager to please all the clients who were submitted to her portfolio. When Malcolm Meadows had asked her to organise a substantial withdrawal from his bank, Poppy's automatic reaction had been to say yes.

She had not given a thought to the divorce case she was handling for his wife.

Her attention was focused on customer satisfaction for Mr Meadows. On his instruction, she had withdrawn five million pounds from the Meadows' joint account. If Poppy had done this with the permission of Mrs Meadows, she knew the pointing finger of blame would not have been so relentless. Instead, she had used her initiative and followed Malcolm's instructions to the letter.

She was still paying for that crime.

After leaving the office, Malcolm Meadows had driven to the coast. No one knew if he was trying to meet his lover and met with misfortune instead, or if he was simply depressed by the acrimonious divorce and had decided to end it all. Whatever the reason, his fate was well documented.

The mangled wreckage of his car was retrieved from the sea bed beneath the shadow of the cliffs. There was no trace of his body or the briefcase with its five million pounds. The notorious currents in that stretch of water were blamed for Malcolm's missing body and, after a rudimentary search, the local authorities quickly stopped looking.

No trace of him, or his money, had been seen since.

'Sky Meadows could have taken us for ten million or more,' Arthur said, closing his eyes and pushing himself back into his chair. 'She still could. Did I ever tell you that?'

Every week, whether I wanted to hear it or not, Poppy thought miserably, as she answered, 'No, Mr Knight, I don't think you did tell me.'

Arthur grunted dourly. 'It also thwarted our chances of making a lot of money out of that divorce. We could have still been working our way through the paperwork, and taking a tidy profit from the account at that.'

Poppy closed her eyes and chewed on her lower lip. Two years of listening to this, and mumbling apologies in response, had left her inured to the words. She could sense that Arthur Knight was building up to something, and wondered if he was going to turn down her request for a holiday. It would not be the first time and she was already prepared for the disappointment of his refusal.

'Does this mean I can't have the fortnight off?' Poppy asked boldly. She dared to meet his gaze when she asked the question, then looked away quickly when she saw he was watching her.

'Poppy, Poppy, Poppy,' Arthur said, shaking his head sadly. He slapped the seat next to his, and waited until she had settled herself there before continuing. 'I'd love to let you have a fortnight off,' he began seriously. 'No one deserves a fortnight off more than you – I mean that in all sincerity – but you're a victim of your own success.'

Poppy felt like a victim, but not of her own success. 'How do you mean?' she asked, not sure she wanted to hear.

Arthur laughed and clapped a friendly hand on her leg as he spoke. Poppy knew there was no intimation in the touch. Not only was Arthur Knight an ugly, balding, fat bastard, he was also married to Mrs

Knight and, therefore, Poppy knew he would have no interest in her. Also, she had seen her own reflection when she dressed that morning. The whey-faced, shapeless thing that had stared back was so dull and uninteresting it was incapable of inspiring sexual feelings in anyone.

Despite all these assurances she was making to herself, she noticed that his hand remained where it was, against the coarse fabric of her long, all-concealing skirt. He rubbed a fat thumb against the top of her thigh as he spoke. His fingers occasionally squeezed her leg for punctuation. 'You really do deserve a break. And I really want you to have one, too. No one deserves time off more than you do.'

Poppy could sense the word 'but' was about to raise its ugly head. She braced herself for its impact, as though it would hurt like a slap.

Still stroking her thigh, Arthur Knight went on. 'But you do too much around here. Far too much. And the thought of having to cope without you for a fortnight is quite frightening.' He shivered theatrically, as if to show her just how terrifying the ordeal would be.

Poppy lowered her head and sighed heavily. She could tell a refusal when she heard one and would rather he had simply said no, rather than trying to dress it up as though it was a compliment. She considered pushing his fat, sweaty hand off her leg and telling him to stick his job where he shoved his Anusol, knowing she would not dare to do either.

Arthur Knight was still talking. 'I suppose you think I'm being foolish, saying that I'm frightened by the prospect of a fortnight without you. But I guess that's part of the problem.' He smiled easily.

Poppy frowned, uncomfortable with the cool appraisal of his stare.

'The idea of having to manage without you makes

me so upset that I get very, very tense,' Arthur told her. His fingers squeezed her leg as though he had just made a point.

Poppy wished she understood what he was talking about. He was not making sense. His sweaty hand was making her leg uncomfortable, and the anticipatory air in the conference room was so thick and unsettling that she felt quite ill.

Arthur smiled at her. 'Now, if only I could find some way of releasing all that tension, then perhaps I could let you have your two weeks off.'

An unsettling thought occurred to Poppy and she glanced into his face. He was grinning broadly and dared to wink at her when she looked at him. The hand on her leg squeezed hard again and Poppy could feel her fears being confirmed. She swallowed thickly and tried to take a deep breath. Staring hard at the conference table, she said quietly, 'I'm not quite sure I understand what you mean.'

In all honesty, she felt certain that she had guessed exactly what he meant, but the idea was so unexpected, and at the same time so repulsive, she dared not contemplate it until Arthur Knight had said the words aloud.

'Tension has different ways of affecting people.' Arthur's fingers inched ever so slightly further up her leg. Poppy could feel the flesh of her thigh was warm and wet where his hand had been. She did not feel particularly excited by his touch but she had to admit it was not an unpleasant sensation.

'Some people need massages.' Arthur was struggling to affect a casual tone. 'Others need to smoke. But with me –' He paused and studied her face for a second. 'Can I be honest with you?'

'Of course,' Poppy told him. The words came from her mouth like a sigh. She could tell where this was leading and the muscles in her stomach were knotting frantically.

'Of course,' he repeated, laughing. He squeezed harder on her leg for a brief moment before pushing his fingers a little higher. 'Well, to be totally honest with you, tension gives me an unbearable stiffness.' His voice had fallen to a conspiratorial whisper that made Poppy feel distinctly uncomfortable. 'The thought of being without you for a fortnight makes that stiffness even worse. But if I could find a way of relieving it, then I'd be happy to let you have the time off.'

'You want me to relieve your stiffness?' Poppy asked dully. She felt certain she was misinterpreting his meaning but she could not quite contemplate how.

He was grinning lasciviously. 'Relieve my stiffness and you can have your fortnight's leave,' he said. His bottom lip protruded heavily and his eyelids had lowered into a sleepy leer.

Poppy glanced at his face and could not recall seeing anything less sexually exciting in her entire life. His hand was still inching its way up her thigh, while the other was buried deep in his pocket. Even though she was trying not to notice, she could see the large swell of his arousal distorting the front of his pants. The slow rhythmic action of his hand, shuffling up and down over the erection, left Poppy in no doubt as to what he was doing. With a rising wave of revulsion, she realised that, as he spoke to her, Arthur Knight was intimately caressing himself.

He was still considering her with his repellent, roguish gaze and Poppy saw that something was expected of her. 'Do you need a massage or something?' she asked, wishing she did not sound so childishly naive.

He growled soft laughter. 'You could start by

massaging it,' he told her. The hand inside his trousers began to work up and down faster and his salacious grin widened.

With her heart pounding nervously, Poppy stood up and brushed his hand away. She could feel her breath coming in bursts and it was an effort to speak to him in a coherent, sensible voice. 'Could you please stop speaking in riddles and rhymes? I don't know what you want from me but if you'd –'

'I want you to suck my dick,' Arthur Knight said sharply.

His words struck Poppy like an open palm against her face. She dared to meet his gaze, then wished she hadn't. The sincerity she saw in his dark-blue eyes was chilling.

'I want you to get down on your knees, beside this table, then suck on my dick,' Arthur told her. His gaze never left her face as he spoke. His hand was moving up and down even faster than before and she wondered if she was enduring some bizarre work-related dream. The thought seemed unlikely and she crushed it before its hopes could hurt her.

'Come on,' Arthur said encouragingly. 'Kneel down, do as I've asked, and you can have your fortnight's holiday.' As she watched, he moved his hands from his pocket and stroked himself through the silver-grey fabric of his trousers. His fingers reached the top of his zipper and she watched him tug it slowly down. The length of eager flesh he had been holding inside strained against the opening slit. Poppy could see a glimpse of pink skin struggling to escape through the fly. He reached a pair of fat fingers between the zippered teeth and eased his length out.

Poppy heard herself gasp. She was staring at his cock with wide-eyed surprise, not sure what she should be doing. She knew exactly what was expected of her now and, although she harboured so many reservations, her overriding instinct was to kneel down and do exactly as Arthur Knight had asked.

It was not that she particularly wanted to suck his cock, or that she found the idea extremely exciting. In all honesty, she considered Arthur Knight to be a repugnant, self-seeking bastard, as sexually exciting as furniture polish. However, she desperately wanted her fortnight's holiday and, if this was the only way of acquiring it, she was determined to do as he asked.

She glanced into his face, desperately searching for a trace of compassion that would allow her to escape the office without having to suffer this indignity. Even before she had looked at him, Poppy knew it would be a fruitless search.

Arthur licked his parched lips as he stared at her. His hand openly massaged his fat, pink length as he shifted his gaze from her face to the front of her long, baggy jumper. 'Get your titties out before you suck me,' Arthur told her, sliding his fist idly over the tip of his cock. 'I've always wondered what your titties look like.'

Poppy risked a nervous glance at his face. 'Could I still go on my holiday if I didn't do this?'

He shrugged. 'I couldn't stop you from going really,' he said with infuriating self-confidence. 'But I promise you now, you wouldn't have a job to come back to.'

Those words were enough for Poppy.

Jobs were difficult enough to come by at the best of times and things were currently moving slowly in the legal world. Since the cock-up with the Meadows case, she had made regular enquiries with local employment agencies. The response she had received left Poppy feeling trapped and cold. While she did not particularly like her job with Knight & Knight, she had to admit that it provided a regular income. Arthur's threat of unemployment was all the impetus she needed to do his bidding.

She lowered herself to her knees and moved her head over his lap. Staring at his exposed cock in such close proximity, she could smell the scent of his excitement.

She had not been expecting to feel any arousal herself, but the act of kneeling seemed to have tickled some subconscious erogenous zone. A nervous thrill caused a ripple of gooseflesh to prickle her forearms. She reached a tentative hand forward and felt the warm pulse of his cock against the tips of her fingers.

Arthur Knight's hand was suddenly in her hair and she felt her head being tugged roughly backward. She stared up at him with a helpless expression as she wondered what she had done wrong.

'I told you to get your titties out,' Arthur reminded her. 'Get 'em out,' he growled. As his excitement mounted, she realised the subtle inflection of his Northern accent was becoming more pronounced.

'But I –' Poppy began, trying to find the words to tell him that her breasts were not worth looking at.

Arthur did not allow her to finish. 'I want my dick sucking and I want to see your titties,' he said flatly. 'Anything less, and you'll be getting a damned sight longer than a fortnight away from here.'

Shuddering, Poppy moved her gaze away from his. She crossed her arms over her chest and reached for the sides of her jumper. In one casual motion, she had pulled the garment off. She wore no bra and revealed herself to him topless. The orbs of her breasts swayed provocatively as she straightened up and glanced at him. She did not know if it was her imagination, coincidence, or something else, but, as she removed

53

her top, Arthur's cock seemed to twitch more excitedly than before.

He moved forward in his chair, his fingers eagerly reaching for the dark-brown tips of her breasts. Deciding she had already gone so far, and there was no point being prudish at such a late stage, Poppy allowed him to touch her. She tried to ignore the sparkle of pleasure inspired by his rough, careless fingers, unhappy with the thought of enjoying herself under these circumstances. Nevertheless, a whisper of excitement touched her and she could feel herself being drawn by the heady impulse to indulge her awakening appetite.

'I always wondered what you had under that scraggy bloody jumper,' he growled, tugging her towards him.

Poppy gasped as he took her in his arms, not sure what he intended to do with her now. He moved his mouth over her breasts and took a dark-brown nipple between his lips. The thrill was far greater than she had expected. She released a soft sigh of contentment, suddenly enjoying herself. The whirlpool of her emotions span faster as Arthur teased the sensitive tip with his teeth, playfully biting at the erect pearl of flesh. With his free hand, he squeezed her other nipple between rough, callused fingers, pinching her so painfully that she began to shiver with mounting delight.

'Now, suck it,' he said, releasing her so suddenly it was like a push backward.

Poppy drew a heavy breath, torn between her arousal and her dissipating feelings of revulsion. Not wanting to torture herself with a moment's more thought, she moved her mouth closer to his cock and pushed out her tongue.

Arthur Knight drew a heavy breath. His arms moved over her head and she expected to feel his fingers in her hair. Instead, she saw that he was reaching for the conference table and she suspected he was trying to steady himself, even though he was sitting down. She heard his fingers distantly brush against the intercom console on the conference table, and assumed he had simply caught it accidentally. For the moment there were more pressing matters on her mind.

She placed the tip of her tongue against the swollen end of his erection and drew a wet circle around the bulbous purple head. As soon as she touched the flesh, his cock seemed to leap away from her mouth. She glanced unhappily at him and reached out to hold the base of his length.

Arthur grinned down at her. 'You're doing fine down there, Poppy,' he said loudly. 'Now take it all in your mouth. You know you want to.'

Obediently, Poppy lowered her mouth over the end. She sucked gently, aware of the quickening pulse of his excitement throbbing against her tongue. She could feel the warmth of her own arousal beginning to spread between her legs and she wondered how her body could be capable of such a response. Arthur Knight was incapable of arousing her and she suspected it was only the intoxication of the moment. The bullying way that he had manoeuvred her into this position was reprehensible and she despised him for doing it to her. But she could not deny the mounting thrill that her submission had evoked. She knew that if she slid a hand between her own legs her pussy would be so hot it would scald her fingertips. Trying to brush that image from her mind, she lowered her mouth slowly down Arthur's raging hard erection.

'Good lass,' he muttered, the words coming out in a dry grunt.

Poppy smiled dutifully around his cock, allowing her head to rise and fall. Her lips gripped wetly to his stiff rod and she stroked her tongue against the pulsating flesh inside her mouth. Each time she pushed her head down, she could feel the swollen end pressing at the back of her throat, threatening to climax.

That twitch of excitement was darkly inspirational. Each time she felt the pulse of Arthur's nearness, she could feel her own climax edging nearer. The intensity of her own impending orgasm was so great she did not hear the door of the conference room opening.

'You bastard!'

Poppy heard the voice and turned to see who had spoken. She glimpsed Derek Knight's face, twisted into an expression that went somewhere between shock and lurid intrigue. Then Arthur was gently guiding her head back to his erection.

'Carry on, Poppy,' Arthur said, kindly but firmly. 'We don't want to stop now, do we?'

Poppy felt like doing nothing but stopping. Her own arousal was quickly evaporating and the thought of having both partners of the law firm see her like this was more than just a little humiliating. But despite her own feelings, she continued to suck on Arthur's length as he dealt with his brother.

'How long has this been going on?' she heard Derek demanding.

'About five minutes,' Arthur replied honestly. 'I'll be done soon if you want a go,' he added calmly.

Poppy drew a sharp breath, as though she had been slapped. She tried to glare angrily up at Arthur but it was difficult because of her position. It was also difficult because his casual offer had refuelled the fading embers of her arousal. She listened intently, desperate to hear what Derek would say or do by way of response.

'She's got nice titties,' Derek remarked absently.

'She's good at blowing,' Arthur told him. Poppy could feel the tremor of each word vibrating in the end of his length.

'What's her chuff like?'

'Why don't you find out for yourself. I haven't had a chance to look down there yet.'

Poppy knew she should have felt outraged but her arousal was just too great. Neither of the men was particularly attractive or exciting but their casual abuse was intensely exhilarating. She had never considered herself to be anyone's sexual plaything before today. The image that stared back from the mirror was disappointing and lacking in any sort of sex appeal. Yet here were two men talking about what they wanted to do with her and preparing to compare notes. Poppy could feel the pulse of her arousal beating louder than ever before. Her anticipation was so heated she expected to spontaneously combust at any moment.

She could hear Derek moving behind her before his hands caressed her buttocks through the coarse fabric of her skirt. He traced the shape of her arse, then allowed the tips of his fingers to follow the line of her panties where they pulled taut into the rounded swell of the cheeks.

She held her breath, still sucking hard on Arthur's cock. She felt Derek's fingers tug at her clothing, then wrench hard at it. There was the sound of fabric tearing and then the skirt was being pulled away from her. The coarse fibres seemed to caress her legs as the garment was dragged from her body.

Then Derek's hands were caressing her backside again, this time unencumbered by the skirt. His

57

fingers followed the same path as before, stroking along the edge of her panties where the elastic cut into her flesh.

Poppy drew a shivering breath, sucking harder on Arthur's cock.

Casually, Derek slipped the tips of his fingers beneath the elastic of her panties.

Poppy shuddered. He had carelessly drawn his fingers against the boiling lips of her sex. The pleasure his touch inspired was so strong it was cataclysmic.

Both hands were beneath the panties now. His cool skin was pressed firmly against the warmth of her buttocks. With a sudden, unexpectedly rough gesture, she felt Derek tugging the panties away from her. His hands snatched and tore at the fabric. Each brutal movement was done without any thought for her and this only added to Poppy's arousal. As he tried to tug the rent garment from her, she realised the gusset remained intact and was pressing with uncomfortable accuracy over the heated tip of her clitoris.

She moved her mouth away from Arthur's cock for a moment, giving voice to a groan of dark, guttural satisfaction. It seemed unreal to be experiencing an orgasm so powerful and strong under these circumstances. Nevertheless, a satisfying explosion of pleasure coursed through her body.

With a casual tug at her hair, Arthur guided her mouth back to his cock. 'I'm close to coming, Poppy,' he told her flatly. 'You wouldn't want to spoil your fortnight off by not drinking all of it, would you?'

There was something about his casual dominance over her that made her inner muscles clench hungrily. He had just instructed her to swallow his come and she had pliantly agreed. She did not know which part excited her the most: his arrogant control, or her own yielding submission. She did not have time to contemplate the thought, suddenly distracted as Derek Knight slid his fingers against the moistened heat of her sex.

Poppy released a second groan, this one muffled by the cock that filled her mouth.

'She's good and wet,' Derek noted.

Poppy gasped as he slid a finger deep into her warmth. The broad tip spread her lips wide open and as the end tickled inside she could feel herself on the brink of another orgasm.

'And she's tight too.' Derek spoke to his brother as though Poppy were unable to hear him. 'But I don't really want to fuck her chuff.'

Poppy could feel Arthur shrugging as she worked her tongue against his pulsing length. 'What's her arsehole like?' Arthur asked.

Poppy wanted to scream with excitement. She held her breath, unwilling to experience the joy of another orgasm just yet and struggling to stave off the threatening moment of pleasure. It was a battle that she might have won, if Derek had not picked that moment to test a wet finger against the rim of her arsehole.

Poppy shrieked.

As the rude finger slid deep into the depths of her dark canal, Poppy felt a series of orgasms explode inside her, each more powerful than the last. She sucked hard on Arthur's cock and squirmed her arse eagerly against the intrusion of Derek's finger. Her entire body was shivering with the aftermath of her multiple climaxes.

'Her arse is tighter than a gnat's twat,' Derek said, a grin tainting his words. 'And I suppose I could fuck it at a pinch, but I fancy a blow job.'

'Chuffing typical,' Arthur growled with good-natured annoyance. 'When we were kids, you always

59

wanted the toys I was playing with. Now you're after the blow job that I'm having.'

Poppy sucked hard on Arthur's length, the men's casual discussion exciting her more and more.

'Couldn't she suck us both at the same time?' Derek asked.

Poppy heard him unzipping his pants and stepping out of them. From the corner of her eye, she saw his semi-hard cock swaying close to her face.

'Take a seat,' Arthur growled sullenly. 'And pull it up close to mine. This lass has too good a tongue to waste it.'

Derek did as he was asked and pulled his chair so that he was sitting next to his brother. Poppy glanced at his cock and watched him roll his fist up and down the shaft, forcing it into full erection. Like his brother, he was uncircumcised but his foreskin had rolled right back to reveal his swollen purple end. Without waiting for an instruction, she reached her cool fingers against the man's cock, then moved her mouth over it.

'This is one hell of a way to start the morning,' Derek observed, caressing the back of Poppy's head as she sucked on him. 'What's the celebration for?'

'Poppy wanted a couple of weeks off,' Arthur explained, allowing Poppy to gently stroke her fingers up and down his length. 'She's doing this for me now, and I'm going to let her have the time off.'

'It's a good job you didn't ask for a rise,' Derek said, speaking to Poppy. 'This bastard would be fucking your arse for the next twelve months if you'd done that.'

The two men guffawed together and Poppy felt another sickening wave of humiliating pleasure wash over her. They were still speaking about her with such callous disregard that she might as well have been deaf. Their sexist banter and cold indifference should have been degrading or annoying at the very least. Instead, Poppy could feel herself heading towards another climax at breakneck speed.

She rolled her tongue wetly against Derek's cock, carefully wanking Arthur's with her free hand. As soon as the senior partner deigned it was time for her to move her head, Poppy felt her hair being pulled so that her mouth went over his cock. She sucked both the men, wetting their lengths with her lips and tongue and gently massaging the bases of their erections.

The fact that she was naked only added fuel to the flames of her arousal. She could not recall feeling so excited in her entire life. She was being forced to kneel on the floor and perform fellatio for her employers. The absolute degradation was so sweet she was having difficulty containing another shriek of ecstasy.

'Suck it harder, Poppy,' Arthur growled suddenly. 'I'm just about ready to spunk.'

Poppy had already guessed this much. She could feel the quickening pulse in his cock against her lip. Arthur was so close to climaxing she could almost taste his ejaculation. The salty-sweet flavour of his pre-come was already filling her nostrils and coating her tongue. As she pursed her lips around his length and fondled his balls, Poppy felt Arthur tensing against the threat of his impending orgasm.

'I want you to drink every bloody drop of this, lass,' he growled, swallowing thickly around his cry of excitement.

Poppy could feel herself shaking. She dared to tease the tip of her finger beneath his balls and stroke against the rim of his anus. The gesture was more than sufficient to push him beyond the brink. The pulse of his climax shuddered along the length of his stiff cock, forcing the first thick spurt of semen against the back of her throat.

The sudden explosion in her mouth and the taste of his seed were too much for Poppy. She had been fighting against the onset of another orgasm but the taste of Arthur's come was too much for her. She squeezed her thighs tightly together and felt the warm release of her climax flood in a sticky spray between her legs. If she had not been working so furiously on his length, she would have bellowed as the pleasure tore through her.

Her head was swimming with excitement and she felt more aroused than she had imagined it was possible to feel. She heard a distant cry and, glancing up from Arthur's cock, she realised Derek was close to coming. Acting without thinking, she moved her mouth over the tip of his shaft, just as he exploded.

Before she had finished swallowing the semen from Arthur's ejaculation, his brother's fluid was filling her mouth. The pulse of Derek's cock was not as hard as Arthur's had been, but he was spraying far more semen into her. The white-hot liquid filled her mouth and Poppy almost gagged as she struggled to swallow it all.

'Good lass,' Arthur Knight said, stroking her hair, and guiding her face back to his wilting length. 'If you lick me clean now, then I'll let you take your fortnight's holiday.'

'Can you get her to lick me clean?' Derek asked, his voice shaky with the residue of his excitement.

'When you've finished, lick Derek clean,' Arthur instructed flatly, as Poppy rolled her tongue over his length. She could still feel the buzz of an electric thrill tingling her pussy lips. Poppy had already decided that she would have to play with herself to relieve some of the pent-up feelings this encounter had caused. As she turned her head back to Derek's cock, she stole a hand between her legs and dared to tease her sex. A finger brushed over her clitoris and pleasure began to course through her as she worked her tongue over his shaft.

'You know,' Derek said suddenly, speaking to Arthur. 'We really ought to offer this service to some of our more prestigious clients.'

His words, and the hint of future submissions that they alluded to, were too much for Poppy. It was not only the pressure of her fingertips against the pulsing bead of her clitoris. The euphoria of this threatened humiliation left her squealing as the thrill of another orgasm swept over her. After this, she wondered if her fortnight's holiday might not seem like an anticlimax.

Four

'Bloody hell!' Wendy whispered. She had been about to leave the east wing's storeroom, her duties there concluded for another day, when the sudden movement caught her eye. She stepped towards the window and peered through, wondering if she had been mistaken. With her face pressed against the glass, she stared across the empty lawn towards the partially blinded window in the west wing.

The health farm's main building had been constructed with two great semicircular wings. In the tip of each lay unused rooms almost forgotten by the staff and clientele, and seldom visited. From the pane in the east wing's storeroom, Wendy had a clear view of the scene in the west wing.

'Bloody hell!' she gasped again, equal measures of shock and excitement colouring her words. 'That's obscene.' Without another thought, she rushed from the storeroom, determined to investigate.

It took her less than two minutes to sprint through the building, her pace hurried by a dark intrigue that had not touched her for months. A handful of early-risers greeted her as she trotted briskly through the corridors of Elysian Fields and she acknowledged each with a polite but cursory nod. If she had seen Bryn or Allen she would have encouraged them to join her but the masseurs were not scheduled to start work for another hour. Not giving her own safety any thought, Wendy made her way to the west wing alone.

'Please. No. No more.'

She could hear the man's pitiful cries of protest as she neared the west wing's forgotten room. Normally she would have associated wails like that with pain, discomfort and agony, but this tone sounded different. There was a suggestion of enjoyment in the pleas for leniency and Wendy felt her curiosity deepen. She could recognise John's voice beneath the unfamiliar cries for mercy and she knew he was with the woman they were calling the Black Widow. The only thing Wendy did not know was what the pair of them were doing. She approached the closed door with the stealth of a natural voyeur. Her heart was pounding and she could feel her mood being coloured by the delicious flush of arousal.

'I promise I won't say a word. Not to the police. Not to Faye Meadows. Not to anyone. I promise.'

Wendy stepped closer to the door, wishing it had been left ajar. There were no internal windows to the room and the only glimpse inside was afforded from the eye of the mortise lock's keyhole. Kneeling in front of the door, she pressed one eye to the keyhole and tried to make sense of what was going on. Barely aware that she was speaking aloud, Wendy whispered, 'Bloody hell!'

'I thank you for your promise, John. It's nice to finally hear some compliance in your tone. But the truth is that I can't trust you. That's why I'm going to have to take this measure.'

By squinting, and using a little guesswork, Wendy was able to make out the scene in the room. She could see John was secured to a contraption that looked like a birthing-stool. Towering over him, with a padlock in one hand, the Black Widow was smiling ferociously.

Allen and Bryn, the health farm's male masseurs, had already spoken to Wendy about the new manager. Their reports had been more than a little disturbing. Her name was Sky, although she preferred to be known as the Black Widow, an epithet that both men had thought peculiarly apt. The Black Widow was cruel, merciless and uncaring, they had told Wendy. The words 'bitch', 'cunt' and 'ball-breaker' had been used repeatedly as the two men tried to explain exactly how bad the woman was.

Wendy had treated their comments with polite contempt, determined to make up her own mind about the newcomer. Watching the forbidding blonde woman smile menacingly down at John, she began to suspect the pair had not been exaggerating.

'Please. No,' John begged.

Sky was smiling, her lips twisted into a sneer of contempt. 'You're beyond the begging stage now, John,' she told him. 'You should have realised by now that it does no good. I'm going to do what I want anyway.'

Wendy drew a shocked breath as she studied the couple. John's body was scoured with welts and lines, as though he had recently received a series of vicious and cruel thrashings.

'Look at that,' Sky grumbled. 'You've gone hard again, John. That really isn't helping me, is it?' Not bothering to wait for his reply, she snatched his solid length and began to roll her hand up and down him. 'Should I wank you off, or try and beat the come out of your balls?'

Wendy pressed herself closer against the door. John was struggling in the birthing-stool, beseeching Sky to listen to him.

The woman ignored him. 'I could hit your balls with my crop,' she explained, tapping a finger against the tight swell of his sac. 'I could do it repeatedly, and I bet you'd come, wouldn't you?'

'Please don't,' he begged.

Sky's smile was tinged with malice. She worked her hand up and down his cock in quickening movements. Wendy could see the swollen head appearing then disappearing in Sky's fist. She saw John stiffen in the chair and realised he was close to coming. Sky moved her mouth down to her hand, wanking his cock towards the ripe swell of her lips.

'Not again,' John moaned. The protest was torn from his mouth as the explosion erupted between his legs. Wendy watched Sky drop her lips over the pulsing head of John's cock, greedily lapping up his seed. She could see John struggling unhappily against his restraints as though he was not enjoying the pleasure that Sky was giving him. 'Not again.' Wendy's eyes widened with excitement as she saw John thrashing wildly in a futile attempt to escape the Black Widow's plan.

'Please don't,' John insisted.

Sky had her face over his. If Wendy had not just seen her sucking John's length, she would have expected Sky to kiss him. As she watched, she saw Sky spit John's come into his face.

'Bitch,' Wendy whispered incredulously.

John was twisting from side to side, his revulsion clear in the tortured expression straining his features. A thick string of his seed trailed from Sky's lips and she wiped it absently away with the back of her hand. After forcing him to lick her fingers clean, she held up the padlock and grinned. 'Now that your erection isn't going to get in the way, it's time to use this.'

John gave a sneer of disgust and did not bother

replying. Wendy could see how unhappy he was with the daubing of seed that covered his face. If the image had not been so exciting she would have empathised with his revulsion.

Sky fastened the padlock round the head of his spent cock, pressing the curved steel bar cruelly tight. 'It's not foolproof,' Sky told him as she studied his secured length. 'If you're daring you could use a tub of Vaseline and try tearing your cock out of there, but I guarantee it would hurt.'

From her view through the keyhole, Wendy suspected that Sky was telling the truth. The padlock looked painfully tight, being fastened just beneath the head of John's cock. Even from this distance she could see that the only way to remove it would be with the use of a key. Any other attempt would result only in distress or injury.

'If you're more daring,' Sky continued, 'you could use a hacksaw. I doubt it would work, and I'm not sure if the A and E ward that treated you would be able to do corrective surgery, but it's always a consideration. There is a final option, and this is the one I think you should go for.'

John stared up at her, silently waiting for her to continue.

'If you're sensible, you'll do as I say and stay silent.'

Wendy pressed forward against the door, curiosity pulling her closer.

'I only need your silence for a week,' Sky told him. 'After that, it will be too late to change things anyway. Stay silent for a week, tell me where you're staying, and I'll mail this key to you.' She flashed the padlock's key enticingly in front of his face. 'You'll still be able to take a pee with that on,' she said, nodding casually at the padlock. 'It's just going to make erections uncomfortable and it might hamper any developing relations that you were thinking of embarking on. But if you're a good boy and you leave here now, you can have the key in seven days.'

'OK.' There was no hint of hesitancy or uncertainty in John's reply. Wendy heard him make the promise as though it had been squeezed from his crushed body. She had never seen the manager looking so cowed and submissive before and for a moment she was stung by a wave of pity for him. She pressed herself closer to the door, wishing she could see the scene in more detail without having to kneel and squint.

'I'll unfasten you within the hour,' Sky said briskly. 'You'll be given half an hour to pack your things and leave the building. You can send me a letter with your new address and I'll send the key on to you. Is that acceptable?'

John was nodding miserably.

'That's good.' Sky smiled. 'Then we have an understanding.' She had concluded the morning's business, Wendy thought. That much was apparent from her decisive tone and sudden change in mood. She was virtually dismissing John now that she had defeated him.

Wendy suddenly realised that her position by the keyhole was decidedly vulnerable. If she was discovered watching this scene, the punishment would be swift and unforgettable. Touched by a thrill of fear, she started to ease herself away from the keyhole. Her fingers pressed lightly against the door for balance and she tried to stand up. For the first time, she realised she had been kneeling in front of the keyhole for a long time. The position was uncomfortable enough to have left her body stiff and she heard the wet crack of cartilage as her knees popped in disapproval. The sound was accompanied by a vague twang of discomfort in her legs as they buckled beneath her. With a wail of despair she felt her body lurch forward and press heavily into the door. The door pushed slowly open, allowing her to fall into the room.

'Who the –'

Wendy glanced at the pair of them and watched their faces change. John's eyes were shining with a glimmer of hope, which quickly evaporated into pained despondency. Sky looked shocked for a moment. Then she caught sight of Wendy's look of startled horror and the shock was replaced by a knowing, cruel smile. 'Hello, Wendy,' Sky said sweetly.

Before Wendy could respond, Sky had stepped to her side. Wendy could feel the woman's fingers curling in her hair and then she was being dragged to her feet. She muttered a small, pained scream but Sky seemed oblivious to the sound.

'I've been looking forward to meeting you,' Sky said, holding Wendy's hair tightly. 'And since you've just been eavesdropping I don't think you'll need that much of an explanation as to what's expected of you.'

'No . . . I . . .'

Sky shook her head until Wendy fell silent. 'Don't try and talk your way out of it,' she growled. 'You're coming with me, and I'm going to teach you about your new position at Elysian Fields.'

Pain erupted in Wendy's scalp as Sky dragged her out of the room.

Two hours later, Wendy's scalp still hurt when she touched it, but that was the least of her worries. She was boiling hot. Sweat streamed from her forehead into her eyes, and soaked the few clothes she was still

70

wearing. Her short dark hair was sodden with perspiration, which trickled in rivulets down her temples. She tried wiping her face dry with sweat-drenched fingers, then stopped herself as she realised how futile the attempt was. It coated her entire body. Not for the first time, she glanced at the porthole window on the locked sauna door and wondered what was going to happen next. She was dreading the Black Widow's return.

If her parched throat could have allowed it, Wendy would have cursed her own obsession with duty. If she had not been diligently doing her chores in the east wing, then she would never have glimpsed the intriguing sight of Sky dominating John. But Wendy knew she could not blame her work for this predicament.

The east-wing duties had been given to her six months earlier, when she started working at the health farm. Faye Meadows, the strict but fair owner of Elysian Fields, had impressed on Wendy the onerous importance of this task, stating repeatedly how vital the chore was. Her grave tone, stern expression and obvious trust left Wendy in no doubt that her duties there were crucial. Because of that conversation, she always attended to her work in the east wing before she started her shift. To leave it any later would have been a violation of Faye's trust.

Sitting in the sauna, glaring unhappily at the locked door, Wendy tried to take some solace from the thought that she had done her job well. It was a bitter consolation. The little comfort it brought was overshadowed by her darkening fear for the future.

Since she had started working at Elysian Fields, Wendy had embraced the health farm's hedonistic doctrine. After spending the last six months in a constant state of arousal, she could now feel herself being touched by an unfamiliar emotion. It was a feeling that had no right intruding into the warm, sunny world of Elysian Fields. It was a feeling that she had not known at Elysian Fields until she saw John being punished by Sky. The last two hours had brought it home to her. She was scared.

Wendy chewed nervously on her lower lip, glancing at the porthole window on the locked sauna door. Perhaps it would have been easier to deal with the emotion if she had been more familiar with it, Wendy thought. The last six months had been such a lavish indulgence in pleasure and fulfilment that she felt the fear like a freshly honed knife edge.

She pulled off her sweat-sodden T-shirt and sat awkwardly on the wooden bench, mopping her face with the soaked garment before angrily discarding it. Dressed only in bra and panties, she felt infuriatingly hot and was tempted to remove these items as well. If it had not been for the inevitable return of the Black Widow, she probably would have undressed completely. Wendy did not like the idea of being discovered with her sweat-oiled body completely naked. The thought made her shiver in spite of the heat.

Fanning herself with a lethargic hand, Wendy tried to stop thinking of the luxuries her body craved. Her lips were parched and a raging thirst burnt the back of her throat. Dwarfing that desire was her need for a clean, fresh towel. Sweat coated every millimetre of her muscular body and, while she might have found the sensation pleasurable under other circumstances, fear was dulling the eroticism of the moment. She wanted to enjoy a refreshing shower, then towel herself dry with a fluffy pink bath towel. Her yearning for this was so acute she felt dizzy with anticipation as she pictured it.

It occurred to her that she should try the door

again and see if she could raise the alarm but she stopped herself from wasting the energy. For the first hour of her imprisonment, she had beaten the door until her hands hurt. At the same time, she had screamed for help until her throat felt sore. Admittedly, a further hour had passed since then, but she knew that her attempts would be as hopeless now as they had been then. Her gaoler was in absolute control. It seemed more sensible to rest and conserve her energy until the Black Widow came back. Before locking the sauna door, she had threatened to return, and Wendy did not doubt the woman's sincerity.

Glancing down at her half-naked body, Wendy watched a rivulet of sweat trickle between the orbs of her breasts. She was still wearing her bra, and as the stream of sweat ran over her sun-bronzed flesh the moisture was caught by the fabric. Wendy gasped softly, unable to think of anything other than the intolerable heat.

She did not notice when a face appeared in the window of the sauna's door. The first indication she had of another person's presence was when Sky threw open the door and stepped into the sauna's steamy air. Wisps of pale-grey steam coloured the air around her, adding a dramatic effect to her arrival.

Earlier she had been angry and scared; determined not to be bullied. Now, because she felt so weak and drained, such emotions seemed beyond her repertoire.

A draught cooled her sodden body before the sauna's door was closed. Wendy took a moment to relish the icy blast, then she looked up at Sky and frowned.

Dressed in a short, black dressing-gown and a pair of black heels, the woman looked as forbidding as ever. Her mouth was set firm and her eyes were harsh and uncompromising. She had tied her long blonde hair up, revealing the slender elegance of her neck and emphasising her natural grace. In one hand she held a tray carrying a tall pitcher of water. Its glass sides were thickly marbled with condensation and it chimed musically as ice-cubes, floating on the cool water's surface, danced with one another. Wendy could feel her parched throat begging for a sip of the liquid. She swallowed thickly, then passed a sluggish tongue over her dehydrated lips.

In the other hand, Sky held a glass of water from which she sipped deliberately. As Wendy watched, Sky drank a mouthful of the icy liquid, allowing the ice-cubes to bounce lightly against her sensuous upper lip. She sighed with contentment and smiled at her prisoner as she placed her glass back on the tray.

Wendy glared at her, knowing this showy display of enjoyment was intended to make her feel worse. She wanted to say something: a stark condemnation of the type of woman who tortured people like this. The words were forming on her lips and she was about to give them voice. The only thing that stopped her was the sight of the towel.

Over one arm, Sky was carrying a fluffy pink bath towel.

Wendy stared at it longingly. She snatched back the breath that had been about to vent her diatribe and tried to maintain her composure. At the back of her mind she had been half-expecting Sky to come into the room armed with a pitcher of chilled mineral water, but she had never imagined the woman could be so incisive as to bring a fluffy pink bath towel.

'You saw what I did to John,' Sky growled, glaring angrily down at Wendy. 'So you'll know better than to get on my wrong side. I can achieve my goals with your help or without it. Things will be a lot easier for me if I have your cooperation, but they won't be impossible if you refuse.'

'What do you want from me?' Wendy asked, the words surfacing painfully. Rather than looking at Sky she was staring at the bath sheet. A wistful expression glazed her eyes.

'I want your cooperation,' Sky said. 'I'd thought that John might have been able to help, but he proved to be a little too wilful.' She shook her head, a regret-tinged smile twisting her lips. 'As I'm sure you heard, John has left Elysian Fields now.'

Wendy fixed Sky with a troubled expression. 'What were you doing to him?'

Sky shook her head, smiling cruelly. 'I didn't do anything to him that he didn't end up enjoying,' she whispered. 'I discovered he had a penchant for submission and he's gone away to explore that facet of his personality.' She studied Wendy's half-naked body appreciatively. 'Perhaps, if we use the same techniques on you, we might discover similar masochistic tendencies in your make-up.'

'You're sick,' Wendy whispered.

Sky turned round and took a step towards the door. 'If you don't want to talk in a civilised manner then I can come back in a couple of hours, when the heat has mellowed you some more.'

Wendy watched the woman reach for the door handle and knew that her chances of getting out of this humid hell were quickly dwindling. She reached a hand out to try to stop Sky. Her mouth was now too dry to articulate words, and, instead of making an intelligent sound, she croaked a cry reminiscent of an injured animal's pitiful wail.

Sky half-turned and fixed her with a quizzical expression. 'Are you prepared to act with some civility?'

Wendy nodded, trying to swallow the thick lump in her dry throat.

'Very well,' Sky said, moving her hand away from the door. She glided gracefully back into the sauna and settled herself on the stiff wooden bench next to Wendy. Casually, she placed her tray and the fluffy pink towel down by her side.

Wendy studied the iced water and the towel as Sky started talking. Those items seemed far more significant and relevant than anything her captor was likely to say.

'You asked me what I wanted from you,' Sky began, speaking in a brusque, no-nonsense tone. 'And because we're being honest and up front with one another, I'll tell you. I want your help, Wendy. I want someone strong and capable, like you, to run Elysian Fields. If there's someone managing this place for the benefit of the paying customers, then the main business is being taken care of. If that's being done properly, then I can concentrate on my own plans.' She paused, pursing her lips. 'Although I did say that I could manage without any assistance, I'll be totally honest and say that things would be a lot easier if you did help.' As she spoke, Sky lifted the glass of water and raised it to her lips.

Wendy watched the woman sip idly from the glass. She knew that if her mouth had not been a parched desert she would have been drooling as she watched Sky enjoying her drink.

'I'm not asking a lot, am I?' Sky asked, moving her hand close to Wendy's shoulder. Her fingers still held her drink and the base of the glass traced an icy line against Wendy's burning flesh. For one glorious instant her shoulder was cooled by the chill.

Dizzy with exhaustion, Wendy tried to contain her excitement. She could see two melting squares of ice

76

floating on the water. As she watched, Sky drew the glass downward, allowing the cool base of the tumbler to rub into the valley of Wendy's cleavage.

Aware that Sky was waiting for a response to her question, she murmured, 'No. You're not asking a lot.'

Her eyes were closed and she could feel her heart beating fast with a combination of gratitude and arousal. The chilled glass between her breasts was bringing a delicious coolness, its intensity matched only by the growing heat between her thighs.

She was aware that the Black Widow was a dangerous creature who richly deserved her nickname, but that did not seem as important as it had earlier. In her tired and vulnerable state, Wendy was beginning to think the woman's plans to take control of the health farm were almost benign. With the exception of John, she had not hurt anyone in her quest for power and her principal concern so far had been for the welfare of the clientele.

'Look at you!' Sky said, pretending to notice Wendy's near nudity for the first time. 'You're sweating an ocean and that bra looks so uncomfortable.' She smiled reassuringly, placed her drink down, and whispered, 'Let me help.' With dextrous fingers she quickly unfastened Wendy's bra and dropped it to the floor.

Wendy allowed her to do this even though she had already noticed that Sky was lecherously admiring her breasts. As the woman moved a hesitant finger towards her flesh, Wendy held her breath. The tips of Sky's fingers traced over the hardening nub of her nipple and she shivered despite the cloying heat.

'Now, let me help you to cool down,' Sky insisted. She reached for the glass and sipped from it. Her lips were still dripping with chilled water when she put down the glass. Wendy could feel small droplets splashing against her burning skin as Sky moved over her. And then they were kissing.

Wendy drew a grateful breath as Sky's tongue worked its way into her mouth. Rather than the heated exchange she had been expecting, Sky's mouth was ice cool and that much more exciting because of it. Wendy shifted forward, determined to embrace the woman and return the pleasure she was receiving. Her bare breasts rubbed against the coarse towelling fabric of Sky's dressing-gown and one of the woman's naked thighs slid against her sweat-oiled legs. She was kissing Sky with a furious passion, allowing her tongue to delve into the cool haven of her mouth.

'We'll have plenty of time for this later,' Sky gasped, breaking the kiss. She placed a firm hand on Wendy's muscular thigh and said, 'We'll be working on your pleasure first.' Sky reached to her side and dipped her fingers into the glass of water.

Wendy watched as Sky extracted a single ice-cube, held it up to eye level and smiled thoughtfully through it. A bead of water tumbled down her thumb, over the palm of her hand, then down her wrist. Following its journey with her gaze, Wendy watched it disappear inside the sleeve of the dressing-gown.

Sky shivered as the water surprised some intimate part of her flesh. The smile she used on Wendy was suddenly broader. 'It's quite refreshing, isn't it?'

Not knowing how refreshing it was, Wendy shrugged wordlessly. She was staring at the ice-cube with reverential awe.

'Let me show you.' Sky held the cube over Wendy's chest for a brief moment, allowing it to drip twice on to her flesh.

The droplets were icy cold, striking her hot skin like frozen bullets. Wendy gasped as though she had been stung. Her eyes widened as she watched Sky slowly lowering her fingers.

Rubbing one flat surface of the ice between Wendy's trembling breasts, Sky eased the cube lazily over her body. She allowed it to slide over the warmth of Wendy's breast then circle close to the pale-pink flesh of her areola. Wendy closed her eyes and stiffened on the uncomfortable wooden bench. Excited tremors were coursing their way through her entire body and her sighs grew heavier.

The ice was freezing against her nipple, but Wendy relished the sensation. She pushed herself on to the cube, groaning as the pleasure that had threatened to course through her finally took hold. Sky leant forward and placed a kiss on her mouth. She squeezed the ice-cube hard against Wendy's bare breast as their lips met.

Wendy responded excitedly, plunging her tongue into the cool, silky haven of Sky's mouth. The intensity of her arousal was surprising but not unwelcome. When their mouths separated, Wendy smiled into Sky's grinning face.

Sky brushed the melting ice-cube over Wendy's lips. With a wicked expression glinting in her eyes, she rubbed it around Wendy's gaping mouth, then against her tongue.

Gasping, Wendy accepted the ice, relishing the tiny speck of refreshment it provided. The lingering flavour of her own sweat clung to the cube, adding to her excitement. The ice seemed to evaporate as soon as it touched the inside of her mouth but a sliver of chilled water trickled down the arid tract of her throat. She was almost overcome by the intensity of her body's heightened response.

'Take these off,' Sky said. Wendy opened her eyes and saw the woman was tugging gently at her panties.

A warning voice at the back of her mind demanded she show some caution. Perhaps the men had been exaggerating with their tales about the Black Widow, but to the rational part of her mind that seemed unlikely. Mounting excitement and heat-exhausted weariness helped Wendy ignore the internal voice of reason. Without giving the matter any serious thought, she lifted her legs and slid the sweat-soaked panties away from her body. She dropped them to the floor and rubbed splayed fingers through the forest of pubic hairs above her sex.

Sky released a growl of appreciation, a salacious smile spreading across her lips. She had her fingers buried in the half-drained tumbler and was fumbling purposefully in the water.

With a shiver of anticipation, Wendy watched the woman lift a second ice-cube from the glass. Cold droplets splashed against Wendy's inner thighs. The much-yearned-for chill was so acute that she groaned deeply. Sky pushed the flat surface of the ice-cube against the sweat-slicked lips of Wendy's sex. Wendy heard herself scream. The sound came from some place between agony and ecstasy, although she could not decide which emotion was the strongest. As if the pressure of the ice-cube were not stimulation enough, she realised that Sky was rubbing it gently against her. The entire length of her pussy was chilled as Sky stroked the cube deliberately up and down. Then, without any warning, she was forcing the smooth frigid surface against the hood of Wendy's pulsing clitoris.

Wendy pushed a hand down between her legs and clenched her fingers tight round Sky's wrist. It had been her intention to move the woman's hand away. She could sense the ferocious power of her impending climax and its enormity frightened her. She quickly realised that Sky wanted to keep her fingers where they were. There was determination flashing in the depths of her hazel eyes and Wendy knew it would be futile to try to struggle against the woman. She glanced unhappily into Sky's face, wishing there was some way of reasoning with her. Seeing her blank, uncompromising smile, Wendy realised she was at the woman's mercy. Regardless of how intense it was likely to be, Wendy knew she was going to have to endure this orgasm.

A bitter smile twisted Sky's face as she pushed the ice-cube harder against Wendy's sex. With squirming fingers, she twisted the flat surface into the throbbing ball of Wendy's clitoris.

Wendy groaned, snatching a breath as the threat of an orgasm edged closer. The sensation of melting water between her legs was so exquisite she could not contain her excitement. The ferocious explosion of pleasure was welling to a crescendo when Sky moved her hand slightly. Wendy gasped and tried to push it away, fearful of enduring too much pleasure. But Sky held her hand firmly in place, and despite Wendy's protestations, despite her struggling, Sky slid the ice-cube between the lips of Wendy's labia. With one long, graceful finger, she pushed it deep into her cleft.

The scream that echoed around the sauna was so piercing it could have shattered crystal. Wendy was struck by a powerful climax that caused red dots to erupt in front of her eyes. Distantly, she guessed that she had come close to passing out, and the thought unsettled her. She studied Sky with renewed admiration, blinking at her as she tried to clear her vision.

Sky was grinning. If Wendy had known her better she would have realised this was the predatory grin of the Black Widow. But this was the first time Wendy had seen the expression and she did not know what to expect.

Sky circled her arm round Wendy's waist and eased her away from the bench. She embraced her for a second, allowing Wendy the chance to rub her hot, sweaty body against the woman's cool, dry robe. Then Sky was guiding her down, on to her knees.

Pliant and eager to do whatever Sky asked, Wendy moved into position. When she was finished, Wendy was kneeling between Sky's legs, smiling avidly up into her sombre face.

'Are we friends now, Wendy?'

Wendy nodded, a heartfelt sigh shuddering from her chest. 'We're friends,' she agreed.

Patiently, Sky asked, 'Are we friends who help one another?'

Wendy nodded again, unable to suppress her eagerness to agree. 'Of course we are,' she said enthusiastically.

'Of course,' Sky repeated. 'I just helped you enjoy yourself, didn't I? Now, I'm going to help you to a drink of water. Then you're going to help me.'

Wendy did not hear the last five words of Sky's sentence. Her attention was caught by the mention of a drink. She stared past Sky, gazing at the pitcher of ice-cold water with a dreamy smile.

Holding Wendy's face steady with her hands, Sky stared into her eyes. 'Are you going to help me when we've finished?'

Wendy swallowed dryly, then tried to look beyond Sky's shoulder at the pitcher of water and the fluffy pink towel. 'Of course,' she whispered. 'Of course I will.'

Sky smiled to herself. 'Of course,' she repeated happily. 'You're going to run Elysian Fields for me and do exactly as I say?'

Wendy was so desperate to enjoy a taste of the chilled water she would have agreed to any demand that Sky made. Simply promising to look after the health farm and do Sky's bidding hardly seemed a difficult task. It was almost as though the Black Widow was being charitable and, for that, Wendy felt grateful. She had forgotten about the cruel treatment John had suffered and her morning's imprisonment in the sauna. Her earlier antipathy was now replaced by a growing respect.

'You do understand that I'm now in control of Elysian Fields, don't you?'

Wendy swallowed and whispered, 'Yes.'

'And do I take it that you'll answer to me, above anyone else?' Sky pressed.

Wendy nodded again, eager to agree to anything Sky asked. Her gaze kept switching to the pitcher of water and she tried to stop herself from being distracted.

'You'll even accept my instructions over those that Faye Meadows gives you?' Sky asked suddenly. There was a harshness to her voice as she asked the question and Wendy blinked twice before answering.

'I don't know,' she began. Seeing the frown cross Sky's brow, she realised she had given the wrong answer. Wendy shook her head, cursed herself, then nodded, suddenly confused by the difficult task of supplying a yes-or-no answer. 'Of course,' she gasped quickly. She knew she had spoken the words too hastily and too late but once they were said there was nothing she could do. It was not that she wanted to disobey the Black Widow. Right now, she was more than happy to do anything the woman commanded. The furious pulse of her arousal would not have allowed her to respond any differently.

But the idea of following Sky's instruction over

Faye's was something different. Agreeing to that would be a violation of the trust that the owner had invested in her and Wendy felt uncomfortable with that prospect. She had agreed only to appease the Black Widow but she had done so in such a way that they both knew it was a lie. For an instant, Wendy was touched by the fear of Sky's retribution. The thought sent an icy chill through her and she stared miserably into the woman's eyes.

Sky smiled warmly into Wendy's weary face. 'You look ready for that drink,' she observed. Her voice was overly rich with kindness. Her soft smile and gentle tone seemed so sincere that Wendy wondered if her lie had been accepted. Sky seemed to have moved on from her list of demands and Wendy felt her fears ease.

Wendy nodded, her eyes widening as she watched Sky lift the pitcher of water from the tray beside her. 'I'm more than ready,' she agreed. 'I'm desperate.'

Still grinning, Sky brought the pitcher of water between them. With her free hand, she tugged the length of cord from her dressing-gown. Wendy caught a shadowed glimpse of the woman's nudity, but her concentration was centred on the pitcher.

'Desperate,' Sky laughed softly, repeating Wendy's word. With a casual flick of her fingertips, she pushed the dressing-gown open to reveal her naked body. Her nipples were rigid with excitement and her shaved pussy lips were dark and swollen. 'I'm fairly desperate myself,' Sky remarked, her sultry tone making the meaning of her words obvious. 'Should we do something about that before we satisfy your thirst, or do you think we can combine the two?'

A frown crossed Wendy's brow. 'How?'

Smiling into her consternation, Sky stroked long fingers through the hairs at the nape of Wendy's neck. Using the gentlest pressure, she pulled Wendy's head close to her breast, and whispered, 'Let me show you how.'

Wendy allowed herself to be pulled closer, dark arousal churning her stomach as her lips neared Sky's nipple. She was prepared to let the tip of her tongue dance against the woman's flesh, eager to repay some of the pleasure she had just enjoyed.

As her tongue met Sky's breast, she felt the first splash against her face. Glancing up, she saw the Black Widow pouring chilled water on to the heated union between her breast and Wendy's mouth.

Struck by a sudden avaricious need, Wendy began to lick the ice-cold water from the woman's body. She felt Sky tense as the chilly liquid froze her flesh, but the woman's groan of enjoyment revealed her true feelings.

Wendy licked at Sky's body in a furious attempt to satisfy her craving. Her need to taste the water was an overwhelming compulsion. Without realising she had done it, she embraced Sky's narrow waist and held her tightly in her arms. Her tongue and lips rubbed over the feverishly hot flesh of Sky's breast.

The two women sighed as their separate appetites were brought closer to satisfaction. Laughing softly, Sky tipped the brim of the pitcher and poured an icy stream of water over her other breast.

Wendy released an excited shriek and moved her mouth against the cool, wet flesh. She sucked hard on the nipple. Rubbing her lips greedily over Sky's breast, she tried to lick up every last droplet of water. As she pressed her mouth against Sky's body, Wendy squeezed herself close to the woman and moaned softly. She could feel Sky shivering and wondered if it was caused by the icy chill of the water, or her mounting excitement. Listening to the woman's quickening cries of arousal, Wendy supposed it did not take a genius to work out the true source.

'Here,' Sky gasped. She was holding the pitcher at eye level, her hand shaking slightly. 'Try this,' she commanded.

Wendy's lips playfully teased one nipple as she looked into Sky's face.

Sky groaned and splashed water over her body once again. This time the stream of chilled water ran between her bare breasts. Wendy moved to get her mouth against the liquid but Sky held her hair tightly for a moment. The two women exchanged glances: Wendy's hurt and puzzled; Sky's cruel and confident.

Sky waited until the water had pooled between her legs, holding her fingers tightly in Wendy's hair. As the last droplet rolled over her shaved labia, she smiled salaciously and pushed Wendy's head down.

Wendy pressed her mouth against Sky's sex without a word of protest. She stroked her tongue against the glistening-wet pussy lips, lapping greedily at the woman's hole.

Sky groaned. Her fingers were still buried among the hairs at the nape of Wendy's neck and she kept tight hold, continually forcing her down.

Wendy dared not resist as her head was pushed lower. The side of her face was pressed against the bench while she stroked her tongue against the slippery lips of Sky's pussy. And still the woman kept a firm hold of her hair.

'Lick it all up,' Sky gasped, the words broken by her mounting enjoyment.

Wendy could feel an excited tremor shaking the arm that held her. Her own greed for the water would have made her lick Sky's sex happily, but the woman's stern command reminded her that she was not just drinking. Determined to please her, Wendy pushed her tongue into the velvety depths of Sky's sex.

Sky groaned.

Wendy pushed her tongue deeper, sensing the musky fragrance of Sky's arousal. Instead of lapping up chilled water, she was drinking warm, syrupy pussy honey. Its sweet taste and mellifluous scent inspired the return of her own arousal. As she buried her tongue into the slippery warmth of Sky's sex, Wendy could feel the pulse of her own desire beating with renewed vigour.

'My clit,' Sky gasped, passion tearing the words from her throat. 'Tongue my clit.'

Wendy obeyed without hesitation. She slid her tongue from the warm confines of Sky's pussy and trilled the tip against her pulsing pearl of pleasure.

Sky shrieked furious words of elation as the thrill of an orgasm began to gather.

Wendy could feel the woman was tense and ready to explode. The thighs by her face were rigid with pent-up pleasure. The hands that held her head were pushing furiously down. Wendy continued to tap her tongue against the woman's erect clitoris, extracting as much pleasure from Sky's climax as she had from her own. As Sky reached the pinnacle of her orgasm, a misty spray of pussy honey splashed Wendy's nose and lips.

Sky's groan of joy echoed dully around the sauna walls. It was a guttural drawl, filled with dark, meaningless expletives. From between the woman's legs, Wendy watched her rock her head from side to side. Her teeth were clenched tightly in a grimace of delight.

Wendy had expected the woman to release her head when the orgasm struck, but Sky made no attempt to move her hands. Conversely, she seemed to hold the hair in a tighter grip and Wendy was touched by a rising tide of panic that snatched the air from her lungs.

'Good,' Sky breathed quietly, staring down at her. Her voice trembled slightly with the aftermath of her enjoyment, but other than that she seemed to be in absolute control once again. 'You've just proved how useful you can be,' she whispered. 'Let's see if we're still agreed on the terms of our working relationship.'

With her head pressed against the bench, Wendy could do nothing but glance up fearfully.

'Who's in control of Elysian Fields?' Sky asked.

Wendy drew a shivering breath. 'You are,' she said firmly.

Sky smiled. 'And who's going to run this place for me, for the foreseeable future?'

'I am,' Wendy said quickly.

Still smiling, Sky nodded. 'And whose instructions do you follow from now on? Mine or Faye Meadows'?'

'Yours,' Wendy said immediately. She was determined that there would be no trace of doubt or hesitancy in her tone this time. 'I follow your instructions.'

Sky nodded, seemingly satisfied with this response. 'You were a little unsure about that point earlier,' she observed quietly. 'And while I admire your dedication to Faye, I need to be absolutely sure that you're on my side.'

'Of course,' Wendy gasped, trying to nod from her position between Sky's legs, trapped against the bench. 'Of course,' she repeated nervously.

'Well,' Sky began hesitantly. 'While I'd like to believe you, without hesitation, I think we ought to have another little drink together.'

Wendy frowned, not sure she had heard correctly, or if she had understood the woman.

'Another drink,' Sky said, pouring icy-cold water over her chest and on to Wendy's upturned face. 'Have this drink with me, then I'll feel better about trusting you.'

Wendy pushed her tongue against Sky's sex and began to lap furiously at her cleft. The icy water had been a welcoming balm before, but now, as it splashed up her nose and into her mouth, she felt close to gagging on it. The idea of being drowned by a combination of iced water and Sky's pussy honey did not seem particularly outrageous. As her lungs struggled to snatch a breath of air, her rising panic returned with a vengeance.

Sky sucked hungry breath, holding Wendy firmly as her sex was treated to another debilitating session of the woman's kisses. 'Oh, yes,' she growled softly. 'Carry on doing that and I'll have no problem about trusting you,' she told Wendy encouragingly.

With water still splashing on and around her face, Wendy gasped and tried to shake her head. Her tongue was working furiously on Sky's labia. She was blinking the ice-cold liquid from her eyes and snorting it out of her nostrils in a desperate attempt to see and breathe while she performed the task. She knew that the woman wanted proof of her absolute submission but Wendy could not think how to express it. She was prepared to do anything Sky asked and, as she lapped at the woman's hole, she tried to think of the words that would reinforce that point.

'Who's in control?' Sky demanded suddenly.

Wendy slid her tongue from the silken warmth of the woman's pussy. 'You are,' she gasped, injecting her words with such frank sincerity there could be no question of disobedience. 'You're in charge.'

'And whose orders do you follow now?' Sky asked sharply.

'Yours,' Wendy sighed with absolute honesty. 'I'll follow your orders.'

'No one else's?' Sky pressed.

'I'll only follow your orders,' Wendy insisted.

Sky drew a triumphant breath and finally released Wendy's hair from her punishing grip. 'That's what I wanted to hear.'

Continuing to lap at the woman's sex, Wendy swallowed thickly. It pained her to realise it but she had meant every word of her promise. With the exception of her duties in the east wing, she was no longer working for Faye Meadows. Now, she was the devoted subordinate of the Black Widow.

Five

There was an air of barely controlled chaos behind the reception desk.

Still wearing the dark glasses that had protected her from the morning sun, Jo stood by her luggage, smiling patiently as she took in her surroundings. The reception area was pleasantly lit, with full-length windows overlooking the landscaped grounds that surrounded Elysian Fields.

Outside, bathed in the beauty of the early-morning sunlight, a handful of women lazed in robes on polished, wooden benches. The verdant lawn they walked on was a well-maintained carpet of crisp green that looked so sumptuous and inviting Jo longed to walk barefoot on it.

Although it was deserted, the interior of the reception area looked just as pleasant. A sign on the back wall, illustrated by arrows, showed the direction of various gym rooms, pools, saunas and an eatery, but this was the only concession to the practicalities of the health farm. Everywhere else seemed to concentrate on a stylish air of pleasant familiarity. The light, wicker furniture and pale, floral trimmings created an ambience that was spacious but welcoming.

Jo would have thought the reception area a lot more welcoming if the staff had tried to deal with their problems professionally. Instead, the two receptionists had shut themselves in a room behind the desk and were shouting at one another in pantomime whispers. Trying to appear nonchalant and disinterested, Jo calmly studied her surroundings and listened intently to everything they said.

In a way, Jo supposed she was responsible for some of their problems. Yesterday, when she had eventually relented and agreed to work on this case, she had made a hurried booking at Elysian Fields. In an uncharacteristic attempt at frugality, she had asked for the cheapest room with minimum services.

An hour later, after Sam had pissed her off, Jo called back and increased the expense of her stay. Shortly after that, and Jo strongly suspected that Sam had been involved somewhere, Doctor McMahon telephoned the office and lectured Jo at great length about her need for some time away from work. After enduring the doctor's endless tirade, Jo had called Elysian Fields and demanded the most prestigious suite available with all the facilities and features they could foist upon her.

She supposed she should have done as much in the first place. It was not as though she had to pay for any of it. What she did not charge to the client's expenses, Jo knew Sam would happily pay for. With that devil-may-care attitude colouring her view, Jo had actually found herself looking forward to the break at Elysian Fields.

Watching the receptionists argue over the diary in their office, Jo tried to recall if she had cancelled the first or the second booking. The idea of having three rooms waiting for her did not seem that improbable and she cringed from the thought of having to explain her mistake to the two dour-faced bitches who worked behind the reception desk. It was much easier

92

to simply pretend she was a victim of the problem rather than the cause of it.

A noise behind her snatched Jo from her musings.

The main doors opened and a tall, willowy woman struggled in beneath the weight of two heavy suitcases. Jo watched her dump the luggage by the door, glance warily around, then walk to the reception desk.

There was nothing spectacular about the newcomer. She was young but a little plain, Jo thought, and her dress sense was so dowdy it looked like she was applying for a job in a charity shop. Her shapeless cardigan hugged small breasts and disguised the shape of her waist and hips. Her ankle-length A-line skirt was so similar in colour to the cardigan that it looked badly matched, and again it disguised more of her figure than it revealed. Like Jo, she wore a pair of impenetrable sunglasses, but as she approached the reception desk she snatched these away from her face.

Jo's interest in the new arrival would have disappeared completely if she had not seen what the woman held in her hand. For an instant the panicked exchange between the two receptionists was forgotten. Jo blinked, then squinted through her sunglasses, trying to see if her eyes were playing tricks.

'Hello,' the woman murmured softly, leaning against the reception desk.

Jo stepped closer to her. 'They're having a bit of a panic this morning.' She nodded in the direction of the office behind the desk. 'I think they've got a couple of unexpected staff absences.'

The woman nodded and rolled her eyes. 'Just my luck to arrive here and find the staff have stopped working.'

Jo smiled sympathetically. 'It's not just less staff

than was expected,' she confided. 'I accidentally booked three different rooms here yesterday. They're still trying to decide which one to put me in.' She glanced at the piece of red plastic in the woman's hand, desperately wanting to get a proper look at it. If her suspicions were correct, Jo thought she could take a step closer to the satisfactory conclusion of this case. Talking to the newcomer could help throw some light on the mystery before she started investigating it properly.

'Is that one of those personal invitations I've heard so much about?' she asked carefully. Speaking quickly, so that the woman did not suspect a motive behind her questions, Jo added, 'I have a friend who received something similar. I could have sworn it looked like that.'

Feigning nonchalant familiarity, Jo eased herself closer to Poppy. The fresh smell of the woman's cologne wafted against her nostrils, and, beneath that, Jo could sense the warmth of her nearness. She could feel the first stirrings of an unbidden arousal tingling between her legs.

Oblivious to Jo's proximity, the woman nodded and grinned. Pride and excitement were shining in her eyes. Passing the piece of plastic to Jo, she said, 'Yes, it is. Take a look at it. I can't believe my good fortune in actually receiving one. Do you know how long I've been working as a solicitor?'

It was a peculiar question and Jo shook her head in response as she studied the invitation. It was identical to the one Faye Meadows had been sent, with the exception of the woman's name. This invitation was made out to Poppy Darling. 'How long have you been working as a solicitor, Poppy?' Jo asked, handing the card back.

'Four years,' Poppy replied, taking the invitation.

'Four long years, and this is the first gratuity I've ever received.' She waved the card in a trembling hand, simultaneously expressing her anger and triumph in the same gesture. Smiling wearily, she said, 'I suppose it's just as well this place is a health farm. A fortnight's break is the one thing I could really use at the moment.'

Jo nodded and tried to look understanding. 'You must have really impressed your client to merit a fortnight's free stay here.'

Poppy shrugged. 'I guess I must have,' she agreed. 'Although, to tell you the truth, I'm not sure who sent it.'

Jo laughed softly. 'You've received your first gratuity in four years and you don't know who sent it to you?'

Poppy smiled awkwardly into Jo's mirth-filled face. The expression stretched awkwardly along her lips and illuminated her otherwise dull features. Jo reprimanded herself for almost dismissing Poppy as plain and uninteresting. There was an allure to the woman's smile that hinted at fantastic beauty, if only she had made the effort to release her potential.

'It didn't even occur to me to think about that,' Poppy explained. 'I know that I've never actually done any work for Elysian Fields. And I don't think I've worked for anyone directly linked to this place ...' Her voice trailed off and her eyes took on a faraway expression, as though she was seriously trying to remember whom she had been employed by over the past four years.

Jo watched her, wishing she did not find the woman so damnably interesting.

Poppy shrugged again and smiled uneasily. 'I had wondered about who sent it but I'd decided not to push it. Once I'd confirmed that the invitation was

95

genuine, and it was going to be honoured, that was enough for me.' A frown crossed her brow and she stared solemnly down at the reception desk. Speaking in a world-weary voice, she said, 'It was hard enough getting the time off work. I've heard about people having to bend over backward to get holidays, but I had to do a damned sight more than that.' She shook her head, laughed darkly, then winked mischievously at Jo. 'I think I can look forward to bending over backward when I return,' she added. 'But what the hell?'

Jo frowned uncertainly, not sure what the woman meant by the comment. Suddenly, she was sure of one thing. Whatever Poppy Darling was like as a solicitor, Jo doubted she resembled the creature who now stood in front of her. It was an unusual thought for Jo, but she felt certain that the idea of a break was allowing this dowdy woman her first chance at self-expression. It occurred to her that her first impression of Poppy might have been unfair and she looked forward to reassessing her over the next two weeks. Admittedly, Poppy was unexciting to look at, but there was something about the mischievous glint in her eyes that Jo found distinctly appealing. She could feel herself being drawn to the woman for no reason other than the light in her eyes and she wondered if Poppy might be the type to reciprocate such feelings. It seemed unlikely, Jo supposed, but she could feel the spreading warmth of excitement between her legs as she mentally pictured herself kissing the woman. The image was so powerful Jo tried to stop herself from succumbing to the feelings of mounting arousal that sparkled in the pit of her stomach.

Seemingly oblivious to this, Poppy waved a flippant hand, dismissing her earlier lapse into melancholy reverie. 'Anyway,' she said, forcing her mood to brighten, 'I'm here now, and that's the main thing.' She struck her hand against the small bell on the reception desk, sending a shrill ring echoing through the room.

One of the receptionists opened the door a quarter of an inch and glanced angrily through the gap. Once she had the woman's attention, Poppy waved her red and gold invitation as though it was a Masonic handshake.

Jo frowned when she saw the look of consternation cross the receptionist's face. The woman turned to face her colleague and Jo heard the words, 'One of them's here. It's one of those cards.'

Then the door slammed shut.

Poppy and Jo exchanged a glance.

'They need to learn a little about customer relations,' Poppy observed.

'That's an understatement,' Jo said softly. 'They're bloody hibernating.' She smiled tightly, her unease suddenly growing. She was about to offer Poppy a word of warning when the door behind the desk burst open and the two receptionists rushed out to greet them.

'Sorry about that,' they said in unison. One of them was speaking to Jo; the other was directing her words at Poppy. Jo glanced at the pair of them and saw that the woman addressing Poppy wore a badge on her lapel bearing the name Wendy.

Jo's receptionist did not have a name badge. 'Thank you for being so patient,' Jo was told by the nameless receptionist.

'Could I see your invitation?' Wendy asked Poppy.

Jo glanced over, trying to make her interest look casual. Her own receptionist was murmuring something about a problem with overbooking, but Jo was happy to ignore her.

'Can you tell me, Wendy?' she began suddenly. 'Those invitations look very special. I was thinking of sending one as an anonymous gift to a friend. If I did, would there be any way of her finding out who sent it?'

The two receptionists exchanged a glance.

'I'll get some information sent up to your room, Miss Valentine,' Wendy said firmly.

Jo turned to stare at Poppy, wondering if the woman was going to ask about the invitation now, while the conversation allowed it. She could see Poppy glancing curiously at her and Jo raised an eyebrow.

'Do you know who sent this one?' Poppy asked after a moment's silence.

Wendy smiled tightly, then rubbed a casual hand through her short hair. She cast a dark glare at Jo before turning to her books. 'I'm sure I can find that out for you,' she said stiffly. 'I'll just organise your room first and then I'll get the information sent up to you.'

How peculiar, Jo thought dryly. This woman doesn't say, 'Fuck off and stop bothering me;' she says, 'I'll get the information sent up to you.' The thought brought a smile to her lips.

'If you'd care to follow me,' Wendy said to Poppy, 'we can go through your needs and requirements for the next two weeks.' She began to usher Poppy out of the reception area and through a door into the main building.

'Will I be seeing you around, Poppy?' Jo called softly.

Poppy turned to her and smiled happily. 'Count on it.' The mischievous glint shone in her eyes again and, for the second time, Jo was touched by a wave of longing for the woman. She realised Wendy was glaring at her, but for the moment that did not matter. All that mattered was the alluring hint of wickedness in Poppy's smile.

Watching the door close on Poppy and Wendy, Jo wondered why she could feel her stomach muscles tightening nervously. Something was giving her serious cause for concern and she wished she could put her finger on the source. Frowning darkly, she realised the remaining receptionist was studying her sullenly. 'Where are they off to?' Jo asked.

'Wendy is taking Miss Darling for the standard induction,' the receptionist explained. 'Allen will be down to induct you shortly.'

'I can hardly wait,' Jo said, rolling her eyes sarcastically. 'Who sent Poppy that invitation?'

The receptionist snorted haughtily. 'I can't tell you that.'

'Of course you can,' Jo assured her. 'Poppy will tell me before the end of the day, so you'll just be cutting out the middleman.'

The receptionist shook her head. 'If Miss Darling's going to tell you, then I don't need to jeopardise Elysian Fields' reputation for discretion, do I?' A knowing smile crossed her lips and she added, 'You just wait until she tells you what you want to know. That way, we'll all be happy.'

Bitch, Jo thought sourly. In an uncharacteristic display of tact, she did not give voice to the thought.

Jo had not expected a proper answer from the woman but the one she had been given was far more detailed than she could have hoped. The receptionist was determined not to share her knowledge about the invitation but Jo could tell the woman was bursting with some private secret that she longed to divulge. The nastiness in her tone and the wicked lilt to her smile left Jo fearing for Poppy's safety.

If it had not been for Allen's timely arrival, she might have pursued the matter further. However, Allen was gorgeous and Jo could feel his presence causing an undeniable distraction. As he bent over to pick up her luggage, she studied the rounded swell of his tight, pert buttocks and allowed herself an indulgent smile. It took willpower to stop her hand from reaching out and stroking his arse, but Jo managed to resist. She had already decided there would be time to play once Allen had taken the cases up to her room.

He grinned at her and whispered, 'Follow me.' Jo found herself unable to resist. His voice was tinged with the unmistakable lilt of a Welsh brogue and, while it was not an accent she usually found exciting, Jo could feel herself warming to the easy familiarity in his tone. For the moment she was able to dismiss Poppy, and the receptionists' unusual behaviour, from her thoughts.

Allen closed the door of her suite and stepped into Jo's arms. She wanted to embrace him warmly and rub her flat stomach against the urgent bulge at the front of his shorts. Instead, she took a step back from him and graced him with a sceptical frown. 'Say that again,' she said doubtfully. 'I'm not sure I heard you correctly.'

He smiled with such arrogant confidence it bordered on conceit. His gaze swept over her and Jo knew he was not just picturing her naked: in his mind's eye he had already fucked her twice and was making himself hard for a third attempt. She knew she should have found his egotism annoying or infuriating and, under other circumstances, Jo knew she would have dismissed him or put him in his place.

But, she could feel the quickening beat of the pulse

between her legs. The spreading warmth of her arousal was exhilarating and undeniable, striking her with a force so strong that Jo thanked God she did not have the willpower to resist.

'You heard me correctly,' Allen grinned. He had a broad frame with long blond hair spilling over his shoulders. His matching shorts and T-shirt hugged his body with the closeness of a lover, revealing every subtle nuance of his figure. His face was youthful and handsome. Allen grinned at her with obvious appreciation. Daringly, he stepped closer. 'Don't try and tell me that you don't know about Elysian Fields, because I won't believe you.'

Jo shook her head, still feeling certain that he was trying to use a line on her. She did not mind if he was trying to chat her up. He was the type of long-haired, muscular guy whom she was happy to have as a lover. However, she had detected a hint of truth in his words and the notion had piqued her interest. 'I didn't read the literature,' Jo explained. 'What was that you just said about attaining physical perfection through . . .' Her voice trailed off and she shook her head, not wanting to embarrass herself if she had misunderstood.

'Attaining physical perfection through the efforts of the most satisfying exercise.' He raised his eyebrows knowingly, then winked at her. 'Normally at this stage, you'd be taken for an induction and your exact needs would be assessed. But the girls behind the desk are a tad busy this morning.' He smiled lecherously and took another step closer. 'I thought I could tempt you with a little induction of my own.' His hand reached out and boldly stroked the swell of her breast through the taut fabric of her blouse.

Jo shuddered, not surprised by the wealth of

pleasurable sensations his fingertips inspired. She tried to study the sincerity of his pale blue eyes. When she realised he was telling the truth, the excitement flared inside her with breathtaking intensity.

'I'm not sure,' she began, hesitantly. Thoughts of how Sam would react if she was unfaithful suddenly troubled Jo's little-used conscience. She wondered if her new partner was as ignorant of the Elysian Fields doctrine as she had been. Surely she had to be, her rational mind insisted. If Sam had known about the hedonistic regime at the health farm, Jo felt certain she would have said something. With mounting panic, she quickly tried to backtrack over each of her conversations with Sam from the previous day.

The entire afternoon had been peppered with so many pointless arguments Jo realised that Sam could have said anything during one of the periods when she was deliberately not listening. Angrily, she cursed her own pigheadedness and wished she had not been behaving like such a child. She could not decide whether Sam would have approved and for a brief moment that seemed like a very important consideration.

Then Allen moved closer.

Jo could feel the bulge at the front of his shorts pressing firmly against her stomach. She tried not to think of the slow, deliberate pulse that throbbed there. The stimulation was already proving too extreme, but she knew she could maintain some of her resolve if she did not try to form a mental picture of his eager length. Seeing the length of long, pink flesh in her mind's eye would have pushed her willpower beyond breaking point.

'What is there not to be sure about?' Allen coaxed. His lips were hovering inches above her mouth and Jo yearned to feel his kiss. One hand brushed against her waist before moving on to caress her buttocks. His other hand stroked softly against the ample rise of her breast. Through the sheer, satin fabric of her blouse, the ball of his thumb carelessly rubbed across her aching nipple.

Jo sighed heavily, trying to think of a reason why she should fight against the sultry appeal of his words. Her concern for Sam's opinion was rapidly dwindling, helped by the ardent thrill that Allen's touch inspired. It was no great deal, she assured herself. Sam had actually sent her to Elysian Fields and if she could not cope with what was about to happen then that was her problem, Jo thought decisively. She was still trying to rationalise this argument, and reach her own level of comfort with it, when Allen kissed her.

Jo pushed herself against his exploring tongue, wrapping her arms tightly round his waist. She raised one leg and rubbed the tactile flesh of her inner thigh against him. Her short skirt rose slightly, allowing her to feel the smooth fabric of his shorts daringly close to the top of her leg.

She could feel his heightened response as he kissed harder. All thoughts of stopping him had fled from her mind. She had quickly come to the conclusion that fidelity was a little like history. It was only important to someone who knew all the dates and all the facts. As she pushed her tongue into Allen's mouth and explored the hot, excited wetness, Jo felt certain that Sam would not learn all the facts about this impending escapade.

As Allen pushed himself gently forward, Jo could feel the world being snatched from beneath her feet. She knew he was pushing her towards the bed. She had been half-anticipating this action, but the fall still caused her a moment's unease.

'This is where you start on the path towards a better body than you've ever dreamt of,' Allen whispered reassuringly. His fingertips traced an eager path down her side. He spoke the words between intimate kisses, each one more arousing than the last.

As the flames of desire fanned her body, Jo drew a shuddering sigh of mounting excitement. She could have argued with him about the bodies she had dreamt of, but Jo knew this was not really the appropriate time. She could also have demanded an explanation as to what was wrong with her body, but there were other matters that were far more urgent and pressing. Perhaps afterwards she could take issue with that comment but for the moment she had needs that insisted on satisfaction.

Lying on top of her, Allen's erection pressed into her stomach with an urgency matched only by the pulse between her legs. As his hands caressed her body, Jo pushed herself up against the thrust of his length. Teasing her fingers against the rigid flesh of his cock, she traced the bulging outline of his arousal.

Allen made a soft groaning sound. His hand had moved down to her thighs but was now travelling upward, beneath the hem of her skirt. Jo could feel the warm pressure of his fingers trailing against the silky flesh of her inner thigh. She trembled as he stroked ever closer to the top of her leg. He obviously wanted to touch her and she found it difficult to contain her need for the caress of his fingers against her sex. A shuddering breath of anticipation trembled over her lower lip.

'How do I start on this path to a better body?' Jo murmured, indulging herself in the heady pleasure of Allen's intimate kiss.

He laughed, moving his kisses lower. 'Should we start like this?'

Jo gasped and arched her back away from the bed. He was exciting her beyond the realms of anything she had anticipated. His mouth moved over her breasts, warming the hardened tips of her nipples through the fabrics of her bra and blouse. After extracting a furious response from her, he moved his mouth lower.

Jo shivered as Allen tugged her skirt up: she knew he was staring at the triangle of pale cotton fabric covering her pubic mound. Glancing down at him, Jo saw his smile broaden. She felt the furious clenching of her inner muscles quicken. Her anticipation of what was about to come heightened as she felt his fingertips tease closer to the cleft between her legs.

Allen teased a finger inside the gusset of her panties and treated her to a broad smile. 'You feel pretty wet down here.'

'I'd be a damned sight wetter if you shoved your tongue there,' Jo told him, her words shaking over trembling lips.

He laughed softly, teasing the tip of his finger up and down against the slick wetness of her labia. Jo could feel the satin-like friction of his finger against her flesh. The intensity of her arousal was so furious she could feel herself welling up like a balloon with the ferocity of her desire. She felt sure that as soon as he actually plunged his cock inside her she would explode in a gigantic, torrential orgasm.

Allen eased the crotch of her panties to one side. He toyed with the lips of her labia using two careful fingers.

Jo moaned softly. She felt him easing a third finger against her eager hole. The first two were holding her lips apart, the third was tracing up and down the centre of her exposed cleft. Each time he rubbed softly against the protruding tip of her clitoris, Jo fought against the urge to scream with elation.

'You want me to shove my tongue in here?' Allen asked carefully.

Jo gasped harshly, wishing she did not feel so close to orgasm. 'I want you to shove something in there,' she told him honestly. 'Your tongue will do for a start. We'll see what else you have later on.'

Shaking his head from side to side, Allen said, 'You wouldn't be burning many calories if I started doing that, now would you?'

Jo frowned and shook her head, confused by his sudden interest in calories. She was about to say something, ask him what he meant, or why he was so interested, when Allen drew his finger upward. Slowly and deliberately, he rolled the tip against the pulsing bead of her clitoris.

Jo released a hoarse scream as the first tickling threat of an orgasm swept over her body. Each nerve-ending felt as though it had been stretched taut and she could feel herself shaking, as though she was caught in the shockwave of an earthquake.

Allen stroked a gentle circle against her throbbing clitoris, then applied a tiny, subtle pressure.

Jo stared up at him with wide-eyed shock straining her features. The force of the orgasm rampaging through her was excruciating. She pushed herself up and on to the pressure of his teasing fingers, then collapsed heavily back on to the bed. Her heart was racing and the pulse behind her ears hammered like the rhythm of a heavy rock concert. Closing her eyes, she could feel the beat of her heart. It was pounding so hard she wondered if its rhythm might be visible on her chest. When she opened her eyes, she saw Allen stepping out of his shorts and grinning down at her.

Jo smiled back into his handsome face.

His erection lived up to the promise of his bulging

shorts. He was long and thick, with a swollen end that pulsed in eager anticipation of entering her. As Jo watched, he stroked his hand against himself, teasing his shaft to a state of absolute readiness.

'For someone who doesn't know what we do here, you seemed bloody responsive just then,' Allen noted dryly.

Jo grinned. 'I'm a fast learner,' she assured him. 'Besides, it's not just your regular clientele who have the right to be horny, is it?'

He shook his head, each movement forcing his smile to widen. 'No, the staff have that right as well.' Lying on top of her, he used a hand to hold her panties to one side while he probed the tip of his length against her eager sex. 'And it's just as well with customers like you coming here.'

Jo could feel the pulsing end of his shaft resting at her pussy hole. She wriggled vainly, trying to slide herself on to him, but Allen was holding her body in a firm, commanding embrace. She stared curiously into his face, wondering why he was stopping her from enjoying herself fully. Admittedly, she was able to glean some pleasure as she rolled the lips of her sex against the end of his cock, but she knew that having him inside her would be a damned sight more satisfying.

'This is going to be the last time you enjoy sex so effortlessly in this place,' he told her seriously.

Jo frowned, not sure what he was talking about. She writhed against him again, enjoying the subtle stimulation of her labia.

'Over the next two weeks, you'll enjoy a lot of good, satisfying encounters,' he reassured her. The tip of his length trembled against her labia with each word, increasing her excitement. 'But each time you enjoy it after this, you'll have to really work for it.

Sex is one of the most efficient ways of burning calories and, if it's approached in the right way, it can be one of the finest ways of exercising and toning the body. Over the next two weeks, you'll learn all about that.'

Jo smiled up at him. 'Shut up, and fuck me, Allen.'

Laughing softly, he did as she asked.

He pushed forward and plunged into her. His length slid deep into her velvety warmth while the pads of his fingers brushed softly against the febrile flesh of her cleft.

Jo shivered as her body eagerly accepted him. Her lips were stretched wide apart as he ploughed his long, thick length inside. With their bodies joined, they began to groan together. Joyous sounds of passion filled the air as their intimacy grew and their excitement intensified.

Allen was only half on the bed. He had one hand between her legs and the other wrapped round her waist, but his feet were planted firmly on the floor. This position was giving him the leverage to thrust into Jo with a powerful, commanding force that threatened to push her off the bed.

For the moment, Jo did not care that he was controlling the pace and the tempo. She allowed Allen to ride her roughly, enjoying the relentless vigour of his lovemaking. He lifted her legs high into the air, forcing himself deeper, then pushed her legs down so that he could kiss her as he ploughed his cock into her.

Allowing him to use her however he pleased, Jo lay limp on the bed. It was refreshing to feel herself being taken by such a skilled, male lover and she was determined to enjoy every intense, delightful moment. It did not matter to her how he pushed or pulled her legs. When they were pushed back, towards her chest

108

he was able to force himself deeper into her tight, wet warmth, filling her canal with his glorious shaft. When he pushed them down, against the bed, the length of his rigid cock was allowed to rub enticingly against the sensitive nub of her clitoris as he rode in and out.

All the time, his hand remained close to the heat of her sex, teasing her labia whenever he cared to. Each time she gasped, he brushed his thumb against her pulsing clitoris.

Enjoying every second of his cock's intrusion, Jo screamed cries of joy into the room. Occasionally she would buck her hips against him, but this was mainly an involuntary response and she struggled to suppress it. Remembering Allen's words before he began to ride her, Jo was determined to extract as much effortless pleasure as she could from this session. He had already said this would be the last bout of lovemaking that she would have without exerting herself. If that was to be the case, then Jo was determined to enjoy it.

Allen continued to rock backward and forward, filling her with his long, thick shaft, then pulling himself slowly from the tight, clenching grip of her inner muscles. While the fingers of one hand teased the lips of her sex, he used his other to reach inside the buttons of Jo's blouse and fondle her breasts. The tips of his fingers reached the aching thrust of her nipples and he teased each one with brutal tenderness.

Jo could feel herself heading towards an orgasm of bewildering intensity. Her entire body was humming as though it had been charged with electricity and she knew that when the climax finally did strike it would be more explosive than she could cope with. The prospect left her shaking with anticipation.

She longed to embrace him, rake her fingernails down his back then pull him on to her. The thought of feeling his chest pressed against her breasts was darkly exciting and she yearned to enjoy that sensation. But because he was doing such a good job of pleasuring her, Jo allowed him to continue riding her.

Her fingers curled into fists, the tips of her nails burying themselves deep into the soft flesh of her palms. She screamed with passionate fury as the threat of her impending climax increased.

And then she felt the throbbing pulse of Allen's explosion.

It was enough to spark her own orgasm. The movement of his twitching cock caused a furious climax to erupt through her body. Jo heard herself shrieking happily, the sound barely audible over Allen's cry of pleasure. With each long, languid pulse of his cock, she felt the boiling wetness of his explosion spurt deep inside her.

A triumphant, satisfied grin contorted his features and Jo realised his expression was a mirror-image of her own. They gripped one another tightly, sharing the warmth of their simultaneous climaxes in a groaning, giggling embrace. Jo could feel him kissing her face and she pressed her mouth over his, enjoying the taste of his excitement and the intimacy of his exploring tongue. His hand cupped her breast and she pulled away from him, surprised by the intense eruption of pleasure that his touch evoked.

'Enough,' she whispered, her voice shaking. Seeing the frown on his face, she said, 'Enough, for the moment.'

Allen grinned and slid himself from her. He rubbed the tip of his finger over the tingling nub of her clitoris as he drew his spent cock from her. 'I suppose

I should get on with some of the chores that I have to do up here,' Allen conceded, stepping into his shorts. 'It's not all fun working in this place, you know. Doctor McMahon has faxed me some instructions.'

Jo nodded and smiled, not particularly listening to him. She was thinking to herself how convenient it was to have sex without getting undressed. All she needed to do now was straighten the line of her skirt, adjust the gusset of her panties, and then she was fully clothed and ready for the rest of the day. She idly wished more men were as considerate as Allen, and then stopped herself from following that train of thought, feeling certain he had said something about Doctor McMahon.

She turned, about to ask him to repeat what he had just said, then cried indignantly, 'What the hell do you think you're doing?'

Allen grinned at her. He was kneeling on the floor, unfastening her case with deft fingers. 'I've been told to search your luggage for contraband,' he explained. 'I was just looking to see what you had in this case that keeps clinking.'

'That's none of your damned business,' Jo told him sternly.

He shook his head. 'Your GP sent a fax, warning us that you might try and smuggle certain items in here,' Allen explained. 'I'm removing them for your own good.' He threw open the lid of her case and stared inside. His eyes widened and a dark frown crossed his brow. 'Bloody hell,' he gasped. 'This isn't a suitcase. It's a fucking distillery.'

'It's not that bad,' Jo said defensively. 'And, like I said,' she added with renewed indignation, 'it's none of your fucking business.'

'There must be fourteen bottles of Jack Daniel's in

111

here,' Allen said, unable to stop himself from sounding incredulous.

Jo shrugged. 'Fourteen is about right,' she said. 'I'm here for a fortnight.'

Allen shook his head and closed the suitcase.

'Are you leaving it?' Jo asked, a smile breaking her lips.

'I might as well take the whole case,' Allen replied. 'What little clothes you have in here, I'll get sent up to you later.' He started towards the door, with the suitcase in one hand.

'Hold on,' Jo said desperately. 'You can't take all of them. What am I supposed to drink?'

Allen shook his head. 'Your doctor seems to think that you don't need the whiskey, and your boyfriend, Sam, seemed quite concerned about your excessive drinking.'

Jo chewed her lower lip angrily, not bothering to correct his mistake and wondering what sort of warnings her 'boyfriend' Sam had been faxing through to Elysian Fields. She suddenly found herself hoping for an early end to this case, so that she could get back to the office to exact some revenge.

Allen placed his hand on the door handle and tugged it open. 'I'll get someone up here to sort out a more detailed induction for you,' he said solemnly.

Jo stared at him. 'Will they bring me my whiskey back?' she asked sharply.

He shook his head.

She snorted a harsh, unladylike sound. 'In that case, they needn't bother.'

As soon as he had closed the door, Jo fell to her knees and took a glance under the bed. Her handbag was there and she was pleased that Allen had not thought to look through it. Reaching inside, she pulled out her newly purchased hip flask and treated

112

herself to a long, satisfying swallow from the silver bottle.

The whiskey burnt her throat with a long, satisfying sweetness that was so perfect it was almost medicinal. She stared at the hip flask with reverential gratitude and sighed happily. This was how life was supposed to be, she thought idly. Whiskey was burning her throat and her pussy lips still tingled with the memory of Allen's excellent cock. She even had the mild intrigue of a case to occupy her. What more could a person want out of life? she thought.

Going to the window of her suite, Jo squinted across the grounds of Elysian Fields, idly wondering where the nearest wine bar might be.

Six

The Black Widow grinned down at Poppy.

The sauna whip in her hand was almost forgotten. Its short leather tendrils dangled limply from her fingers, barely swaying even when Sky took the most determined step around the room. She circled the exercise machine, reassuring herself that Wendy was fastening the woman's wrists and ankles securely. She knew there was no reason to have any doubts, but Sky had dreamt of this moment for months and she wanted to be sure of every last detail.

'Why are you doing this to me?' Poppy wailed.

Sky slapped the sauna whip hard on the PVC bench between Poppy's legs. The sound of the leather tendrils striking the surface was as brittle as snapping ice. The dry crack was almost lost beneath Poppy's startled cry in the flat acoustics of the small gym. 'You've been told not to ask questions, Poppy,' Sky hissed sharply. 'Do as I say. Don't make me force you.'

Poppy sighed unhappily and slumped against the padded metal tubing of the pec deck. She did not move, even when Wendy had finished tying her bare ankles to the metal pipe above the footrest. Her secured wrists hung limply against the padded arms of the exercise machine and her shoulders rolled forward in a defeated slouch.

'Get her to sit properly,' Sky growled in Wendy's ear. The barely controlled malice in her voice left no room for dissension.

Wendy moved quickly and without question. She nodded curtly, then took a step to Poppy's side. With calming words and a strict tone, she made the solicitor grip the handlebars of the machine with her hands. At the same time, she forced Poppy to sit upright with her shoulders back and her chest out.

Sky watched with a frown of disapproval as Wendy helped to shape Poppy's posture on the pec deck. All the time her anger was growing. It was a basic weights bench, Sky thought angrily. She had seen the most simple-minded muscle-heads working effortlessly on these machines. There was no great trick to operating it.

And here was Poppy, a supposedly intelligent solicitor, who could not even sit on the bloody contraption without looking as though she had been asked to juggle and tap dance simultaneously. Under other circumstances Sky might have found the solicitor's awkwardness amusing. However, these were not other circumstances and Sky could feel her black mood darkening as each moment ticked by. Watching Poppy's guileless fumbling was only making her vile temper worse. The woman's innate clumsiness reinforced Sky's belief that she was dealing with an idiot. Each struggled attempt that she made to sit properly on the exercise machine fortified Sky's low opinion of her.

Shaking her head in disbelief Sky paced around the mirrored gym and cursed Poppy's stupidity. The woman had been trusted to handle something as important as her divorce yet she could not handle sitting down at a bloody exercise machine. Admittedly, Sky knew part of that was her own fault. She had elected to use Knight & Knight Solicitors, and she had said she was comfortable with the junior partner, Poppy Darling, handling her affairs. But at the time she had not known Poppy Darling was a clinical imbecile.

Over the past two years, she had spent a lot of time berating herself for that mistake; for trusting her affairs to Poppy. Now she realised the time for such self-recrimination was over. Now it was time to berate Poppy.

'... Move your arms together,' Wendy was saying, 'and you'll be toning your deltoid and your pectorals.' Her fingers went to Poppy's arms and shoulders to illustrate the two muscles she referred to. 'For best results, press your knees together and clench your lower body while you're using it. You'll be exercising your gluteus maximus and your adductor longus.' She tapped Poppy's bottom lightly, then stroked her fingers over her inner thigh by way of explanation.

'That'll do for the moment,' Sky said firmly. She could not see the point of Wendy explaining how to use the pec deck. At the moment, it was weighted so heavily that a team of trained elephants would have had difficulty trying to operate it. Sky had deliberately overloaded the weights so that whoever was tied to the machine would be unable to move. After her first day at Elysian Fields with John, Sky had realised how attentive a person could be when they were unable to move.

Now, she wanted Poppy to be that attentive.

Wendy obeyed Sky's instruction instantaneously and took a step back. She glanced uneasily at the whip in Sky's hand, then frowned at her. 'You're not going to hurt her with that, are you?'

Sky graced Wendy with an icy glare. She was aware

116

that Poppy was watching her miserably, waiting for an answer to this question with the same expectant hesitation. 'Lock the door on your way out,' Sky growled softly. 'I'll expect you back here in two hours to assist me.'

Wendy glanced uncertainly from Sky to Poppy, then back to Sky. The unhappiness in Wendy's eyes made it obvious that she wanted to disobey the Black Widow's instructions, but they both knew she would not. After all that had happened between them in the sauna, Wendy still felt indebted to her and Sky knew it. The thought of disobeying her, even under these circumstances, was bound to be unthinkable.

Sky widened her cruel smile in an unspoken challenge. She reached out a hand and stroked her fingers gently against Wendy's cheek. Her smile widened when she saw the woman struggle not to flinch from her touch. 'I assume that you do have other duties to perform,' Sky said loftily.

Wendy nodded. She cast an unhappy frown in Poppy's direction, then turned back to Sky. 'I have duties to attend to in the eas –' She stopped herself abruptly. 'I do have other duties,' she amended.

Sky frowned, wondering why Wendy had stopped herself so suddenly. Before she could question her about it, Wendy was already gliding through the gym's doors. Sky mentally backtracked over her parting words and wondered what the woman had stopped herself from saying. She could only imagine it was one part of Elysian Fields, and that puzzled her. Although Sky knew she was building a reputation for being a stern task master, she did not think any of her staff should be frightened of saying that they were off to the eatery.

She thought of taking a step after Wendy, or calling the woman back with a barked command.

Then she changed her mind. She could see that Poppy was staring at her with growing fear and she knew that now was the time to capitalise on that emotion.

It did not surprise her that Poppy was so scared. Sky had caught sight of her own reflection in the mirrored walls of the gym and she had to admit that she was looking fiercely intimidating. Her black seamed stockings clung to her legs and shone like polished glass beneath the gym's lights. Not that there was much of the stockings to see with the thigh-length boots she had on. The lacy edges appeared over the top, then there was simply the smooth expanse of the tanned flesh that stretched from her inner thigh to the zippered crotch of her black panties. She was wearing a stiff, black leather basque, tied tightly at the sides by a lattice-work of leather straps, revealing diamonds of the bare copper-coloured flesh beneath. The tightness of the basque emphasised her broad hips and slender waist and added volume to the swell of her breasts. Long, black leather gloves covered her slender forearms, contrasting starkly with her lightly tanned skin. The gloves were fingerless, revealing the blood-red polish of her manicured nails. To complete the ensemble, she had torn a length of leather from the many-tipped tongue of the sauna whip, and used it to tie back her long blonde hair. The reflection that glared back at her from the mirror was simultaneously exciting and threatening.

Secretly, she thought that Poppy had every right to look frightened. This was an outfit she had worn in the past for her husband and he had jokingly referred to it as her 'psycho-bitch' costume. Now, more than ever before, Sky was determined to live up to that reputation.

She slapped the sauna whip between Poppy's legs,

118

shattering the expectant silence. 'You look scared, Poppy. Do you think you should be scared?'

Poppy snatched a trembling breath and stared miserably at her captor. 'I don't know,' she whispered meekly.

Sky shook her head, her anger mounting. 'You don't even recognise me, do you?' she snapped.

With watery eyes, Poppy stared at her then shook her head.

'Bitch!' Sky exploded. She slapped the sauna whip down hard against Poppy's inner thigh, extracting a shriek of surprise. The sound gave her a grim satisfaction and she slapped the whip against the other thigh, provoking the same result. 'You lousy bitch,' Sky growled. 'How dare you not remember me?'

Poppy tried to shrug but her tied arms made it impossible. Her lower lip quivered as she struggled to say something, but terror held her mute.

Sky was pacing furiously up and down in the small gym. Each forceful, stamping step on the wooden floor embodied her absolute outrage. 'I honestly don't believe you,' Sky gasped incredulously. 'You fucked over my entire life. You turned me from a woman with wealth and resources to a virtual pauper, and you have the audacity not to remember me.' Again, Sky slapped the sauna whip against Poppy's inner thighs, extracting a modicum of grim pleasure from each anguished cry she inflicted.

Poppy was shaking her head from side to side, tears spilling copiously over her reddened cheeks. She tried to say something but the words were made unintelligible by the high pitch of her fear-strained voice.

'The strange thing is,' Sky said suddenly, 'I remember you perfectly. Seeing you now, it's like seeing you the last time I was in your office.'

With an obvious lack of comprehension still straining her features, Poppy shook her head miserably as she sobbed.

Sky ignored the woman's misery, suddenly lost in her own thoughts. 'You're still dressed like a woman with a lost-property box for a wardrobe,' she said nastily. 'And you still have all the style and coordination of a road accident.' She stepped closer to Poppy, glaring down at the woman. The sauna whip was still in her hand and, although she had no intention of using it, Sky had raised it to shoulder height, to scratch the back of her neck thoughtfully. Poppy cowered as though she expected to be struck, but Sky, lost in her own reverie, barely noticed. 'Do you know what I always wondered?' Sky asked suddenly.

Poppy shook her head. Her eyes were wide and staring.

'I always wondered if you were as artless and uncoordinated as your dress sense.'

Poppy was frowning unhappily, not following the meaning of Sky's words. She shook her head again and blinked back the latest welling of tears that threatened to spill down her cheeks.

'My late husband always spoke in your favour,' Sky said, a wistful smile teasing her lips. 'He said you would be dressed like a lingerie model under those shitty clothes that you wear. At the time, I told him he was just being a tosspot, but I'm beginning to wonder now.'

Poppy swallowed thickly and shook her head. She began to stammer something, then seemed to stop herself. Fear of the woman who stood above her was apparent in her meek gaze.

Sky was warming to her theme, encouraged by the look of mounting terror on Poppy's face. She took the sauna whip in both hands and moved it towards her victim's face. 'I want you to hold this between your teeth,' Sky explained carefully. 'If you drop it to the floor, I'll punish you with it.'

Poppy opened her mouth and Sky could not decide if the woman was trying to accept the whip or about to protest. Whichever was the case, Sky took advantage of the moment and pushed the handle of the whip between Poppy's lips.

Poppy closed her teeth against the leather and glared mournfully upward.

'Drop it,' Sky repeated firmly, 'and I'll punish you.' Without waiting for a response, she moved her hands down and traced her fingers against the beige polyester of Poppy's cardigan. The modest swell of her breasts filled Sky's hands and she allowed herself the pleasure of caressing the little orbs. She could feel the shape of a stiff bra beneath the unpleasant fabric of the cardigan. Beneath the bra, there was the familiar pressure of a yielding breast. Her fingertips pressed through both layers of fabric and she spent a moment tracing the rounded swell.

Poppy drew a startled breath around the sauna whip that gagged her.

Sky smiled cruelly, moving her fingers to the line of beige buttons. As soon as she had hold of both edges of the garment, Sky gripped tightly, then tore it open. Cheap plastic buttons sprayed against the mirrored walls and wooden floor of the gym. The sound of them striking glass and wood was almost lost beneath Poppy's cry of surprise.

Sky smiled tightly.

The rent cardigan hung from Poppy's shoulders like a rag. The vision of her breasts, clad in only a stiff white bra, was revealed to Sky. Trapped in the unflattering fabric, her orbs trembled in perfect rhythm with her self-pitying sobs.

Sky longed to touch the gently quaking flesh but she exercised a moment's self-restraint. She placed a crimson fingernail against the pale skin below Poppy's breasts and trailed it slowly downward. The firm pressure she employed left a dark-red line in its wake. When the nail reached the waistband of Poppy's sandy-coloured skirt, Sky paused and graced her victim with a cruel smile. She hooked her nail beneath the fabric and moved her other hand to Poppy's knee. A line of buttons went up one side of the skirt and she squeezed her fingers between the holes. With a sudden, vicious motion, Sky ripped the garment open. The fabric gave far more easily than she would have expected and she was surprised to find herself holding two pieces of torn cloth.

Poppy made a startled sound around the whip but it was little more than a choked tremor. She stared up at Sky with an expression that silently pleaded for leniency.

Sky glared down at her, her brow furrowing ominously. The firm set of her jaw made it obvious that she was in no mood to offer a reprieve. 'Black knickers,' Sky growled sullenly.

Poppy glanced wordlessly down at herself, then stared back at Sky. With the sauna whip still trapped between her teeth, the woman looked like a dog holding a bone, Sky thought.

'A white bra, and black knickers,' Sky repeated, unable to hide her obvious disgust at this transgression of the unwritten fashion laws. She reached forward with a fast hand that made Poppy flinch from the threat of a blow. Instead of striking the woman, Sky pulled the whip from between her teeth. She brandished the weapon menacingly as she glared down at Poppy's underwear. 'A white bra and black knickers,' she growled again. The tips of the whip trembled, as though they were expelling some of the furious electric charge fuelling her vile mood. 'And neither of them look as though they fit properly,' she observed critically. Her hazel eyes had darkened to a dull brown colour that barely hinted at the true depths of her worsening mood. 'Is that a deliberate attempt to look cheap and nasty? I don't believe you've come to this place dressed in such a way.' She shook her head with disdain. 'My husband was so wrong about you, wasn't he?' A look of genuine sorrow seemed to taint her features, although it was gone in the blink of an eye.

'I don't know who your husband is,' Poppy sobbed. 'I don't know who your husband is, and I don't know who you are. I'm sorry,' she wailed, 'but I just don't know who you are.'

'My husband was Malcolm Meadows,' Sky explained stiffly.

Poppy's face crumpled like a paper handkerchief in a merciless fist.

'Since the last time we met, I've earned the nickname "the Black Widow", but I doubt you'd be aware of that. You probably best remember me as Sky Meadows, Malcolm Meadows' penniless widow. Have I helped to jog your memory a little yet?'

'Oh! No!' Poppy cried. Realisation had struck her like a fist. 'I never meant to ... I mean, it was a genuine mistake and ... I am so sorry –'

'You haven't begun to know what sorry is yet.'

'I thought the invitation here was a simple gratuity,' Poppy moaned. She leant her head on the padded rest near to her tied right arm. Miserably, she sobbed against it, her entire body shivering with each cry.

'Who the hell would give you a gratuity?' Sky asked nastily. 'You're totally worthless. There's only one thing you need, and we both know that it's not a gratuity, don't we?'

Poppy glanced up at her with eyes that swam behind a veil of tears. 'What do I need?' she whispered.

Sky's grin was predatory and dangerous. 'You need punishing,' she said quietly. Because she spoke without obvious anger, she realised her words carried a lot more menace. 'It's as simple as that, Poppy. You need punishing. You've needed punishing for a long time now, and I'm just the woman to do it for you.'

Poppy recoiled from Sky's words. If she had not been tied to the pec deck, they both knew she would have fled the room. 'It was an accident,' she moaned. 'I never meant to cause you any upset and I never meant to lose your money. I was just trying do the right thing and –'

'The road to hell is paved with good intentions,' Sky observed darkly. 'Now shut up.'

'But I –' She got no further.

Sky slapped her face, cutting her off cold. She pushed the handle of the whip back into Poppy's mouth, making her hold it there before letting go. 'Remember,' she hissed, 'drop it and you're really going to be in trouble.'

Gagged again, Poppy nodded. She was doe-eyed with fear and in no position to disobey.

'Good,' Sky said encouragingly. A dark smile flitted across her lips, then she turned her attention to Poppy's bra. Her frown reappeared. 'White bra and black pants,' she murmured with blatant disgust. She reached for the cups of the bra and tugged them in opposite directions with powerful urgency.

Poppy grunted unhappily around the whip. Her moan was barely audible above the sound of tearing fabric. She tried to distance herself from Sky as the woman tore the bra away from her body but Wendy had tied her tightly to the pec deck. Poppy could do little more than twist and flinch against her bindings.

With a grunt of satisfaction, Sky hurled the torn fabric into a corner of the gym. She glanced at Poppy's exposed breasts and made a noncommittal sound by way of appraisal. Her hands cupped the warm flesh and she rubbed the tips of her fingers against the raised ridge of Poppy's dark-brown areolae. Before either of them could extract pleasure from the intimacy, she snatched her hands away and guided them deliberately downward.

Unhappily, Poppy stared at her.

Sky deliberately ignored the woman. Her fingers hooked under the waistband of Poppy's panties and she treated her to an evil grin.

Poppy shook her head in silent refusal of what the Black Widow intended. The tendrils of the sauna whip brushed lightly against her cheek as she moved her head from side to side, but she ignored their gentle caress.

Glaring triumphantly into Poppy's fearful eyes, Sky continued. She slid her hands inside the warmth of Poppy's panties, touching the hidden flesh with cool, exploring fingers.

So intense was her fear and distress that an uncontrollable pulse shivered through Poppy's body.

Ignoring her tremors, Sky worked her hands down through the thatch of flattened hairs. Her fingers moved purposefully toward the lips of Poppy's sex and, when the tip of one nail grazed against the nub of Poppy's clitoris, she smiled at the woman's discomfort with malicious cruelty.

Around the whip, Poppy snatched a shuddering breath.

Still smiling, Sky tore the panties from the woman's hips.

With the tearing fabric cutting against her intimate flesh, Poppy gasped sharply. A dull shriek wailed at the back of her throat but the noise was lost behind the whip in her mouth. A ragged sigh shook its way out of her body.

'There,' Sky muttered, satisfaction colouring her words. 'Now you're a step closer to being coordinated.' She studied her victim for a moment, admiring the shapely curves of Poppy's bare body. Her breasts were not overly large, but they were pert and tipped with gorgeous dark-brown areolae that silently begged for Sky to touch them. Still sitting in the posture Wendy had shown her, her narrow hips and her lithe legs possessed an appeal that had been well and truly hidden while she was clothed. Although she dressed in the most unflattering way imaginable, Sky had to admit that, naked, Poppy looked quite alluring. She remembered how her husband had joked about the dowdy solicitor's lingerie and wondered if he had suspected she was hiding such a beautiful figure beneath her wretched clothes.

Not even aware that she was doing it, Sky reached out a hand and brushed her knuckles against the swell of Poppy's breast. She caressed the dark-brown areola of one orb and allowed the tips of her fingers to tease the flattened nub of the woman's nipple. A sensation like electricity passed through her fingers.

Both women studied one another suspiciously. That they had both experienced the sensation was undeniable.

Sky glared warily down at Poppy, as though she suspected her of trying some clever ploy to gain release from her bindings.

Poppy was staring unhappily up at Sky, not masking her obvious fear at this new turn in events.

Without warning, Sky gripped the woman's nipple and squeezed hard. The tips of her manicured fingernails buried themselves into the soft tissue, almost cutting into the flesh. Wanting to inflict more discomfort than the tips of her fingers could manage, Sky twisted her wrist and tugged hard at the same time.

Poppy barked a sharp exclamation of surprise. Her jaw dropped as she stared at Sky with an expression of absolute disbelief. The whip tumbled from her mouth, bounced lightly against Sky's wrist, then fell to the floor. When Poppy dared to glance up at the Black Widow, her face was contorted by mixed emotions. Above the pain and the hurt was a fearful frown. Poppy realised she had dropped the whip and that went directly against Sky's orders.

Wordlessly, Sky released her grip on Poppy's breast. She bent down to pluck the sauna whip from the floor and tested it thoughtfully with a flick of her wrist.

As the tendrils of the whip brushed through the air, Poppy flinched.

Sky studied her solemnly.

'What do you want from me?' Poppy whispered. 'Why have you brought me here? And what are you going to do with me?'

Sky shook her head. 'You're in no position to ask questions,' she remarked stiffly. 'But, since you're so curious, I suppose I should tell you. I'm not going to do anything to you that you haven't done to me,' she explained enigmatically.

Poppy shook her head, not bothering to hide her lack of comprehension. 'I don't understand,' she sobbed. 'What are you going to do to me?'

'I'm going to do the same thing to you as you've done to me. I'm going to fuck you over. I'm going to fuck you over and I'm going to make you desperately unhappy.' Sky's smile broadened as she watched more tears well in Poppy's eyes. Before the woman had a chance to protest, Sky raised the sauna whip. With a harsh cry of satisfaction, she brought it swiftly down against Poppy's bare breast. The whip's sharp-edged tips bit cruelly into her exposed nipple.

Poppy's cry of despair echoed hollowly against the mirrored walls of the gymnasium. She tugged against the restraints at her hands and her feet, shaking her head in refusal of the pain flaring in her chest.

Her discomfort was so obvious that Sky almost felt a twinge of sympathy. It was only a short-lived emotion – Sky quickly killed it before it could develop. Not trusting the threat of her own good nature, Sky stopped herself from empathising with the woman's plight. She reminded herself how much suffering she had been forced to endure because of Poppy's stupidity and incompetence. Thinking of the hardship she had lived through during the past two years was more than enough to quash her compassion. Sky raised the whip high in the air and struck Poppy on the other breast. She scored her victim with pinpoint accuracy, flicking the whip adroitly against Poppy's nipple.

The leather tips of the sauna whip cracked like autumn twigs.

Poppy's mortified cries turned into agonised shrieks.

With bitter satisfaction, Sky began to laugh. Poppy was staring at her with hurt, tear-swollen eyes and that only added to her good mood.

'Does that make you feel better?' Poppy asked miserably.

Sky snapped the sauna whip twice through the air. The first blow scored a direct hit on Poppy's left breast. The second grazed the areola of her right.

Each blow extracted anguished cries from Poppy. With her smile tightening, Sky slapped the sauna whip down between her legs. The tips bit hard against the PVC bench, landing so close to the bare lips of Poppy's sex that both women flinched. Glancing at the end of the whip, Sky could see a handful of Poppy's dark-brown pubic hairs caught in the leather tendrils. She had not intended to go so near to the woman's pussy with the weapon and realising how close she had come to properly hurting her sent a thrill of excitement coursing through Sky's body.

'Damned right that makes me feel better,' Sky murmured honestly. She glanced at Poppy's nipples, swollen from the barrage of blows they had just received. She supposed that they were standing so proudly simply because of the abuse they had endured. She doubted it could be attributed to anything else. Nevertheless, when she placed an inquisitive finger against the thrust of one nipple, she knew that Poppy's cry was not made from discomfort.

'You have a submissive side, don't you?' Sky muttered, rolling the hard button of flesh between her thumb and forefinger.

'Isn't it just as well?' Poppy replied sharply.

Sky squeezed the swollen tip hard. With her other hand she raised the whip and brought it down smartly against Poppy's other breast.

'Don't talk back to me, you dumb bitch,' Sky hissed. 'You have a submissive side, which means you might get off on some of the stuff I have planned for you. But if you start trying to talk back to me, I'll make sure you suffer through every long minute of this afternoon. Do I make myself clear?' As she asked the question, Sky squeezed hard on the delicate nub of flesh she was holding.

Poppy had her eyes squeezed shut, as though this would combat the flare of pain emanating from her breast. Snorting air through her nostrils like a panting mare, she nodded her response to Sky's question, unable to manage the words.

'Good,' Sky growled. 'I'm pleased that we understand one another.'

Poppy stared miserably at the Black Widow, the pain still torturing her features even when Sky had removed her hand. 'I'm sorry for talking back,' she murmured unhappily. 'I didn't mean to cause offence and I didn't mean to –'

'Shut up,' Sky said softly. 'Or I'll whip your tits again.'

Poppy held her tongue and stared at the woman in fearful silence.

Sky grinned at her eager obedience, warming to the dual roles of dominatrix and disciplinarian. She turned the sauna whip round in her hand, holding the top of the handle, close to the tendrils of the whip. After studying the rounded base of the handle for a moment, her grin widened.

Watching her, Poppy frowned in horror, recoiling from the idea that had so obviously occurred to Sky. 'No way,' she gasped.

'I told you to shut up,' Sky reminded Poppy absently. She was still staring at the rounded end of the whip's handle, a fond smile teasing her lips as she considered its smooth phallic shape. 'Don't make me warn you again,' Sky added meaningfully.

Poppy looked as though she was about to say something but she caught a glint of the malice in Sky's hazel eyes. The unspoken threat of punishment was more than enough to silence her. Even when Sky brandished the end of the whip in front of her face, she remained obediently silent.

'Suck it,' Sky said simply. She pushed the edge of the whip against Poppy's lower lip. 'Suck it, and get it good and wet,' Sky instructed her.

Rolling her lips around the phallus-shaped handle, Poppy sucked on the rounded end. Watching her, Sky could see the woman's tongue distorting the soft flesh of her cheek as she valiantly attempted to wet the entire length. Sky was surprised by how stimulating she found the sight. Poppy did not look particularly pretty as she sucked on the whip, but Sky thought she was a vision of servility as she tried to accommodate all of it in her mouth.

It was an unconscious reaction when she reached a hand into Poppy's hair and pulled her head against the phallus. Because Poppy was seated and she was standing, Sky was struck by the realisation that this was how it would feel for a man to get a blow job. The idea brought a peculiar excitement and inspired a sudden appetite that she had not expected.

The need to have Poppy's tongue was sudden but overwhelming.

Sky snatched the handle of the whip from Poppy's mouth and held it up to the lights beneath the gym's ceiling. The black leather glistened with the coating of Poppy's saliva.

Sky released her hold on Poppy's hair, moved the whip down and pushed it between Poppy's legs. The end pressed rudely into her cleft, forcing itself roughly against the lips of Poppy's labia. Because she was tied hand and foot to the pec deck, and because she was sitting in the correct posture for exercising, the handle of the whip could not penetrate her. However, Sky knew that the phallic end of the handle would be exciting the sensitive flesh between her legs.

Not that Sky was particularly bothered about Poppy's enjoyment of their afternoon in the gym. The solicitor's pleasure was so unimportant it was barely worth contemplating. Nevertheless, Sky felt she would extract far more satisfaction from this afternoon if she forced her victim to endure a thrill of the pleasures that she was probably unfamiliar with.

Poppy sighed as the handle of the whip was pushed between her legs. Sky rolled the rounded end hard against the eager lips of her hole. As she did this, Sky pressed the rigid handle slightly upward, so that its hard length brushed firmly against the thrust of Poppy's clitoris. Again, Poppy made a small sound of protest, but now it was a half-hearted noise. Her eyes were open wide and she was staring at her tormentor with a newly developed respect. Her cheeks were tinted with a darkening blush and her eyes, still dewy with tears, now shone with an excited sparkle.

Sky rolled the length of the handle harder, wedging the implement between the lips of Poppy's sex and the PVC bench. She allowed herself a brief smile of satisfaction when her handiwork was complete, then studied Poppy's confused face.

It was obvious from the way she shook her head, and the way her breathing had suddenly changed, that Poppy was torn between conflicting emotions. On the one hand, Sky could see that she was loath to enjoy herself sexually under these circumstances, especially as the victim of another woman. But Sky could also see that Poppy's body was responding eagerly to the combination of pain, bondage and intimate stimulation. Sky could have happily watched Poppy struggling to deal with her dilemma through the rest of the afternoon. There was something exciting about the woman's naivety and her innocent manner. It was obvious that her pleasure was mounting but she seemed incapable of dealing with it under these circumstances. If Sky had not felt the

132

urgent pull of her own longing, she would have happily teased Poppy for the remainder of the day.

She reminded herself that Poppy's humiliation was only one aspect of the revenge she had been planning. Sky was willing to forsake some of the pleasure now, knowing that she could enjoy delivering a long, drawn-out punishment when her main victim finally arrived. Reaching between her legs, she grabbed hold of the zipper at her crotch and carefully tugged it open. The teeth pulled slowly back, then parted, revealing the shaved lips of her pussy. They glistened slickly with excitement.

Poppy stared at her nervously. Her blatant unease was like a soothing balm to Sky.

Sky stroked an idle finger against the pulsing nub of her clitoris, surprised by the sudden fury of her desire. Her touch inspired a shiver of delight that scurried to every nerve-ending in her body. She could feel the slickness that moistened her cleft and the sensation of sliding her fingertip against the yielding folds of her sex produced a wonderful *frisson*. If it had not been for the sight of Poppy nervously licking her lips, Sky could have happily rubbed herself to a climax.

The sight of Poppy's dark-pink tongue, stroking apprehensively against her lips, reminded Sky how urgently she needed to experience the woman. She teased the zippered sides of her gusset wide apart then placed one foot on the PVC seat of the pec deck. The side of her boot was dangerously close to the handle of the whip she had wedged against Poppy's sex. As she stood up, Sky deliberately pushed it hard against her victim.

Poppy gasped, 'What are you doing to me?'

'What the hell do you think?' Sky growled softly. She reached for the metal bars that hung above the exercise machine and gripped tightly. Still standing on the PVC bench, she placed one leg over Poppy's shoulder and thrust her heated mound against the woman's face. 'Lick me, Poppy,' she said forcefully. 'Lick me, and make me come.'

For a moment, Sky did not think the woman was going to respond. She could feel the lips of her sex bristle with excitement as she pressed them against her victim's face. She could feel Poppy's warm breath against her shaved lips, but she could not yet feel the intrusion of the tongue that she so desperately craved. Not that it really mattered: Sky could feel the threat of an orgasm building simply from the pleasure of experiencing Poppy's nervous breath against her sex.

Since her change in circumstances, she had discovered there were a lot of pleasures to be had from dominating a sexual partner. There were pleasures that she had never suspected could be so satisfying. Even if Poppy refused to use her tongue, Sky knew that she would gain even more joy by punishing the woman for her disobedience.

She was so surprised to feel Poppy's tongue pushing against her pussy that, at first, she did not realise it was the source of her pleasure. The tickle of electric excitement sparkled upward from the lips of her labia, causing her to shriek with mounting euphoria.

Between her legs, Poppy made an unintelligible sound as she lapped her tongue up and down against the heated wetness of Sky's sex. Poppy dared to tap the tip of her tongue against the eager thrust of Sky's clitoris, inspiring an excited groan.

Sky rocked her hips gently forward. She kept hold of the pec deck's upper bar with one hand and used her other to stroke the back of Poppy's head. As her fingers entwined in the brunette's long tresses, she forced the woman's head harder against her sex.

Poppy gasped, the sound muffled by the labia pressed over her mouth. She worked her tongue into Sky's tight, wet hole and wriggled it forcefully.

With a scream of pure pleasure, Sky pulled Poppy's head closer. The orgasm tore through her body like a hurricane, stirring her nerves into an intense, chaotic jumble. Her muscles were straining with the furious exertion of her climax. But still her body demanded more.

Poppy was struggling to move her head away, but Sky held her tightly, keeping her where she was needed. She knew that Poppy was close to gagging. The woman was making a desperate attempt not to drink the juice Sky's climax had delivered. However, Sky was determined that Poppy would swallow every drop. She was also determined that the woman was going to enjoy herself while she did it, whether she wanted to or not. Deliberately, Sky pushed the heel of her boot against the whip. She glanced down and smiled, happy with the way the whip's handle was rubbing at Poppy's sodden cleft.

The woman between her legs suddenly gasped, and, with her fingers still buried in her hair, Sky felt a sudden change sweep through Poppy's body.

She heard Poppy release a low moan and then felt her straining against the bindings at her wrists. Surprisingly, Sky saw the weights on the pec deck move a little as Poppy struggled physically against the intensity of her orgasm. Before Sky had a chance to comment, she realised Poppy was lapping greedily at the spent wetness between her legs. Her probing tongue rubbed over the tingling lips of Sky's sex, deftly rekindling the embers of her desire.

Seemingly oblivious to the effect she was having on Sky, Poppy continued to lap up her pussy honey with an avaricious tongue. Within moments, Sky felt the blissful delight of a second orgasm tearing through her. She screamed as the waves of pleasure cascaded over her. Furiously, she rocked herself against Poppy's tongue.

Poppy's mouth was working hungrily against the lips of Sky's sex and her cries were a-mixture of protestation and delight. As Sky's body approached the pinnacle of pleasure, she twisted her heel hard against the whip between Poppy's legs, forcing the handle roughly against the woman's sodden lips. Sky's excitement was momentarily intensified by Poppy's squeal of elation, but the woman's enjoyment was still peripheral to Sky. Her own satisfaction was of far more importance.

To add excitement to her domination, Sky snatched the whip from Poppy's sex and climbed down from the pec deck. With a malicious grin, she began to strike at Poppy's bare breasts again with the tip of the sauna whip.

This time, instead of shrieking and crying out in complaint, Poppy moaned with joy. Instead of cowering away from the punishing tendrils, she thrust her breasts forward as though she was relishing the whipping. Her enjoyment was infectious.

Breathing heavily, Sky stopped flogging the wanton woman.

Poppy continued to groan, thrashing herself from side to side as her body visited planes of unimagined euphoria.

Watching Poppy's body being racked with tremors of delight, Sky teased the tip of the whip's handle against her own sex. After having the woman's tongue tease her pussy so adroitly, Sky's need for penetration was intense. With a firm hand, she guided the rounded head of the whip against her eager hole, and pushed it upward.

The handle slid effortlessly inside. She could feel her own urgent wetness soaking the length of hard leather, facilitating its smooth passage into her warmth. The sensation of its wide girth, parting her and filling her, was intoxicating. The thrill of an orgasm rushed through her before she had pushed the handle all the way inside. As soon as the last quivers of the climax had subsided, she drew the handle slowly out of her sodden pussy.

With a cruel smile, she pushed it in front of Poppy's nose and forced her to lick the leather clean. Again, she found herself excited by the sight of the woman's mouth accepting the phallic-shaped length. The arousal was so swift and sudden that, before she could stop herself, Sky had snatched the whip from Poppy's mouth and jumped back on to the pec deck. Thrusting her sex against Poppy's tongue, Sky held the woman's head and forced her once again to lap the wetness from between her legs.

She lost count of the number of orgasms Poppy gave her. The woman's gift for submission and her squirming tongue were enough of a distraction to make the morning pass without Sky noticing. Sky did not realise she had lost track of time until she saw Allen appear in the gym's doorway.

Her first thought was that a problem had occurred. 'No problem,' Allen replied simply. He seemed torn between staring at Sky in her psycho-bitch costume and admiring Poppy.

Strapped to the exercise machine, her hair plastered with sweat and pussy juice, and her exposed nipples thrusting forward, Poppy looked beautifully vulnerable, Sky thought. She could appreciate the lingering look that Allen bestowed on Poppy and concurred with his good taste.

'Where's Wendy?' Sky asked sharply. 'I asked her

to call back here for me when I'd finished. Why are you here? Where is she?'

'Wendy has some duties to attend to in the east wing,' Allen said simply. 'She asked me to call and do whatever you asked.'

Sky nodded thoughtfully, frowning to herself. Thinking back to the previous morning, she remembered that Wendy had spotted her with John from a room in the east wing. It occurred to her that there was something in that part of Elysian Fields that she knew nothing about and she supposed that she ought to try to learn exactly what it was. Considering the way that Wendy had been trying to keep it secret, Sky guessed it had to be important. She was about to ask Allen if he knew what was in the east wing when he spoke, destroying her train of thought.

'Wendy asked me to go to the reception desk and see if anyone else had called with one of your special invitations, but there haven't been any,' he told her.

'There's only one other card,' Sky replied darkly. She was frowning, unconscious of the disturbing effect this had on Allen. 'If the recipient hasn't arrived yet, it doesn't look like she's going to.'

'Only one other?' Poppy asked curiously.

She was still tied to the pec deck, looking weary and defeated, but her eyes sparkled with a dull lustre of excitement. She fell silent until Sky looked at her, and the Black Widow realised she was waiting for permission to carry on. That thought alone brought a wide smile to Sky's lips. Relishing her position of power, Sky nodded at her.

'That woman I met at the reception desk seemed to know all about those special invitations,' Poppy explained. 'She said that a friend of hers had received one and she was trying to find out who sent mine.'

Sky frowned. 'Who's this?' she demanded. She switched her glare from Poppy to Allen, then back to Poppy. 'What woman?'

Poppy furrowed her brow in serious concentration. 'Jo Valentine,' she said suddenly. 'That's her name.'

'Jo Valentine,' Sky repeated thoughtfully. She pursed her lips and frowned unhappily. 'I think that I'm going to have to meet this Jo Valentine. The woman seems to know more about my special invitations than is healthy. When I've finished with her, she'll have told me all she knows, and a whole lot more.' The sound of the Black Widow's malicious laughter echoed against the mirrored walls of the gymnasium.

Seven

There were two reasons why Jo thought it was best to start investigating the case at midnight. First and foremost, her hip flask was empty. Jo stared at the silver bottle with the hurt look of someone who has been betrayed. She pulled the cord on her dressing-gown tighter, stepped into a pair of slippers, then reached for the door handle.

She was desperately trying to convince herself that her other reason for leaving the room had something to do with the case. When she had climbed out of a restless bed two minutes earlier, the case had been an overriding factor in her thoughts. Now, with her fingers brushing the polished brass of the door knob, she could not recall exactly what she had intended doing in order to make some progress. All that seemed important was her insatiable craving for a drink.

Dismissing the case as being unimportant, Jo stepped out of her room and into the hall. She walked quietly through darkened corridors and unlit areas, knowing it would be most prudent to start her investigation in the kitchen. Perhaps there would be fewer pieces of helpful or incriminating documentation resting in the pantry, she realised, but Jo suspected they were bound to have a bottle of cooking sherry, or something. Even a miniature

140

bottle of rum flavouring would have sufficed for the moment, she thought miserably.

She quietened her pace as she neared the kitchen doors, aware of a sliver of light sliding beneath the bottom. It seemed peculiar that someone was already there, especially at this late hour. Walking silently and stealthily in her carpet slippers, she pressed her head against the door and listened intently for any telltale sounds.

Strains of muted laughter reached her ears but the muffling door snatched all traces of gender from its lilt. Jo pressed her face closer to the lacquered wooden surface, listening hard. She was trying to guess who might be laughing in a health-farm kitchen at such a late hour. She supposed it could have been the cook. She did not know the person, but she felt sure that whoever had prepared the afternoon's meal was blessed with a sense of humour.

Jo caught the murmur of words mingled with the laughter as she strained her ears, but there was still no revelation. After taking a deep breath to steady her nerves, she pushed the door ever so slightly ajar. With squinting eyes, she tried to make sense of the slice of room that became visible, but the door was suddenly snatched from her hand and pulled sharply open. Jo stumbled towards the floor, shifted her feet to steady herself, then realised she was standing in the centre of the kitchen.

There were three people sitting round a circular table and they studied her in sudden silence. Laughter was caught in throats, and drinks hesitated against lips. Jo glanced from one face to the next. Her heart beat fast and for an instant she wondered if she had made a grave mistake.

'Good evening, Jo,' whispered a male voice from

behind her. 'I thought you might come down and join us. You look the sort.'

She turned and found herself staring at Allen. His long blond hair was tied back in a ponytail and an easy, welcoming grin rested on his lips. Jo could sense no hint of a threat in his expression and she gave him a smile. Her fear of any danger quickly evaporated. 'Allen, what are you doing in here?' she asked. Turning to glance at the others, she found her curiosity getting the better of her, and asked, 'What are you all doing in here?'

'The same thing that you are,' a woman at the table replied sharply. They all chuckled among themselves and Jo took a moment to study them.

Sitting furthest away from her, she recognised the dour-faced Wendy from reception. Rather than looking surly and unpleasant as she had that morning, Wendy seemed relaxed and almost approachable now. There was a sparkle in her dark-green eyes that reminded Jo of Sam's constant allure. The thought brought the stirrings of a warmth between her legs as she nodded polite acknowledgement to the woman.

Beside her sat Bryn, the health farm's other male masseur. He had the same magnificent physique as Allen but most of his face was hidden behind a full, luxuriant beard of the same rich, dark-brown colour as his hair. Jo had already seen him at work after her induction with Allen. At the time she had promised herself that she would become better acquainted with the man.

The other woman was also vaguely familiar, Jo thought. She had seen her dining in the eatery. As Jo recalled, the woman was the same one who had been offering loud opinions about the 'rabbit food', on her plate. The combination of belligerence and arrogance was an unpleasant blend that Jo would have been happier avoiding.

'This is Violet,' Allen said, introducing the woman. 'You know these other two, don't you?'

Jo nodded at everyone and allowed Allen to guide her towards a seat. She was still confused as to why they were all down in the kitchen. She was also wondering why they were all wearing dressing-gowns. Admittedly it was late, but still the attire seemed very informal. The only saving grace she could find in their common uniform was that she did not feel out of place. 'So what are you all doing down here?' Jo repeated. 'Or shouldn't I ask?'

Violet spoke before anyone else could offer a reply. 'After that crappy excuse of a meal this evening, I came down here to see if they're hiding the food from the paying customers.'

Jo smiled.

'Allen said if I was still hungry at midnight he and Bryn could fill me up,' she went on. The room was filled with the sound of shared laughter.

Jo smiled dutifully at the woman's rudimentary sense of humour, prudishly deciding that she did not approve of such coarseness. As she settled herself in the seat that Allen offered, Jo tried to keep the disapproval from her face. She had met women like Violet before and knew that they could behave like bitches when they believed themselves to be slighted.

Allen sat next to Jo and quickly began to shuffle a deck of cards between his long, broad fingers. 'We all know the rules,' he told them. Casting a kindly glance at Jo, he added, 'You'll pick them up as we go along.' He turned to face the rest of the table. 'The game's pontoon, because Bryn here is too thick to know how to play poker.' The two men cursed one another playfully but there was no real antagonism in their words. 'We all know the stakes too,' Allen went on. 'So, if someone could pour Jo a drink, then we'll begin.'

Jo glanced at the centre of the table and her face lit up. Staring back at her was a familiar, square bottle, filled with golden nectar and labelled in stark black paper with distinctive white lettering. 'I'll have a Jack Daniel's, please,' she said. 'No.' She quickly amended her hasty decision. 'I've changed my mind. I'll have a large Jack Daniel's.'

'Jo will have a mineral water,' Allen said firmly. 'She hasn't won a real drink, yet.'

Jo frowned. 'We're playing for drinks?'

'Amongst other things,' Allen replied, grinning.

'We're playing for whatever is at the table,' Violet explained tersely. 'You don't have a problem with that, do you?'

Jo sensed the woman was implying something more than just food and drink, but she let the matter go for the moment. There was a challenge in Violet's voice that Jo did not want to rise to. An atmosphere of anticipation hung over the table and her natural curiosity was insisting she find the cause.

A small voice at the back of her mind wanted to remind Allen that this was probably one of the bottles he had stolen from her room. If that was the case, then she did not need to play games to win the right to drink it and she felt justified in mentioning this. However, she knew that such a statement would sound churlish in front of the others and she stopped herself from voicing the sentiment. Nodding morosely at Wendy, Jo said, 'I'll have a delicious glass of your finest mineral water. Hold the flavour.'

'Ice and lemon?' Wendy asked, pouring water from a pitcher into a glass.

Jo nodded. 'And scotch,' she attempted weakly.

She was warmed by a murmur of soft laughter as she took her drink.

Wendy placed the bottle back in the centre of the table between an unopened litre of vodka and a half-empty carafe of red wine. Littering the remainder of the table were a couple of dozen bars of chocolate, various bags of flavoured crisps and a couple of packets of biscuits. Jo saw a brimming fruit bowl as well. She guessed that these were the prizes they were playing for and wondered whose idea this midnight feast had been. She thought of asking, then decided it was of no consequence. All that mattered was winning her first hand, and getting a proper drink. It occurred to her that if she hit a lucky streak she might indulge herself in a bar of plain chocolate, but she could not anticipate that luxury with the same degree of excitement as the whiskey inspired.

Allen flicked cards briskly across the tabletop, sending two to each of the players. Because she was sitting on his left, Jo was able to watch everyone else play before she took her turn. Violet smiled confidently and said she was happy. Bryn twisted, then threw his cards down in disgust. Wendy took two cards, then shook her head when Allen offered her a third.

'Go on,' Bryn encouraged her. 'A five-card trick beats everything.'

'It doesn't beat a pontoon,' Wendy reminded him.

Violet made a tired sound. 'Are we going to have to explain the rules of how we're playing again?' she demanded.

'I meant it beats everything except a pontoon,' Bryn growled defensively.

'Whatever it beats, I'm not having another card,' Wendy said firmly. She glanced at Allen and said, 'I'll stick.'

Jo studied her cards with a frown. 'Am I meant to be getting twenty-one?' she asked.

Violet sighed heavily. 'Should we be playing snap, or is that one over your head too?' She shook her head in exasperation and leant across Bryn so she could speak to Wendy. 'This is like playing cards at a chimp's tea party,' she confided loudly.

Allen waved a silencing hand at her. He glanced over Jo's shoulder and studied her cards. 'Bitch!' he cried softly. 'You've got a pontoon.'

The other players threw their cards down and muttered with annoyance.

Jo grinned at each of them while Allen studied his own cards. He shook his head as he looked at his losing hand. 'Pour the lady her Jack Daniel's,' he said simply.

'Are you sure that's what she wants?' Wendy asked quietly. She smiled suggestively at Jo. 'There's an awful lot on offer at the game tonight.'

Jo studied the woman with a curious frown. 'What else could I have?'

Laughing, Allen shook his head. 'Pour her a drink,' he said firmly. 'She'll soon get the hang of how we play things here.'

Wendy shrugged and poured the drink, exactly as Allen had instructed. He dealt the cards again, and, as Jo took her much needed sip of whiskey, she listened to the idle conversation being passed around the table.

'How did you get on with the Black Widow?' Wendy asked, directing the question at Allen.

He shrugged and shook his head. 'That woman has got a screw loose. I can understand why you're doing everything she tells you.'

Wendy took offence at the comment. 'I am not doing everything she tells me,' she declared indignantly. 'I'm simply trying to keep hold of my job under bloody difficult circumstances.'

Allen dealt the last card and raised a pacifying hand. 'I didn't mean that as it sounded,' he apologised. 'I guess the new regime here has got us all on edge. She didn't even seem to understand me when I said you were attending to your chores in the east wing.'

Wendy groaned loudly. 'Say that you didn't,' she growled unhappily. 'Say that you didn't really tell her I was in the east wing.'

'Wasn't I meant to?' Allen frowned.

'Even I've worked that one out,' Violet said, laughing sourly.

Wendy shook her head and glared sullenly at Allen. 'You're an arsehole, Allen. An absolute arsehole.' She raised her fists and beat his arm angrily, her lips curled with exasperation.

'And I'm a winner,' Violet said suddenly. Her words cut through the argument and she placed her cards on the table so that an ace was showing over a face-down card. 'If anyone can match a pontoon, speak now . . .' She allowed her voice to trail off as the others good-naturedly cursed her luck. 'And as for my prize,' she continued thoughtfully. 'I'd like to see Wendy and Allen kiss and make up.'

'You bitch,' Wendy growled.

Violet's wicked grin broadened. 'And, when I said "kiss and make up", I didn't mean you should kiss mouths,' she elaborated.

Jo expected Wendy to refuse. She could see an angry frown on her face and Allen had not looked happy when his colleague called him an arsehole. Nevertheless, she watched Wendy climb out of her seat, walk over to Allen and tug the cord free on her towelling robe. The robe fell open, revealing a glimpse of her naked flesh.

Allen shifted his chair round so that he was facing her.

Sitting next to him, Jo could see the eager bulge of his erection pushing at the front of his robe. She watched him pull his dressing-gown open as he stared lewdly at Wendy.

'Kiss and make up?' he said.

Wendy glared angrily at his stiff cock. 'Careful I don't bite it off,' she hissed. Kneeling down in front of him, she placed her lips round his shaft and began to suck on him.

Jo could feel the warmth of her arousal spreading between her legs. The sight of such blatant sexual intimacy, so unexpected and so close to where she sat, triggered a tingling wetness in the pit of her stomach. She watched Wendy work her mouth over Allen's cock, then move her lips from him so that she could lick his entire length. Before she had finished, his shaft glistened with her saliva.

'Isn't it about time you kissed Wendy?' Violet asked. 'You're meant to be kissing and making up, not getting a blow job.'

Wendy moved her mouth away from him and wiped her lips dry on the back of her hand. She stood up slowly and began to spread the folds of her pussy with splayed fingers.

'No, no, no,' Violet chastised, shaking her head and frowning.

Jo glared at the woman for her intrusive behaviour. Her earlier animosity returned and she decided that she really did not care for Violet. Prudently, she kept the opinion to herself.

'Allen can kiss your tits,' Violet went on, oblivious to Jo's unkind thoughts. Her smile twisted wickedly as she glared at Wendy. By way of an explanation she said, 'I still owe you for the lack of towels in my room this morning. I said I'd get you back for it.'

'You really are a bitch, aren't you?' Wendy commented.

Violet laughed in wholehearted agreement. 'It takes one to know one,' she replied tartly.

The entire group fell silent as Allen moved his mouth over Wendy's bare breasts. He teased one nipple between his lips, then the other, nibbling playfully on the erect buds until Wendy was gasping.

Jo envied the woman her good fortune at having Allen please her in such a way. After having enjoyed the pleasure of his lovemaking that afternoon, she knew how adept he was at intimate teasing. She could empathise with Wendy's mounting moans and groans and wished Allen had been told to kiss and make up with her. She knew this simple stimulation would not have been enough for her own burgeoning appetite, but it would have been a delightful piece of foreplay.

Not that Allen was content with just stimulating Wendy's breasts, she realised. He had slipped one hand between her broad, muscular thighs and was easing his finger into the wetness of her hole. The long digit was slippery with the honey-like dew of Wendy's excitement. Seeing this, Jo realised the heated warmth between her own legs was burning with an infuriating passion.

'Enough,' Violet said abruptly. Her single word stopped the pair of them.

Reluctantly, Wendy moved her breast from Allen's teasing mouth. She graced him with a smile, wrapped her robe round herself, then glided gracefully back to her seat.

Allen covered his stiff, unsatisfied erection and turned back to the table. After briskly shuffling the cards, he began to deal again. He glanced at Jo and gave her a knowing, lecherous wink. 'Do you think you have an idea about the rules we're playing to?'

She grinned back at him. 'I've got an understanding of the situation,' she conceded. Remembering the argument that had forced Allen and Wendy into that situation, she wondered if it might have some bearing on her investigation. It was annoying that she should have to put her arousal on hold as she tried to find out more about the case, and Jo silently cursed Sam for accepting this assignment on her behalf. She leant closer to Allen and asked, 'Have you and Wendy got a problem with the management here?'

'A problem?' Wendy snorted. 'The woman's a psychopath.'

Allen considered this damning opinion for a moment, then nodded wholehearted agreement. 'Wendy's right,' he agreed. 'Our new owner is a little bit on the volatile side.' He frowned and squinted at Jo. 'Didn't she call in and visit you this afternoon?'

'Didn't who come and visit me this afternoon?'

'Mrs Meadows,' Allen explained. 'She said she wanted to call in and see you when I saw her in the gym.'

Jo shook her head, a puzzled frown creasing her forehead. 'No. No one's been to see me today.' She tried to work her way through what she had just learnt, wishing it was not quite so confusing. There were plots in American soap operas that did not seem quite as involved and complex as the happenings at Elysian Fields. Jo strongly suspected she was missing something but it was awkward trying to ask glib questions when her client had given her so little to begin with.

'Anyway,' she said, speaking quickly so that the topic was not brushed over. 'I thought Mrs Meadows had been the owner since this place first opened. Didn't you just say she was the new owner?'

'It's quite a coincidence that,' Bryn noted. 'Both

the new owner and the old owner being called Meadows. Do you reckon they might be sisters?'

'More likely it's a pseudonym,' Allen said thoughtfully.

'Or it could be a false name,' Bryn suggested, trying to appear sage as he made this suggestion.

Jo glanced at him. She wondered if he was joking but was unable to decide. His beard hid any wry smile he may have been wearing while his eyes remained clear and untouched by any trace of mirth. Mentally dismissing Bryn, she tried to decide which of the two Mrs Meadows had employed her. After a moment's thought, she decided it was unimportant as long as she had the correct invoice address.

'Are you ever going to deal those cards?' Violet asked sharply. There was a touch of petulance in her tone that grated on Jo's nerves. 'If you shuffle them much more the spades will fall off.'

Startled back into action, Allen tapped the deck twice on the table, then flicked a pair of cards to each player.

'So why did Mrs Meadows want to come and see me?' Jo asked, staring nonchalantly at a pair of threes. She placed the cards face down on the table and glanced from Wendy to Allen as she sipped at her drink.

'You ask a lot of questions, don't you?' Wendy observed. Her tone was innocent and without accusation, but Jo still felt an unsettling pang when she heard the words. This case had not seemed to merit anything as grand as going undercover but, with her usual sense of caution, Jo had elected not to leave her business cards on the reception desk. A case was always safer when less people knew about it. She realised that her natural curiosity had come close to giving her away.

'She asks too many fucking questions,' Violet snapped irritably.

Jo held her breath, biting back the vicious retort she had been about to bark. Something was amiss at Elysian Fields and she felt close to finding out what it was. It would be a shame to distance herself from those round the table simply because of Violet's truculence.

Violet was glaring defiantly at Allen as she barked, 'Twist.' The harsh tone of her voice was enough to let them all know that she was in a bad mood and not to be trifled with. Quite how the woman could be irritable in the company of such easy-going people, Jo did not know, and she wondered if Violet had been this abrasive before she arrived.

'Stick,' Violet said tersely after examining the card Allen had given her. Glaring at Jo, she added, 'You'd better hope I don't win another hand. If I do, I'll put something in your mouth to keep you quiet.'

Jo studied her with unperturbed equanimity. 'Has your dentist ever fallen in?' she asked softly. The comment was enough to make a tense silence fall. Allen tried to lighten the mood by joking with Bryn about his next card, but the mounting tension prevailed. Smouldering glances from Violet added to the darkening mood and Jo wished she could do or say something to disperse the atmosphere. The evening had the potential for so much more.

When Allen actually won the hand, Jo saw Violet was glaring at him. She could tell from the woman's steely expression what thoughts were going through her mind and she found herself in complete accord with Violet's unspoken warning. 'Don't suggest that Jo and I kiss and make up,' Violet's threatening gaze insisted.

Sensibly, Allen chose to heed the unvoiced

warning. 'My win,' he said with a sly smile. 'So why don't we all make ourselves a little more comfortable.' To demonstrate exactly what he meant, Allen stood up, tugged the cord on his dressing-gown, then shrugged it off. He stood over the table for a moment, allowing them all to study his broad muscular body and his long, meaty erection. When he saw that no one was moving, Allen clapped his hands together smartly and gestured so that the others would follow his lead. 'Come on,' he insisted. 'I want to see some nudity round this table.'

Bryn and Wendy stood in unison and began to ease their gowns off.

Jo cast a cursory glance at each of them, noting the powerful physique of Bryn's body and the exciting breadth of his erection. Unconsciously, she licked her lips as she studied him. To disguise her obvious excitement, she took a small sip from her glass.

She had intended to grace Wendy only with a fleeting glance, but her attention was caught by something enticing in the woman's nudity. Wendy held herself with an athletic grace and poise that Jo found infuriatingly arousing. Her full breasts swayed gently as she stretched her body out of the dressing-gown. Jo could feel herself drawn by an irresistible impulse to reach out and touch one of the woman's nipples. She knew that, among company like this, such a breach of life's normal protocol would not trouble anyone. However, her hand remained round her glass and she struggled to resist the urge. She was not a hundred per cent confident that Wendy would allow such a caress. Jo's first impression of the woman had not been inspiring. Wendy had initially struck her as cold and surly. Admittedly that had been during the middle of a busy morning when a person was least likely to seem approachable, but the negative image still lingered. Reluctantly, Jo denied herself the indulgence of touching Wendy, for the moment.

Snatching her gaze away from the woman's desirable figure, she realised Violet was glaring at her threateningly.

Jo had known the woman was staring at her while the others undressed. If she had been the first to undress, Jo knew that Violet would have dismissed her as a slut. Now, if she waited until everyone else was naked, Jo felt certain that Violet would decry her prudishness. Normally Jo would not have cared about the woman's low opinion of her. She sensed, though, that this evening held a lot of possibilities, and did not want to miss out on a single one of them.

Primarily, she found she was learning more and more about the case. Even if all this information seemed to be adding to the confusion, she supposed that was not really a bad thing. Cases invariably became more confusing before they were resolved. There was also the additional excitement of what might happen in the next few moments. Allen's suggestion that they all disrobe seemed to move the evening closer to something exciting but indefinable. Jo could sense a glorious tension building in the air around them and she knew that something spectacular was about to happen. Whatever that was, she had already decided she wanted to be a part of it. She was also reluctant to move out of the same room as the open bottle of Jack Daniel's.

Because of all of these factors, she was determined not to be intimidated by Violet and her antagonistic, bullying behaviour.

As Jo watched, Violet stood up.

Jo eased herself out of her seat at exactly the same moment. She moved her hand down to the cord of her dressing-gown as Violet did the same. In unison, the two women shrugged their robes off then glared defiantly at one another.

Jo studied Violet's nudity, trying to maintain a scornful, disparaging scowl. It was not easy. The woman had a splendid figure with creamy pale flesh and the alluring contours that Jo always found irresistible in a woman. Her breasts were full and round. Her stomach, while it could not be described as flat, was only slightly too large, and Jo suspected that the remaining layer of fat would have been worked away by the end of the week.

Violet snapped her fingers, snatching Jo's attention. 'See this?' Violet said, teasing her fingers through the fringe of curly hairs that covered her sex. The blood-red colour of her manicured nails contrasted with the pale-pink flesh of her pussy. Her voice was low and sultry, taking on a harsher inflection as she repeated the question, hissing threateningly: 'See this?'

Jo nodded. Her face was impassive and calm. She studied Violet with a stony gaze.

'If I win the next game of cards, you're going to eat this,' Violet declared firmly. 'Do you still want to stick around for the next hand?'

The obvious challenge in her voice was something Jo could not turn away from. She met Violet's defiant glare with more poise than she would have believed possible. 'I'll look forward to it,' Jo replied. Annoyed by the woman's unpleasant attitude, but determined not to show it, Jo eased herself back into her chair. She chewed her lower lip thoughtfully as she glared across the table at Violet.

Allen flicked cards to each of them, trying to frown firmly at Jo and Violet as he dealt. Both women ignored him.

Tired of trying to appear threatening, Jo glanced at her cards, then turned to Wendy. 'I'm surprised Poppy hasn't shown up for this card game,' she began carefully. 'Then again, I haven't seen her all day. Do you know where's she been hiding?'

Allen grunted soft, humourless laughter. 'She's probably still with the Black –'

'We don't know where Poppy might be,' Wendy broke in suddenly. She fixed Allen with a firm, silencing glare that equalled the threatening force of anything Violet had been administering.

Sensibly, he did not take issue with her interruption.

Wendy tried to remain oblivious to the curious stares that her harsh tone had inspired, but it was an impossible task. Her cheeks turned a flustered red and she no longer had the courage to meet anyone's questioning expression.

Seeing the way Wendy's cheeks coloured, while the rest of her naked body remained a gorgeous creamy white, Jo felt the familiar flutter of excitement tickling deep inside. It was an intense feeling; a delicious, tingling pleasure that left her mouth dry and her pulse beating ever so slightly faster.

She had been wondering if Sam might consider her recent behaviour to be adulterous. Now that thought was dismissed. Jo was on a case and she realised that Wendy had information she could use. Under these circumstances there was no such thing as infidelity; there was only the investigation. If a certain method got results, then it was the right way of working. Judging by the way Wendy was blushing as she tried to remain silent about Poppy's fate, Jo felt certain that the woman had information she could use. Besides, Jo thought pragmatically, Wendy has the most alluring green eyes. They reminded her of Sam's and she momentarily felt a pang of guilt at the salacious thoughts she was entertaining. She did not allow the guilt to intrude for long, caught by the glint of a promise in Wendy's smile. Her athletic body was such an enticing vision it was impossible not to look at her and want her. The idea of taking Wendy somewhere discreet, so they could be alone, excited Jo fiercely. She could feel the lips of her sex tingling with anticipation at the prospect. Jo reached a tentative hand towards Wendy's leg, intending to caress the top of her thigh with gentle, but suggestive fingers.

Her fingers were just about to touch the milky-white smoothness of Wendy's upper thigh when Violet spoke.

'I win,' Violet declared triumphantly. She laughed wickedly.

Jo turned to glare at the woman and saw she was brandishing an ace and a king. Unhappily, she snatched her hand away from the intimacy of Wendy's legs and lifted her cards to see if she had come close to beating the woman. The two picture cards that stared back were of no help.

'I win,' Violet repeated. Her broad grin widened. She smiled knowingly at Jo and winked. Sitting back in her chair, she laughed softly to herself.

'Pick something nice,' Allen growled softly.

'I've already decided what I'm having,' Violet told him. The stiffness in her voice was as yielding as an iron bar. She winked at Jo again and placed a hand between her legs. Although the table hid what she was doing from everyone's view, it was obvious that her fingers were toying with the lips of her own sex. With a lewd smile, she raised one finger to her red-glossed lips, drew her tongue wetly against the tip, then lowered it back between her legs. All the time she kept her wicked grin fixed on Jo's frown.

'Remember,' Allen insisted, 'this is Elysian Fields. We encourage better physical health through the enjoyment of sex.' He stressed the word 'enjoyment' with the full inflection of his Welsh accent. 'Even during a midnight card game, we don't encourage sexual punishment.'

'I bet the new owner would,' Wendy whispered quietly to herself.

Jo heard the words and studied the woman curiously. In spite of the radiant beauty of Wendy's sensational body, she again found her gaze being drawn to the allure of her sparkling green eyes. There was something disturbingly exciting in those emerald depths and Jo could feel her need for the woman growing. The need to know her, physically at least, hit Jo with the force of a punch.

'I've decided what I'm having,' Violet said firmly. 'Would you care to come around here, Jo?' she asked, sliding her chair away from the table. Her voice was rich with artificial sweetness.

Still enticed by the vision of Wendy, Jo barely glanced at Violet. She drained her glass of Jack Daniel's, stood up and walked purposefully round the table. Staring down at the seated woman, Jo was struck by a peculiar contradiction: the woman's nudity should have inspired a wave of excitement but Jo felt nothing. Violet was powerfully attractive with a pretty face, and, while her naked body was not perfect, it had enough allure to make it more than desirable. Yet Jo studied her nude form with casual indifference. Her thoughts were locked on the enticing contours of Wendy's athletic body and her mind was already indulging itself in the carnal pleasures of knowing the health farm's assistant manager.

Violet was as stunning as Wendy, if not quite as

158

athletic. She was resting back in her chair. One hand was teasing the hard bud of her nipple, while the other toyed deliberately through the hairs around her pussy. Jo thought she looked like a picture of sensuality but that did not help to arouse any feelings inside her. She knew that the flutter of wet excitement between her legs had been caused by Wendy and she intended satisfying that warmth with the woman who had inspired it.

'Kneel down,' Violet suggested graciously. 'I'm sure you'll be far more comfortable if you do that.'

Jo smiled and moved closer. Her mind was working quickly as she tried to think of a way out of this situation. She did not want to be with Violet; she wanted to be with Wendy. Not only did Jo find the other woman more appealing, she also believed that Wendy would be able to help her with the case.

An idea struck her and she smiled thoughtfully to herself.

She was barely conscious of her own nudity as she stepped closer, even when her legs brushed lightly against the intimate flesh of Violet's inner thighs. The fact that they were both stark naked was so far from her mind it was almost peripheral. Rather than simply kneeling, as she had been instructed, Jo lowered herself down slowly. She held Violet's gaze with her own, unintimidated by the woman's silent, wilful challenge. Her bare breasts rubbed gently against Violet's shoulders as she moved. By the time she was actually at eye level, Jo could feel the hardened nubs of her nipples dancing coolly against Violet's.

Their lips were kissing distance apart and Jo could feel the woman trembling with excitement. She saw the intensity of Violet's arousal reflected in her shining eyes.

With a gentle flick of her head, Jo nodded backward, encouraging the woman to sit up in her chair.

Warily, Violet eased herself forward, moving her mouth closer to Jo's.

Jo lowered her lips to Violet's cheek and delivered a soft, delicate kiss. Encouraged by the gentle shudder of the woman's body, she moved her kiss on to the slender smoothness of Violet's neck. At the same time, the tips of her fingers rubbed over the swell of the woman's nipples. Pressing her lips below Violet's ear, Jo allowed the tip of her tongue to trace against the sensitive flesh. Quietly, so that the others could not hear, she whispered, 'Why don't we do this some other night?'

Violet sighed softly, warmed by the combination of Jo's kisses and the stimulation of the fingers at her breasts. 'Why not tonight?' she asked, breathing the words in the same low, inaudible tone.

'Because tonight,' Jo reminded her, 'you can have Bryn and Allen. If you don't win another game of cards this evening, you might not get the chance to have them, like you wanted.' As she said the words, Jo dared to tease a finger against the heated wetness between Violet's legs. 'And from what you said before,' Jo went on, 'I think I know just how you wanted them.'

Together with her words, the gentle stimulation of Jo's finger was encouragement enough. Violet took a long, lingering look at Jo, her gaze seeming to dwell on the rise of her breasts. With a smile that could have been tinged with sadness, Violet turned her head away and glanced at Allen. 'Did you tell me to pick something nice?' She held a hand up, effectively pushing Jo away from herself as she spoke.

'I think I did make some suggestion like that,'

Allen conceded. He studied Violet with a cynical frown. 'Have you decided that what you were planning wasn't nice?'

Violet dismissed his patronising tone with a wave of her hand. She glanced at Bryn, then stared directly at Allen. Jo realised she was forgotten in the midst of all this and slid easily back to her chair.

'You told me the pair of you would "fill me up" tonight,' Violet reminded Allen. 'Was that just an idle threat or am I likely to see some action?'

Allen laughed softly. 'You know how to lay down a challenge,' he observed, reluctant admiration tainting his words. Because she was sitting next to him, he was able to reach out a hand and touch her as he spoke. The tips of his fingers caressed her shoulder, moving down to her arm, then to the swell of her breast.

Violet caught a breath in her throat. She studied Allen with the glint of renewed excitement shining in her eyes. Her hand reached out to the eager length that sprouted from between his legs. Curling her fingers round his erection, she began to tease his foreskin slowly backward and forward.

'Are you sure you want to try this?' Allen persisted. His fingertips were tracing a lazy circle round her smooth areolae.

Jo realised that his calm voice and earnest tone were carefully calculated tools. The more he asked Violet if she was sure about what she wanted, the more she was being forced to think about the pleasures that lay ahead. Listening to Allen's dulcet voice, Jo could picture both men in action, rubbing their naked bodies furiously against any woman lucky enough to be wanted by them. She could only imagine how exciting that thought was for Violet and she envied the woman her good fortune.

161

Reaching from behind, Bryn placed a tentative hand on Violet's shoulder.

She turned her head so she could face him, then their mouths were locked and they were embracing one another in an awkward kiss.

Transfixed by the scene, Jo watched the woman being teased by the two men. As Bryn kissed Violet's mouth, Allen dropped from his chair and knelt in front of her. Her naked body was completely exposed to him and he hesitated for an instant before placing his lips against her breast. Jo could see him grinning as he did this, sliding a finger against the wetness between Violet's legs as his tongue did a dance against the proud thrust of her nipple.

Not that Violet was resting idly while the two men pleasured her. Allen had moved his cock out of her reach so now she was having to content herself with playing with Bryn's erection. Her hand went quickly over his shaft, tugging him to full hardness, then rolled up and down in long, languid strokes.

Bryn sighed heavily, still kissing Violet as she wanked him.

'We have to talk.'

Jo was surprised by the urgency of the words whispered in her ear. She tore her gaze from the scene of Violet's pleasuring and glanced into Wendy's concerned face. She frowned at the seriousness she saw there. 'Is there a problem?'

Wendy seemed to consider this question, looked doubtful for a moment, then nodded her head anyway. 'Mrs Meadows sent you, didn't she?'

Jo rolled her eyes. One of these days, I'll get through a case without being spotted, she thought. She nodded by way of reluctant reply and, in the same whispered tone that Wendy was using, she said, 'Yes. The real Mrs Meadows sent me.'

Wendy did not seem surprised by the way she said this. She pushed her chair back, held out her hand, and waited for Jo to take it.

'Where are we going?' Jo asked quietly.

'We have to talk,' Wendy reminded her. 'And it really should be in private.'

Jo glanced at the others. Violet was locked in the throes of euphoric bliss and would not have noticed if Jo and Wendy had suddenly grown additional heads. Although they did not seem to be enjoying the same exaggerated degree of bliss, both Bryn and Allen also seemed wrapped up in the excitement of the moment.

'We won't be missed,' Wendy assured Jo, 'and this is important.'

Nodding sombrely, Jo shrugged her robe back on, then snatched the bottle of Jack Daniel's from the centre of the table. Caught by Wendy's disapproving frown, Jo exercised a conciliatory smile. 'We can drink and talk,' she assured her.

Wendy shook her head from side to side. She took the bottle out of Jo's hand, patently intending to put it somewhere safe. Jo was attempting to retrieve the bottle when she felt the electric spark of Wendy's touch. The woman's fingertips seemed to brush exactly the right spot on her wrist, creating a sensation so intense that Jo felt as if she had been slapped. It was clear that Wendy had experienced the same sensation. Jo saw the woman was staring at her with wary excitement.

Leaving the whiskey bottle, Jo took a brave step towards Wendy and pressed herself close. Her desire to touch the woman and hold her naked body was burning uncontrollably. After tugging the cord of the woman's dressing-gown, then unfastening her own, she pulled the layers of fabric from between them.

Wendy gave a small gasp.

Jo barely heard the sound, busy making a similar noise herself. Wendy's warm, nubile body was touching hers and the excitement it generated was infuriating. Jo could feel the rise of her own breasts being pressed against the delightful, unfamiliar contours of Wendy's. Unable to stop herself, she placed a hand on the woman's slender waist and stroked the soft, silky flesh.

Again, Wendy sighed.

Jo realised the woman was sharing her immense excitement even before Wendy touched her nipple with a tentative fingertip. The woman's tortured breathing and her eager smile were giveaway signs. Unable to resist the urge, Jo pushed her mouth forward and they kissed. Their tongues met in a furious, wet exploration. At the same time, they caressed each other's bodies with the deft strokes of inquisitive intimates. Jo could feel her excitement intensifying and wondered vaguely if she might achieve orgasm from something as simple as a kiss. She supposed it was possible, but the demands of her growing sexual appetite assured her she would not attempt such an experiment this evening. Grinding her hips against the woman, Jo moved her hands to Wendy's buttocks. She allowed the tips of her fingers to caress the peachlike orbs before kneading the flesh in a subtle lover's massage. Holding her gently, Jo continued to ride her pelvic bone up and down. She was purposely rubbing her clitoris against Wendy's leg and she doubted the woman could remain unmoved by the intimacy.

Her suspicions were confirmed when, after breaking their kiss, Wendy whispered, the tremor of dark arousal tainting her words, 'Let's go to a bedroom.'

Jo nodded. 'Mine or yours?'

Wendy shrugged, as though the matter was of no consequence. 'Yours,' she began, then stopped herself. A frown creased her brow and she studied Jo thoughtfully. 'The Black Widow didn't get a chance to visit you today, did she?'

Jo shook her head.

Wendy nodded and said, 'Then, if that's the case, we'll go to my room. We wouldn't want her to come looking for you and have her disturb us, would we?'

Seeing the exciting promise that lurked in Wendy's eyes, Jo knew that she did not want anything to interrupt this evening. She cast a last, hesitant glance at the bottle of Jack Daniel's and then decided there were more important things. Squeezing Wendy's hand affectionately, she took an appreciative glance at the woman's nudity before she fastened her robe. Wendy was right, Jo agreed. Nothing should disturb this evening for them.

Hand in hand, smiling eagerly at one another, the two women left the kitchen.

Eight

The deafening beat of the music rolled in waves all around her. Sam was lost in the rhythm of the music. As she rocked her head from side to side, her wig of long blonde hair whirled about her face in chaotic tresses. Beneath the pulsing lights of the nightclub, each strand shone with a million different colours.

Because her job at the Good Night Club called for it, she was topless. Her small, pert breasts swayed with each flounce of her hips, jostling provocatively for anyone who cared to look. She was wearing stockings and a short skirt, allowing the hem to rise and fall with each rhythmic sway. She did not know if any of the clientele had noticed but she had removed the cutting G-string that was meant to be a part of her costume. Rather than wearing the flimsy piece of fabric, her sex was completely naked beneath her skirt. She had felt exciting and daring in doing this. Not only was her pussy bare but she had gone to the trouble of shaving the lips so that they were now a thin pouting line of pink. Unused to the sensation of being shaved, she had spent an entertaining morning exploring the pleasure that came from touching the silky, smooth flesh of her depilated sex.

A man snapped his fingers, summoning her presence with uncouth arrogance. Normally Sam would have feigned deafness and not even considered allowing him the pleasure of watching her dance. However, he was sitting at Faye Meadows' table and Sam was glad of the opportunity to dance near there. Faye Meadows seemed to do most of her business from this table and Sam felt it was the right place to find out more about the current case. There was something about the limited information she had given that did not ring true for Sam. Because the workload for the new office was sparse, Sam had been able to spend several hours researching the client. Some of the things she had uncovered about Faye Meadows were quite surprising and added to the growing mystery. Because she wanted to be a good private investigator, and because this was her first real case with a wage at the end of it, Sam wanted to do things properly.

Also, there was something irresistible about the prospect of dressing up in a wig and stockings and taking a job as lap dancer. The whole idea was so seedy she felt herself being drawn to the job's lurid charms. Using the excuse that an undercover operation was necessary, Sam had thrown herself into the role.

She glanced at the man who had called for her, aware that his face seemed vaguely familiar. Stepping over to the space in front of him, she continued to rock and sway in time with the music's calypso beat. She did not think she had seen him in the nightclub before: she knew him from somewhere else. For the moment, exactly where eluded her. At the back of her mind, she knew she would have had a better chance of recognising him if she had worn her glasses. However, they were tucked away in the single pocket of her skirt and she did not want to break the eroticism of the moment by pulling them out, putting them on and peering owlishly at him.

The dancing was proving to be a surprising amount of fun for Sam. While she had always believed herself to be slightly daring, she had never considered herself an exhibitionist. Having spent the previous night, and most of this one, displaying herself to anyone who cared to watch, she found herself thrilling to the unexpected pleasure of such perversity. The smiles of approval and the expressions of unabashed lust were more than just reward. Since starting work at the Good Night Club she had found herself in a state of almost constant arousal. Throughout the day, as she manned the office and took care of the day-to-day requirements of the business, her thoughts were constantly turning to the pleasures of her undercover work. Admittedly, it could have been a lot more fulfilling. There were times, like this one, when she was having to dance in front of someone she did not particularly like, but there were worse things in the world, she told herself pragmatically.

And the situation was not completely lost. She was working as a lap dancer and knew that her performance was not just being admired by the men at Faye Meadows' table. A couple of broad-shouldered guys at the bar had already passed her knowing winks, and she thought she had been graced by a daring smile of approval from one of the waitresses. It was Sam's intention to try to find out later if the woman had been giving a come-on, or if she was simply the annoyingly friendly type. Fervently, Sam hoped it was the former of these two options. She had not enjoyed sleeping on her own since Jo went to Elysian Fields. The thought of going to sleep in someone's arms appealed to her and the waitress's warm smile had seemed genuine and reassuring. Determined to find the young woman once she had finished this dance, Sam threw herself into her work. She smiled disarmingly at the man who had summoned her, allowing her grin to encompass the second man sitting beside him.

'Get rid of her,' the second man complained unhappily. 'We have to talk.'

The man who had summoned Sam shook his head. 'We'll talk when Faye gets here. For now, I want to enjoy myself.'

'You've been enjoying yourself too much lately. You were enjoying yourself with Poppy, and that could have led to problems. We're going to end up in serious trouble here. I know it, Arthur.'

Arthur waved his hand in an impatient gesture, silencing his companion's worries. All the time his gaze was fixed on Sam as she rocked her hips provocatively in front of him. His eyes flitted shrewdly from side to side as he followed the mesmerising sway of her breasts.

Sam grinned lewdly. She watched the man reach into his jacket pocket and produce a crisp note. Wafting it in front of her, he beckoned for her to move closer.

Smiling, she moved forward.

'I don't like this, Arthur,' the other man mumbled unhappily. 'We could get into a lot of trouble. If Faye finds out what we're doing with her money –'

'She won't find out anything, Derek,' Arthur broke in firmly. 'Not unless you keep opening your stupid big mouth in the wrong place.' Arthur fixed him with a silencing glare, momentarily ignoring Sam. 'We've been running the risk of suffering some catastrophe since we started working for the bloody Meadows clan. Sky could have screwed our practice with a bigger fucking lawsuit than we've ever dealt with. Instead, she's being fair with us. She just wants us to help her get what she thinks is rightfully hers.'

'It's called stealing, Arthur,' Derek insisted. He folded his arms and frowned heavily. 'No matter how you dress it up, it's still stealing.'

Arthur shook his head. 'You're a pious twat,' he muttered. Turning back to Sam, he reached out with one hand and stroked the top of her stocking-clad leg. Raising the hem of her skirt slightly, so that he had access to the elasticated band of her black garter, he pushed the crisp note against her leg.

Sam jiggled her breasts for him, forcing the sound of happy laughter to rise up from her throat. She had no idea what the two men might have been discussing, but she doubted it had any bearing on her case. Admittedly, they were talking about Faye Meadows, but most of the customers who used this exclusive table referred to Faye at some point in their conversation. As soon as the money was safely against her leg, she started to back away from him, lowering her cleavage down to his face as her legs danced backward.

Arthur reached a hand up for one of her breasts. He stroked the sensitive flesh, and his corpulent face broke into a smile.

Sam allowed his sausage-like fingers to remain against her as she tried to decide what was going to be the best course of action. Normally it was against the rules for any member of the nightclub's clientele to touch the lap dancers. However, the rules were subject to a broader interpretation on Faye's table and Sam was very much aware of this. Arthur's fat fingers traced the swell of her orb. He gently massaged her breast, smiling into her eyes as he touched her. His caress was disturbingly intimate; more exciting than she would have expected from a man who was so unremarkable he was on the verge of being repugnant. With a well-practised skill, he teased the puckered flesh of one areola before rubbing his nail roughly over her nipple.

Unwittingly, Sam heard herself gasp with surprise. The brutality of his uncouth caress was delightful and exceptional. He grinned lewdly up at her, seeming to sense her enjoyment. Without breaking eye contact, he flicked open his wallet and pulled out another note. After stroking the crisp edge against her erect nipple, he gestured for her to come closer.

Excited by his touch, Sam was happy to comply. Over the past few days she had been manhandled and mauled by a dozen or more of the nightclub's customers. Such touching was a clear breach of the regulations but Sam felt certain that such restrictions would not apply to undercover private investigators. As soon as she was close enough, Arthur reached for her leg. His cool fingers, still wet from holding a pint of bitter, reached for her inner thigh. The gentleness of his hand was surprisingly subtle and Sam felt her heart skip a beat. The tips of his fingers were exciting the silky flesh close to the crease of her sex. The stimulation was so delicate she did not know if it was intended or accidental. She only knew that the man was arousing her intensely. She continued to dance for him as he tucked another note underneath the elastic of her black garter.

'Have I seen you somewhere before?' he asked, when she had placed her ear close to his face.

Sam felt herself smiling at the obviousness of his line. Even though she had thought she recognised him earlier, his words still had all the transparent charm of an oft-used chat-up line. 'You could have,' she told him blithely. 'I've been places before.'

She saw him frown, shake his head and prepare to reiterate his question, before giving up on the whole idea. His blatant lack of familiarity with talking above the deafening music made her certain that he was not a regular patron of the Good Night Club.

He summoned her close again, reaching back to his wallet at the same time. Plucking out two of the largest notes he could find, he tucked them carelessly into the waistband of her short skirt. His cool fingers chilled the warm flesh of her stomach. Their intimate intrusion against the fabric of her skirt moved her excitement to a new and unexpected plateau. Gesturing at his companion, he said, 'Dance for my brother. If you can make him hard, there's an extra tenner in it.'

Sam kept her expression blank, not wanting him to see how truly uninspiring the thought of an extra ten pounds really was. She reminded herself that she was working undercover, and her character was supposed to react excitedly at the thought of earning such a pitiful sum. The reminder did little to help her enthusiasm, but she smiled dutifully at Arthur and began to gyrate her body in front of Derek.

'I don't really –' Derek began.

Sam stepped closer to him. She placed her legs on either side of his and bucked her hips forward in time to the music. The hem of her skirt was flying upward and she suspected it was the sight of her exposed sex that silenced him. One moment he was raising a half-hearted protest, trying to say something to Arthur as he smiled apologetically at her. The next, he was giving her his devoted attention. His gaze was fixed on the vision between her legs, although she noticed that he did occasionally glance up at her breasts. The pleasure of being admired struck her again and Sam felt a gratifying tingle of pleasure wash over her.

The thought of having men desire her as she flaunted her naked body was more enticing than she would have believed. She supposed they would have found her total nudity even more alluring but she suppressed the urge to snatch off her skirt and test the theory. She was not just there as a lap dancer, Sam reminded herself. She also had another job to do.

Staring into Derek's flustered features, another sparkle of recognition nagged at the back of her mind. It seemed odd that these two men should seem familiar in any respect. From the way he was studying her, beneath the surface expression of lust and lasciviousness, she guessed Derek was harbouring similar vague recollections. Dismissing the vague memory for a moment, she concentrated on her dance, trying to arouse and excite the man as much as she was able.

Using her biceps, she pushed her arms together and forced her diminutive breasts forward. The small orbs seemed to grow as she pushed the cleavage deeper. Still writhing her hips from side to side, Sam offered Derek her sexiest pout as she bent over him.

As she was bending forward she distantly realised her uncovered sex was likely to be revealed. It did not seem to matter at first and it was only when she felt the intrusive exploration of fingers between her legs that she realised how exposed she actually was. The cool, wet pad of a fingertip rubbed deliberately against the lips of her sex. The excitement of dancing for so many of the nightclub's clientele had already inspired a delicious wetness and Sam had felt more than a small stirring of passion when she caught herself thinking of the waitress with the alluring smile.

Judging by the cool chill that accompanied the moist finger against her shaven mound, she guessed she was being touched by Arthur's beer-wet hand. He drew a line against the febrile lips of her depilated labia, easing her pussy open and daring to press inside the boiling velvet of her hole.

Shocked and thrilled by the urgency that his touch inspired, Sam drew a shivering breath. She had been offering her breasts towards Derek in an attempt to arouse and stimulate him. Now the nubs of her nipples had hardened as the finger penetrated her sex. The subtle, circular caress of Arthur's gently probing fingertip evoked sensations that she could only describe as awesome. The thought of lowering herself back on to the intrusive finger was appealing but she dared not act upon it. With an effort of will, Sam tried to ignore the hungry tingle that flared from the depths of her cleft. Purposefully focusing on her dancing, Sam continued trying to excite Derek. She pushed her breasts close to his face, enjoying the sight of nervous sweat glimmering on his forehead. It was not difficult for her to maintain a sexy pout. The meaty fingers that teased her hole were already inspiring tiny, electric sparkles of pleasure. A second finger had joined the first and this one stroked wetly over the hardened nub of her clitoris. The pearl was pushed rudely from its hood and rubbed with slow deliberation. Sam could feel herself hurtling closer to the brink of orgasm. The easy way in which she was transported to such a state of bliss left her gasping for breath. It was a physical struggle to stave off the threat of an impending climax.

'Having fun, gentlemen?'

Sam glanced up at the sound of the voice, then quickly looked down again. In an instant all thoughts of arousal and pleasure were wrenched from her mind. An untapped instinct for self-preservation took over and she eased one of Arthur's hands away from her sex.

Because she did not attempt to move the other,

Arthur allowed his finger to remain on the edge of Sam's pussy lips, still maintaining the threat of penetration.

Barely aware of his intimate touch now, Sam tried to think of a casual way to extricate herself from the table. She hoped that the blonde wig would cover her face from Faye's view, or that the woman would be too blasé about her lap dancers to bother looking at any of them. This was Sam's second evening at the Good Night Club and, while she was already aware of the rules that surrounded Faye's table, she had only dared visit it while Faye was absent from the building. This was the first time the woman had come close to her, and Sam wondered if she should have gone for a more concealing disguise than the simple blonde wig she wore. Mentally, she crossed her fingers and prayed for good luck.

Aware of a stiffening in the woman's posture, she realised that good luck was not going to be on her side this evening. Her hopes of remaining undetected began to dissipate as soon as she felt Faye's manicured fingers touch her bare shoulder.

'Who are you?' Faye asked abruptly. There was a shard of ice in her tone.

Sam was not surprised to see the shocked expressions that crossed the faces of Derek and Arthur: they were clearly worried that she must have heard their conversation. They glanced inquisitively from Sam, then to Faye, then back to Sam again. She felt one of the notes being snatched rudely from beneath her garter and realised it was Arthur who had done this. He clearly did not feel any need to tip her if she was not one of Faye's lap dancers – but that did not explain why he left his finger nestling against her pussy.

'I want to know who you are,' Faye repeated

sharply. 'You're not one of my regular girls, but I know you, don't I?'

Sam raised her head slightly and risked a nervous smile through the fringe of her blonde wig. She tried to remember the name she had given on her application, suspecting she had gone for one of the character names from *Star Trek*. But she had filled out the form two days earlier and trying to recall the name she had glibly scrawled was now beyond her.

'Tell me who you are,' Faye said. The note of anger in her voice was now rising meteorically. 'I know your face but you're not one of my regular staff, are you?' She raised her hand and snapped her fingers, summoning someone from the shadows.

'Who the hell is she, Faye?' Arthur demanded. There was a strong current of panic in his voice which made his tone sound strident and unpleasant. 'Do you allow any strange young woman to come dancing topless in front of your patrons?'

'This wouldn't be your first visit if you thought we allowed that,' Faye remarked dryly. She glared unhappily at Sam, then glanced past her. Her gaze returned to Sam's face. 'This is your last chance. Tell me now or you'll be in real trouble. Who are you?'

Sam realised that the summoned help was closing in and her options were dwindling. She stood up, threw her shoulders back and tried to remain nonchalant about her near nudity. With one careless hand, she snatched the blonde wig from her head and released her own glorious mane of vibrant red tresses. At the same time, she reached into the small pocket of her short skirt, produced her glasses case, then donned her wire-framed spectacles.

Faye Meadows stifled a gasp of surprise. 'Which one are you? Valentine or Flowers? You're one of the investigators, aren't you? You're the senior partner, right? Flowers?'

176

Sam opened her mouth, flattered by the promotion this client had given her. Before she had a chance to reply, Arthur was on his feet and shouting angrily at Faye. 'Are you saying she's a fucking investigator? Why the hell have you got a fucking investigator patrolling us?' He glared furiously at Sam, then turned his attention back to Faye. 'This does it for me. Derek and I are leaving.'

Sam was about to intervene, when she felt two pairs of hands grab her from behind. She glanced nervously over each shoulder, not surprised to see two of the nightclub's doormen staring impassively back at her. Dressed in their uniforms of black suits, white shirts and black bow ties, they looked as cold and uncommunicative as the penguins their clothes had been modelled on. She made a brief attempt to struggle free but their hands held her tightly.

'I haven't had her patrolling you,' Faye explained hurriedly. She was struggling to keep a reasonable tone to her voice, attempting to placate the two men. 'I have no idea why she's here. I'll find that out in a moment, but let me assure you I'd employed her on a completely different matter.'

Arthur waved a silencing hand high in the air. 'Don't try and squirm your way out of it. You can forget about getting any help with your insurance claim now. Derek and I will return your file. You're no longer on our books.'

'No!' Faye declared sharply. 'This is ridiculous. Please, no!' She glared at Sam, then glanced at one of the doormen. 'Take her to my office, and wait in there with her,' she barked. Realising Arthur and Derek were walking past her, Faye quickly tried to stop them from leaving the building.

Sam knew she could not intervene. The two doormen were tugging her away and they seemed determined to follow Faye's instructions explicitly. She allowed them to turn her round and lead her away. The waitress she had been admiring walked past, and Sam was shocked to see the woman was scowling at her. The thought that she had lost all hope of winning the waitress's affections hit harder than the danger of her predicament. Miserably, she cursed the situation she had landed herself in. Around her, the nightclub's music continued to beat from the speakers at a deafening volume. The rest of the clientele continued about the business of enjoying themselves, oblivious to her plight.

'Thank you,' Faye growled as she entered the office. She stared angrily at Sam as she barked, 'Thank you for fucking over that little deal. Thank you for fucking over a business relationship I've been building for over two years and thank you for pushing my business empire one big step closer to the edge of a bottomless precipice.' She slammed the door closed as if to emphasise the enormity of her anger. Glaring at Sam, she pointed a threatening finger and hissed, 'You're going to pay for this, you little bitch.'

Sam studied her with a relaxed expression, unintimidated by the woman's menacing display. The office was a complete contrast to the dimly lit intimacy of the nightclub. This room was lit by bright neon strip lights. The walls were a sterile white hidden behind overladen shelves. Books, box files, plastic trays and bundles of dog-eared receipts completed most of the room's decor. The sound of the nightclub's music pulsed from the walls but now it was a distant murmur.

Sam had made herself comfortable in a padded swivel chair. She was still wearing nothing but the short skirt and stockings, her guard having chosen lechery over chivalry. Between her legs she was holding a book borrowed from one of the shelves. She closed it slowly, allowing Faye to read the title: *Greek Fables and Mythology*.

When she selected the book, Sam's guard had made one or two remarks about her enjoying 'Greek', but she had ignored his comments, aware of an urgent need to look up something relevant. She made a point of letting Faye see what she had been reading before sliding the book back to its space on the shelf. Trying not to be too obvious, she allowed the spine to jut out a little further than the hardback volumes on either side. She had to stand up and lean over a desk to put the book away, unconsciously displaying her backside and sex to Faye and the doorman. Remembering that she was not wearing pants, she realised that her exposed sex was on view to them. Trying not to show any discomfort with this thought, she moved slowly away from the shelf and brushed the hem of her skirt back down with a gesture that was almost casual.

'You,' Faye snapped. Sam saw the woman was talking to her guard. 'Fuck off out of here. I don't want to be disturbed.' There was a crisp note of authority in her voice that defied any challenge he might have raised.

Nodding curtly, he made for the door. Sam noticed that he graced her topless body with one last, rueful expression. In his eyes she could see an unfulfilled yearning that he had obviously hoped she could satisfy. For a brief instant she thought she saw a glimmer of pity in his face, as though he knew she was about to suffer some diabolical misfortune at Faye's hands. And then he was gone.

As soon as the door closed behind him, Faye

flicked the button on the battered Yale, locking them in together. She turned slowly to face Sam, a cruel smile on her lips. 'One question,' Faye said simply. She took a step closer to Sam as she spoke. 'One question, and I want an answer. How much do you know?'

Stepping nervously back, Sam swallowed. 'I don't understand,' she began. 'How much do I know about –'

Faye slapped her face. The sound of her flattened palm cracking against Sam's cheek echoed in the small office. Sam stifled a shocked gasp, raising a hand to her aching jaw. She stared miserably at Faye, aware of the menacing glint in her ice-blue eyes. The hard set of her mouth, the thin line of her lips and the cruel sneer that curled her nose were more than familiar. At school, Sam had once been the subject of a beating from school prefects. The girl who initiated that beating had worn an identical expression to the one she could now see on Faye's face.

'This is your one and only chance to get out of here without really suffering,' Faye told her, pointing a dramatic finger towards Sam's face. 'And I strongly recommend that you grasp it with both hands. Tell me how much you know or, God help you, I'll make you tell me.'

Sam held her ground, standing defiantly in front of the woman. 'If you'd let me explain,' she began, quelling the nervous tremor that threatened to shake her steady voice. 'I only came here because –'

Faye slapped her again. This time the force of the blow was hard enough to knock Sam down. She was fortunate that the padded swivel chair was behind her when she fell, otherwise she would have been staring up from the floor like a broken rag doll. She glared up from the seat, beseeching Faye with a pained and frightened expression. Her near nudity did not seem to trouble the woman and that realisation only added to Sam's fear.

'You know about Malcolm, don't you?' Faye barked. 'You know about him and the insurance claim, and I suspect you've been talking with Sky.' She glared furiously at Sam, the passionate glower in her eyes demanding some sort of response. 'What were the Knight brothers saying?' Faye growled.

Panic was taking over and Sam did not have a clue as to what the woman was talking about. An inner calm had visited her as she sat beneath the doorman's lascivious gaze, allowing her time to think about the complexities of the case, but that calm seemed to have disappeared with Faye's arrival. She wanted to declare her ignorance but a poignant knife blade of terror held her silent. She suspected that any comment that was not a straight answer would merit another punishing blow. When Sam did find the courage to open her mouth, the first sound that came out was a gasp of pain as she tried to move her aching jaw.

'Start talking to me,' Faye hissed sharply. She lifted one stiletto-heeled shoe from the floor and stamped her foot on to the seat of the chair. The heel pushed firmly into the chair between Sam's legs. The tip of her shoe fell against the front panel of Sam's short skirt and the pressure of the pointed toe rested heavily over the lips of her sex.

Nervously, Sam glanced up at Faye, aware of how precarious her situation had become. She had just learnt more about this case than she could have hoped and now she was in danger of getting a beating for it. She supposed the price might have been worth paying, but the things she had learnt did not seem to fit together. Her thoughts were a whirlwind that raged ceaselessly. As she tried to think of a way to placate Faye, she was also trying to work out how this new information fitted in with the other things she had learnt over the past few days.

'What do you know?' Faye demanded.

Her hand moved forward and for an instant Sam thought she was going to be struck again. It was only second nature to back away from the domineering woman, but in the confines of the padded chair she quickly realised there was nowhere to back away to. She wanted to say that she knew nothing. Even with the things that Faye had just told her, she still felt absolutely clueless about what was happening. But she doubted Faye would believe such a claim.

Instead of striking Sam, Faye's fingers reached for her bared breast and stroked one nipple. She was still scowling with the same menacing glint in her eye, but now her expression seemed tinged with something dark and unreadable. Her smile, cruel and threatening before, now seemed more malevolent.

Sam swallowed. Her nipple hardened beneath Faye's touch and she tried convincing herself that it was purely an automatic reaction. She wanted to believe she wasn't feeling aroused. Her days of getting pleasure from being submissive were a thing of the past, she told herself. Glaring defiantly up at Faye, she attempted to slap the woman's hand away.

Faye was fast. With her free hand, she caught Sam's wrist and pushed it back. The fingers at Sam's nipple squeezed hard against the nub. There was no mercy or tenderness in her touch. When Faye pushed the wrist back, it was done to hurt. When she squeezed the nipple, the pressure was calculated to inflict as much pain as possible.

Sam gasped. A flare of pain erupted from her wrist and a piercing bolt of pleasure exploded in her breast.

At the same time she could feel the toe of Faye's shoe pressing hard against her cleft. She glanced down and saw that Faye had managed to slide the tip of the stiletto beneath the hem of her skirt. Although she could not see it, she could feel the shoe pressing against the pouting lips of her sex. Faye's penetrating her seemed more than possible and Sam was chilled by the unspoken threat.

She stared into the uncompromising face that hovered above her and wished she knew what to do. She tried to think what Jo would do if she was in this situation, then stopped herself. Jo would never have been stupid enough to get into such a position, Sam thought. This sort of mistake was so typically Samantha Flowers that she believed she could have applied for a patent.

It was difficult to concentrate on most of these thoughts. There was something cloying about the fear that Faye evoked. There was also the warmth of her own arousal, hampering the clear head she so desperately longed to attain. The toe of the shoe against her sex was touching her with a lover's intimacy. She could not deny she was scared by Faye's domineering manner, but there was also the *frisson* of excitement that the woman inspired. Faye was touching her body in ways that Sam could only think of as intimate and personal. The feelings Faye stirred quickened the eager pulse in Sam's cleft.

Sam drew a frightened breath and beseeched Faye with a silent plea. She did not expect any response to her helpless expression, but it was the penultimate line of defence in her armoury. When she realised it was doing no good, she knew it was time to play her last card. Frowning miserably, she allowed a single tear to roll down her cheek.

Faye studied her, the menace in her expression

intensifying. She still held Sam's nipple between merciless fingers, while her other hand pinned Sam's wrist uncomfortably back into the chair. Faye shook her head from side to side, twisting Sam's nipple as she glowered down. 'You don't know a fucking thing, do you?' Faye growled.

Sam struggled to suppress a miserable sob. It was one thing to be humiliated and punished like this, she thought. It was worse to have that happen while someone pointed out your inadequacies. Shaking her head in agreement, she sniffed back another tear and stared miserably down.

Faye moved her hand from Sam's wrist to her chin and tilted her head upward. She was smiling, but Sam still regarded the expression warily. 'You know nothing about this case,' Faye said pointedly. 'Yet you've come here, fucked over one of my business deals, lost me my solicitors and screwed up an insurance claim I was working on.' She shook her head, smiling with bemused wonder at the depths of Sam's incompetence. 'You're a walking fucking disaster.'

Unhappily, Sam tried to look down. She had wanted to use the tears as a device to extricate herself from this situation but now, as Faye pointed out her ineptitude with clinical accuracy, Sam found that the tears were caused by a genuine wave of misery. They brimmed heavily on the lower lids of her eyes and she no longer wanted this overbearing woman to watch her cry. It had been uncomfortable when she began and at that point she had been faking.

Faye did not allow her the privilege of lowering her face. She kept her fingers beneath Sam's chin, pushing upward so that they were forced to stare at one another.

'You're going to prove yourself good at something

before this day's out,' Faye growled. 'One way or another, you're going to prove yourself good at something.' The tip of her toe pushed forcefully against Sam's sex, as though she was pressing home her point.

Sam gasped, shocked by the suggestion. She could feel that her nipple was no longer being squeezed. Instead, Faye was caressing the tip with an intimacy that was disturbingly gentle. With mounting disquiet, Sam watched as Faye moved her fingers away from her chin to the tip of her other breast. She caught a startled breath when the woman's fingertips brushed the swell of her nipple. An electric shock of pleasure erupted in the erectile tissue and an unexpected bolt of delight coursed from the spot where Faye had touched. Breathless and startled, Sam stared wistfully up at the woman, aware that her cheeks and forehead were glowing dully with the sudden warmth of her blushes.

'I thought you'd be the sort who liked this kind of thing,' Faye remarked calmly. 'I figured you were on with your business partner. But I could see you had a need for this sort of game too.' Her cruel smile tightened as she pressed her fingernails cruelly into the soft, pliant flesh of Sam's nipples.

Sam gasped. She was shocked and hurt by the contrast of pain with the pleasure she had been enjoying. She glared into Faye's unimpassioned features and tried to think of something she could say to make the woman forget her thoughts of punishment.

'I said I'd find a use for you before this evening's over,' Faye said, releasing her hands from Sam's breasts. 'And I think I've just thought of one.'

As Sam watched, Faye stroked the palm of her hand over the swell of her own breast. The sensation through the thick gabardine fabric of her jacket was obviously pleasing, Sam guessed, because Faye sighed contentedly. Her other hand rubbed against her hip, the fingers easing purposefully towards the crease at the top of the legs. Half-expecting the woman to start playing with herself, Sam held her breath and tried not to stare.

Faye took a step back from the chair, moving her toe downward and pressing hard against Sam's sex before taking the foot away. She glided gracefully to one of the shelves and reached into a plastic tray.

Sam frowned, not knowing what to expect. She wiped the tears from her cheeks with the back of her hand and blinked miserably through her glasses. She was surprised to see the woman remove a bulky stage microphone from the tray, and for an instant she wondered if Faye had given up on the idea of punishing her. The hope only lasted for a moment, quickly replaced by a realisation of what the woman intended.

If Jo had been there, Sam knew she would have been asking Faye if they were going to do some karaoke, or have a private singalong. The thought was meant to be cheering, but it only served to remind Sam that Jo was not there and she was having to endure this on her own. Considering the cruel smile on Faye's lips, Sam could see that her punishment was about to begin and she shivered uneasily.

Faye shrugged the jacket from her shoulders and then unfastened the zip at the side of her skirt. Stepping out of the garment as it pooled at her ankles, Faye tugged the long length of electrical flex that trailed from the base of the microphone and moved closer to Sam. She was still wearing her blouse, the long hem discreetly covering the tops of her legs, but as she bore down she began to unfasten the buttons at the neck.

'You'd better not hurt me,' Sam said quietly. 'I won't tolerate that and my partner won't tolerate it either.'

Faye shook her head. 'That doesn't really intimidate me,' she replied. She held the microphone in one hand and the long length of black flex in the other. With an almost casual flick of her wrist, she brought the end of the cable spinning through the air in a broad arc. Sam was startled to feel the end of the cable strike her leg. The gold-tipped jack-plug cut a line across one of Sam's black stockings, splitting the sheer denier to reveal a raised red line beneath.

Sam drew a shocked breath and stared at Faye with renewed respect. Thoughts of trying to intimidate or bluff her were now gone from Sam's mind. She could see that Faye was not the sort of woman who delivered idle threats. The danger of the situation impressed itself upon her. Trying to squeeze herself back into the chair, away from Faye, Sam stammered the beginning of an apology.

Faye was not listening. Still grinning, she brought the end of the microphone cable down hard again. This time it cut higher on Sam's leg. The sharp tip of the jack-plug bit into the flesh above the top of Sam's garter.

Wincing with the sudden explosion of pain, Sam snatched her leg into the chair and tried to caress the grazed lines of flesh that Faye had just caused. She realised that by sitting in such a position she was openly displaying herself to the woman. The knowledge that she was exhibiting the lips of her exposed sex did not seem as important as stopping Faye from hitting her leg again.

'You've pissed off the wrong person,' Faye said.

Her voice was like acid. With a casual hand, she slapped Sam's legs down, so that they hung beneath the chair. 'Your one chance to redeem yourself is by doing exactly as I say.'

Sam dared to pluck up the last of her courage and glowered defiantly back at the woman. 'And if I don't do exactly as you say?' she demanded.

Faye shook her head and smiled with infuriating arrogance. 'You don't have a choice.'

Before Sam could stop her, Faye had wrapped the cord of the microphone round one wrist and fastened her to the chair. Sam started to say something but her protests were silenced by a back-handed blow to her mouth. It was as close as Faye came to acknowledging her struggles, and it ended them abruptly.

In the stunned silence that followed, Faye fastened Sam's other arm to the chair. With a well-practised flick of her wrist, she tied the remainder of the cord round Sam's ankles, securing her feet to the centre pole of the swivel chair.

'You won't get away with this,' Sam whispered, wishing she felt as defiant as she sounded. She could taste blood on her lower lip and her tongue detected lingering pain beneath the swelling where she had been struck. More frightening than either of these sensations, she could feel the inner muscles of her pussy throbbing with eager anticipation.

Faye laughed sardonically. 'Stay quiet or I'll slap you again. You no longer have a say in things.' Kneeling down in front of Sam, she traced one long, manicured fingernail against the sensitive flesh of Sam's breast. 'Right now, I can do whatever the hell I please,' Faye explained. With a cruel smile, she added, 'And I intend to do just that.' She hooked the tip of one finger into the waistband of Sam's skirt.

Sam tried to recoil from her touch. She was excited

by the intimacy of Faye's intrusive finger but there was something menacing in the woman's smile that left her chilled at the same time. The fact that she was tied to a chair and at the woman's mercy would have been enough to frighten her. The evil glint in Faye's eye left her cold and fearful. 'What are you going to do to me?' Sam demanded, swallowing a nervous lump in her throat. Her heart was beating so fast she could feel the pulse pounding in her temples.

With a sudden lunge, Faye tore Sam's skirt open. She glared at her bare sex with an angry frown that quickly faded into a wicked smile. Faye growled, 'I issue my lap dancers with G-strings and *you're* not wearing one.'

Sam tried to think of an appropriate response but nervousness held her tongue. She studied Faye through a miserable veil of tears, loving and loathing the intimidation.

Faye stroked the tip of her finger against Sam's hole. One nail trailed softly against the pink folds. Sam could feel herself responding to the caress and wished her body was not so easy to arouse. The heated pulse between her legs quickened and she could feel an anticipatory dryness in her throat. The tips of her nipples burnt with a tingling pain that demanded they be caressed. Her entire body was quickly becoming more and more responsive. Faye continued to draw her finger along the gentle pout of Sam's pussy lips. The subtle friction was lubricated by the warm wetness of Sam's arousal.

As much as she hated herself for responding to the woman in such a way, Sam could not deny her rising excitement. She glared truculently into her captor's face, hating her and wanting her in the same moment.

Faye returned the expression blithely, continuing to stroke at Sam's intimate flesh. 'If you had been wearing knickers I could have gagged you with them,' she explained. 'Not that anyone will be able to hear you in here,' she added quickly, 'but just for my own peace of mind.'

Sam felt her heart beat faster. She wished that her fear and arousal had been separate emotions. If that had been the case, she knew she would have been able to cope with at least one of them. As it was, she could not decide if the threat of being gagged had caused terror or excitement. Her desperate need for release was no longer confined to the desire to be free from the chair. She was overwhelmed by the urgent longing to give her body the fulfilment it so desperately craved. The pulse between her legs beat with a frenzied desire that craved the release of satisfaction.

A thought occurred to Sam and she tried to dismiss it. The sensation of Faye's finger sliding against the dewy folds of her pussy lips was disturbingly good. She could feel herself creeping closer to the brink of an orgasm and her body had already warned her that the release would be monumental. The thought that had occurred to her threatened to destroy the pleasure of release and she cursed it for being so intrusive.

Faye eased the tip of her finger inside the velvety warmth of Sam's sex.

Simultaneously, both women drew startled gasps of pleasure. They studied one another with mixed expressions of excitement and longing. Sam could see the shine in Faye's pale blue eyes and knew the woman was as passionately aroused as she was.

With her other hand, Faye reached up and stroked the heel of her palm against one of Sam's breasts. The dry flesh rubbed smoothly over the hard nub. Sam groaned, wishing she had the time to enjoy all of the woman's beautiful, rude caresses.

'Untie me,' Sam whispered reluctantly.

Faye shook her head. She teased the end of her finger against the pulsing pearl of Sam's clitoris. The gentle pressure inspired a shriek of elation from Sam. She pushed herself back into the chair as far as her bindings would allow, then shook her head in joyous refusal of the pleasure her body was suffering.

'Too much,' Sam whispered happily. Her fear had suddenly dissipated as she realised she had the upper hand. She vowed to point this fact out to Faye as soon as she had made the woman release her. 'Please. Stop and untie me.'

Pushing her finger gently in and out of Sam's eager cleft, Faye shook her head in slow but firm refusal. A second finger joined the first and within a moment she was sliding them both into the tight confines of Sam's slick wet hole.

'This is your last chance,' Sam urged her. She could feel her pussy lips being excited by the gentle stretching pressure of having to accommodate two squirming fingers. The sensation was debilitating and the breath was being torn from her lungs in excited pants. 'Untie me now and I promise not to lose my temper,' Sam insisted.

Faye smiled softly and eased a third finger alongside the first two.

Sam pushed herself far back into the chair. She had been tied in such a way that it hurt her ankles to make any physical movement. Actually bucking her hips back and forth against the woman's probing fingers was a bitter agony for her ankles, but she did it just the same. The fingers slid roughly into the warm wetness of her sex, pushing her to the brink of a cataclysmic orgasm. She knew that it would only take a few more thrusts and she would be beyond the point of no return. The anticipation of that release was so strong that Sam could almost taste the triumphant satisfaction.

'What on earth makes you think that your temper would worry me?' Faye asked curiously.

For an instant, Sam could not answer. The explosion of pleasure between her legs was so great that she could do nothing but groan incoherently. Each nerve-ending seemed taut and hyper-charged. Her mind was soaring to sensational heights of ecstasy and as she shook her head against the back of the chair she gasped words of elation.

After the orgasm, it took a moment for her to get her thoughts back in order. When she did, the woman was standing over her, a disparaging frown creasing her brow. She had given up her hold on the microphone and was now holding a roll of packing tape. Sam shivered when she saw the impassive coolness of the woman's expression. Nevertheless, she knew that she now had the upper hand and only hoped that she would get a chance to explain this much before the woman gagged her.

'Untie me,' Sam instructed firmly. 'I think I've worked all this out now. But it would help if you confirmed something for me.'

Faye stared at her scornfully. 'And what might you have worked out?'

'Why did you call the health farm Elysian Fields?' She noticed the flicker of uncertainty in Faye's eyes and her smile broadened. Shaking her head, she waved one bound hand to show that she did not need a response. Glancing at the spine of the book she had been reading earlier, she smiled triumphantly to herself. 'Don't bother,' Sam said magnanimously. 'I've just worked it out.' It all made sense now. The talk of an insurance deal, the name Elysian Fields and all those other things she had learnt about the woman during her research of the past few days. She fixed Faye with a knowing expression and said, 'You were planning on taking a trip to Elysian Fields this evening, weren't you?' The startled expression in the woman's eyes was confirmation enough for Sam. She grinned broadly and continued. 'I think that you should untie me and we'll take that trip together.'

Sam could tell from the hesitant frown on Faye's face that she was teetering on the brink of control. She needed to mention only one more thing and then she knew the woman would release her. Without hesitation, Sam asked, 'Do we go and see your husband together? Or do I go to the police on my own?'

Faye Meadows knelt down and began to unfasten Sam's restraints.

Nine

Sky slammed the telephone down so hard she cracked the handset. A shrill ring jarred her ear as the phone protested against such abuse, but she ignored the sound. Her face was a darkening thunder cloud. 'Bastards,' she hissed angrily. She whirled round and glared at the woman on the floor, not bothering to mask the fury contorting her features.

Poppy stared meekly up. A wave of unhappiness washed over her tear-reddened cheeks as she flinched from the sound of Sky's voice. Kneeling on the floor, her naked body quivered with nervous apprehension. She was still holding the striped cheeks of her arse high, just as Sky had instructed. Her breasts swayed gently beneath her and, if Sky had taken the trouble to indulge in a closer examination, she would have seen that both nipples were scored with the fading scarlet memories of all her earlier whippings. The tremor that shook Poppy's body caused a ragged moan to fall from her lips.

Until she had taken the telephone call, Sky had felt the stirrings of some sympathy for Poppy. She had gone out of her way to make the day unique for the solicitor. Every moment had been devoted to sexual torture and the mysteries of pleasurable punishment, but Sky could see the woman was beginning to tire of such lessons now. Before the phone call, she had empathised with Poppy's weariness.

The idea for a health farm like Elysian Fields had been devised at a time when she considered the enjoyment of sex to be fulfilling, satisfying and wholesome. Since Malcolm's death, life had shown Sky new aspects of sex. She still found it fulfilling and satisfying but she had begun to realise that her partners did not have to. As long as she was in absolute control of the situation, Sky knew she would get satisfaction. When she was caught in the throes of passion, nothing else mattered.

Throughout the day she had treated Poppy to a working example of this thesis. It had been a revelation, she thought coldly. Poppy's reluctant enjoyment of each sadistic punishment was taking her closer to a new way of life. Sky had no idea what sort of woman the solicitor had been before she arrived at Elysian Fields, but she felt certain she had changed. The naked figure kneeling timidly on the floor of her bedroom may have been pliant and malleable before, but now she had been transformed into a sexual submissive. Seeing the excited shine in Poppy's eyes when she was slapped or whipped, Sky knew that the woman was now the devoted servant to anyone who cared to abuse her. The part of her mind that had longed for this revenge took a good measure of satisfaction from having done the job so well.

While Poppy had obviously relished every orgasm, despite the ruthless way each had been extracted, exhaustion was now beginning to hamper her enjoyment. The telephone call had put Sky's sympathy in check.

She reached down and grabbed a fistful of Poppy's hair. Twisting her head to one side, she squeezed a scream from Poppy and growled, 'That was your fucking employers on the telephone.'

Poppy snatched a frightened breath, the sound rasping harshly in her dry throat.

Glaring down at her, Sky caught sight of her own reflection in Poppy's shining eyes. Her blonde hair was pulled back in the severe way that she favoured for domination, and she still wore the black basque and stockings of her psycho-bitch costume. She knew she looked imposing, and under other circumstances Sky would have enjoyed Poppy's fearful expression as she quivered on the floor, but right now she was struggling to cope with mounting anger and her own appearance was irrelevant.

Using the back of one hand, Sky slapped Poppy across the face. 'Your employers have just given me some distressing news,' Sky hissed. She still held Poppy's hair and pulled it tightly as she bawled the information at her. 'Very distressing news,' she reiterated, stressing her point with spittle-flecked words. 'They've been followed by a private investigator and they think there might be another one in this place.' She shook her head wearily. 'I'm surprised they managed to fuck you,' she mumbled in a disparaging tone. 'I wouldn't have thought they could find a cunt in a whorehouse.'

Poppy released a small gasp.

Sky did not know if the woman was shocked by her use of such base language, or if it was the reference to how the Knight brothers had used her. Staring into the meek plea in Poppy's eyes, Sky's anger darkened. She pushed the woman away with a frustrated sigh and stormed towards the door of her bedroom. She could have happily taken her anger out on Poppy but there would have been no satisfaction in such an act. Poppy was not just beaten and cowed. After the way Sky had treated her, Poppy would be far too willing to enjoy such humiliation.

In her current mood, Sky wanted to exert her anger on someone who was not trained to revel in it. She

196

wanted to hurt someone and have the satisfaction of seeing them suffer properly.

Sky took one last disdainful look at Poppy and scowled. 'I want you to stay right there,' she hissed sharply. 'I don't want you to move until I come back. Do you hear me?' After extracting a reluctant nod of servility, Sky stormed out of the room, slammed the door and left the submissive alone.

Poppy stayed where she had been left, too frightened to move.

After trying Jo's bedroom, Sky was annoyed to find the woman was not there. She remembered her original idea for the health farm and smiled confidently to herself. She marched briskly down the stairs and went towards the eatery, then through to the annexed kitchen.

The scene in the kitchen looked like something from a pornographic movie. As she stood and watched, Sky could not deny the stirrings of arousal that swept over her. She was still filled with a blazing anger that she longed to release, but there was also a furious excitement between her legs demanding satisfaction. Watching the unbridled display of carnal abandon, she felt her need for fulfilment increase.

Bryn lay across the centre of a table that teetered on the verge of collapse. The table's legs were shaking with the pounding it received and Sky could see that most of its contents had already fallen, or been pushed, to the floor. A couple of bottles rested among a pile of crisp packets and sweet wrappers. She could see a pack of strewn playing cards lying amid the debris, but her concentration was not focused on such trivialities. There were two others on top of the table with Bryn.

Violet was straddling him, easing his long cock into

the cleft of her pussy. She had her arse directed towards Sky, displaying her wet sex lips as Bryn's stiff length penetrated her. Her mouth was pressed over Bryn's face, kissing and licking him greedily.

The other person on the table was Allen. Sky smiled confidently up at him, recognising his backside because of the twin stripe marks she had left there that afternoon. She could see him nuzzling the end of his cock against the tight rim of Violet's arsehole, preparing to enter her as Bryn ploughed his length deep into the heated warmth of the woman's pussy.

Violet was groaning and gasping. She encouraged Allen with soft, desperate pleas. Her cries were interspersed with tearful sighs as she begged him to probe the forbidden depths of her backside.

Sky saw the woman's legs trembling and could almost feel the pleasure that she was experiencing. Simply watching the scene was an exhilarating experience. The thought of actually participating stirred a heat in her loins that Sky had difficulty quashing. Standing by the door, she was afforded the perfect view when Allen pushed his hips forward. He held Violet's waist in his strong hands, and guided his length deep into the tight confines of her arsehole. Violet's scream echoed around the kitchen, rattling from the metallic surfaces and threatening to wake every other guest.

This was how Elysian Fields was supposed to be, Sky told herself. Fulfilling and wholesome sex in place of all those other unhealthy distractions that a body could crave. Watching Violet sweat and tense her muscles in absolute enjoyment of the moment, she distantly wondered how many calories the woman was effortlessly burning up. Just watching her, Sky could see that Violet was performing exercises in muscle control that went beyond any aerobic workout she would have normally attempted. She was pushing her body to its limits in an effort to squeeze more of Allen's cock into the dark depths of her arsehole. If the scene had not been so lewd, Sky would have wanted to use it as promotional material for the health farm.

Allen's length slid slowly forward, entering Violet's arsehole and stretching her tight ring wide. Bryn's cock, shorter than Allen's but delightfully thick, was sliding deep into the warm haven of Violet's pussy. The woman was enjoying the pleasure of having two rampant studs fuck her and, although Sky did not consider herself prone to jealousy, she was more than a little envious of Violet's good fortune. Sighing heavily, she turned to the door and started to make her way out of the kitchen.

'Sky? Is that you? Why don't you come in here and join us?'

She turned back to face the three of them when Allen called her. He was still fucking Violet's arse as Bryn rode between her legs, but for the moment his attention was centred on her. Shaking her head, she turned back to the door. 'I'm trying to find Jo Valentine,' she explained. 'That woman and I have some business to attend to.' Even as she said the words, Sky realised she was making her anger obvious and wished she could hide the emotion. It was not a good policy to let everyone know what she was thinking or planning.

'Have you tried Wendy's room?' Allen suggested.

'Why should she be there?'

Allen's knowing smile was answer enough. Sky nodded, flung the door open and marched purposefully out of the kitchen. She wanted to take a last look at the scene before she left. If she was being totally honest with herself she wanted to go back and get involved. There was a part of her that wanted to push Violet out of the way and indulge herself with Bryn and Allen, allowing the pair of them to use and abuse her however they saw fit. The notion of such bliss left her tingling with a mixture of excitement and anticipation.

Wilfully, she suppressed the urge and started down the corridor. Now that she had an idea where Jo Valentine might be, Sky had to act on it. With a cruel smile, she decided that whatever Jo Valentine had to say for herself it would not be enough. Sky had wanted to enjoy herself in the kitchen and she had now decided it was Jo's fault that she could not. Because of that, Sky decided that when she found the investigator she was going to punish her even more severely.

'Stop right there,' Sky hissed. She lowered her voice because of the late hour, aware that there were guests sleeping in rooms that led off from the silent corridor. In spite of her whispered tone there was enough ice in her voice to stop Wendy cold as she came face to face with the Black Widow.

'Where the fuck have you been?' Sky demanded. 'And where is Valentine?'

Wendy stammered for a moment, her hesitant voice revealing her lies before she could give them proper voice. 'Val ... Valentine?' she began. 'I don't –'

Sky reached out with one hand and caught hold of the cord of Wendy's dressing-gown. She pulled her close with a sharp, powerful tug and glared into her eyes. She did not hurt Wendy but the movement was so sudden and unexpected she heard her deliver a short gasp of surprise. When they were close together, Sky inhaled deeply. The air around Wendy was redolent with freshly spent pussy juice. In the darkness, her cruel smile tightened.

'Jo Valentine,' Sky hissed. 'Jo Valentine the private investigator. Jo Valentine the woman whose cunt you've just been eating. Where is she?'

Wendy caught a breath, as though she had been slapped. In the darkness she glared back at Sky. With her voice still faltering, she began to say, 'I don't know what you –'

Sky did not allow her to get any further. She grabbed the lapels of Wendy's dressing-gown and pulled the woman tight against her. There was little light in the corridor, save for the dull green glow of the EMERGENCY EXIT signs. From that emerald glimmer Sky was able to discern the lustre of viscous wetness coating Wendy's lips and chin. Pressing her face close to Wendy's, she whispered, 'I'm giving you one last chance, then I'll lose my patience. Where is Jo Valentine?'

Wendy swallowed. In the corridor's poor light her eyes shone with fear. 'I don't know.'

Wearily, Sky released a sigh. 'That's a lie.'

Wendy shook her head and tried to make her whispered voice more convincing. 'It's not a lie,' she insisted. 'I don't know where she is.'

In the silence that followed, Sky could hear the angry pulse of her own heartbeat. She had checked Jo's room twice this evening and she had checked Wendy's once. The sheets in Wendy's room were used and dishevelled and Sky suspected that whatever had gone on between the two women had occurred in there.

As the darkening cloud of her anger took over, she began to realise that she was beyond caring about the threat of an investigator. She was desperate to make someone suffer and her first choice for that privilege had been the elusive Jo Valentine. However, if she was going to have to pick a consolation prize, Wendy seemed more than suitable. She had already annoyed Sky by lying to her and now she was compounding her crime by trying to maintain that lie. All this came on top of the pledge that Wendy had given her for absolute obedience.

Sky decided she had had enough.

Dragging her by the cord of her dressing-gown, Sky began to pull Wendy down the corridor, back to her bedroom.

'No,' Wendy gasped, trying to remain still and failing miserably as Sky dragged her. 'You can't. I mean –'

Sky paused for a moment. She pushed her face close to Wendy's, enjoying the scent of pussy juice on the woman's breath. The light, exciting fragrance caused her heart to beat faster. The pulse of her arousal was heightened by the thrill of her growing anger. 'We'll discuss this back in my bedroom,' she said quietly.

Without thinking about it, she leant forward and kissed Wendy on the lips. As her tongue explored the woman's mouth she could taste the musky, sweet remnants of love juice. She heard Wendy sigh beneath the intrusion of her kiss and Sky smiled excitedly to herself.

Despite her fear, or perhaps even because of it, Wendy was quivering beneath her touch. Sky could feel her anticipation mounting and wished she could see the woman's face. Wendy was so obviously scared that Sky longed to see the glimmer of fear shining in her eyes. That idea alone was enough to send a pulsing charge tingling through her inner muscles. Barely able to contain her own excitement, Sky growled, 'Follow me.' Without waiting for Wendy to respond, she began to drag her down the corridor.

* * *

Fifteen minutes later, staring down at the two naked backsides, Sky realised again this was not how she had envisioned Elysian Fields. Admittedly, she had not wanted the place to be called Elysian Fields. That was the idea of either her late husband or the manipulative bitch he had married, but the name was the smallest of her considerations.

Poppy and Wendy knelt on the floor in front of Sky, holding their backsides high in the air. Sky had been trying to exercise a little leniency on Poppy's arse. She had whipped, caned and scored it so many times that it seemed to have developed a permanently reddened hue. The orbs were criss-crossed with a spider's web of raised red lines and some were so dark and severe that Sky feared they would tear if she inflicted another beating. To compensate for this she was administering the heavier blows to Wendy.

This was not how it was meant to be, she reminded herself sullenly.

She was struck by a moment's unhappiness amid the pleasure of the punishment she was administering. The health farm was meant to have been developed on a theme of mutually enjoyable sex. Sexual punishment and humiliation went against the belief she had subscribed to when she first conceived the idea of the health farm. Now, as she prepared to take control of the building, she wondered if she had become an unfit person to be in charge.

It would be difficult to resist the pleasures of domination, she thought honestly. The position of control was good for her, creating a powerful excitement that helped her to achieve the most marvellous satisfaction. Yet she knew that if she was going to maintain her position in charge of Elysian Fields she would have to find another avenue for her passions. But she decided to vent her rage first and consider the problem later.

Glaring down at Wendy's backside, Sky blamed the woman for a lot of her problems. She raised the riding crop high in the air, then brought it down against Wendy's arse. The tip connected with a hollow slap, echoing from the walls of Sky's bedroom.

Both Poppy and Wendy cried out in protest.

If Wendy had told the truth earlier this evening, Sky knew she would be punishing Jo Valentine by now. Perhaps that did not make things right, she conceded, but she would have felt justified in punishing someone who was supposedly spying on her. She raised the crop again and brought it down in a swift arc twice, then three times.

Wendy wailed as the crop caught her buttocks repeatedly. The cheeks of her arse were burning a bright red beneath the darkening welts. She trembled on the floor, shivering as though very frightened or very excited. Studying the glistening wetness that coated her labia, Sky suspected it was a combination of these two feelings. The pouting swell of Wendy's lips had peeled open. The moist crease revealed silently demanded her attention.

Smiling darkly as she noticed the woman's wet lips, Sky raised her crop and caned Wendy again. For the moment, it did not matter that sexual punishment was wrong and went against the ethos of Elysian Fields. Wendy seemed to be enjoying it, and, from the surly looks Poppy was doling out, Sky suspected the solicitor was missing the kiss of the crop's tip.

With her good mood restored, Sky began to shout orders at the two women. She pushed the heel of one stiletto into the cheek of Poppy's backside, forcing her to the floor. After barking a list of instructions, she grabbed Wendy's hair and dragged her up from the carpet. As soon as Wendy was standing, Sky pushed her on to the bed. She still held the riding crop and raised it threateningly. With a wicked smile, she glared down at the terrified woman, trying to decide which part of her body to strike.

Wendy lay motionless on the bed. Sky had already taught her how to lie still during a punishment. The natural urge to protect herself had been beaten out of her and she lay rigid beneath the Black Widow, prepared to accept whatever chastisement was administered.

The sight of such submission inspired a wet tingle between Sky's legs. Controlling her mounting excitement with a faltering breath, she tried not to smile as she stared down at Wendy. 'This is going to be your last chance to speak before I punish you properly,' Sky explained. 'Where will I find Jo Valentine?'

For an instant it looked as though Wendy was going to tell her. There was a hesitancy in her green eyes which grew as she glanced from Sky's menacing frown to the wicked tip of the riding crop. Her lower lip trembled and Sky held her breath, waiting for the revelation to spill from Wendy's mouth.

Then Wendy was shaking her head. 'No,' she whispered, and looked away from Sky in a bold act of defiance.

'Bitch!' Sky spat, slapping her riding crop angrily across Wendy's nipple. Ideally she would have wanted Wendy to tell her where Jo was hiding, but the woman's rebellion had its compensations. She slapped the tip of the crop across Wendy's other breast with a sharp, vicious blow. Ignoring Wendy's shrieks, Sky turned her attention to Poppy.

With typical obedience, Poppy had carried out her

instructions to the letter. Sky had demanded a handful of items and Poppy placed each of them on the bedside table. With the task done, she took a step back. She studied Sky with an expectant expression that begged to be given another instruction.

Snapping her fingers and pointing, Sky motioned for Poppy to kneel on the floor. She handed her the riding crop then climbed on to the bed. Positioning herself over the prostrate Wendy's face, Sky grinned down at her victim. Her slit was so close to Wendy's face she could feel the warmth of each exhaled breath caressing her sex. 'I want you to lick me, Wendy,' Sky explained. Her tone was calm and almost conversational. 'I want you to lick me, and lick me well. Once you've made me come, I'll be prepared to listen to you. But I'm not listening until you've made me climax. Do you understand?'

With a fearful expression, Wendy nodded.

Sky lowered herself, pushing the lips of her pussy against Wendy's tongue. She rested herself heavily on the woman's face so that Wendy's only option was to lap at her tight wet hole. Her sodden cleft was treated to a barrage of kisses and the titillation of a broad, hot tongue rubbing against it. Sky could feel her clitoris being teased by the delicious wet friction of Wendy's mouth. The sudden thrill snatched a cry from her throat. Revelling in the heady joy of the stimulation, Sky lowered her body over Wendy's, moving her face towards the submissive's gaping sex. With a casual snap of her fingers, she summoned Poppy to her side.

The solicitor responded instantaneously.

'Suck her tits,' Sky muttered, reaching past Poppy. She waited until the woman was suckling on one of Wendy's nipples. It took only a moment before the two women were moaning. Even with her face buried into Sky's mound, Wendy was still able to make muffled sounds of mounting enjoyment as Poppy teased the sensitive tips of her breasts.

With malicious glee, Sky exercised the pair of bulldog clips that Poppy had brought for her. She stared down at Wendy's glistening lips, tracing a finger against the warm, wet flesh as she followed the line of the woman's pussy.

Wendy's muffled sighs deepened to a heavy pant and Sky heard herself groaning deeply. Wendy's tongue was lapping furiously at the haven between her legs and Sky's entire body was trembling with the elation of a threatening climax. But Sky was extracting her real enjoyment from the prospect of forcing Wendy to submit.

Originally, in the sauna, she had thought that Wendy was cowed and beaten. The woman had seemed to break beneath Sky's domination and she had not anticipated being troubled by any hint of disobedience. Wendy's defiance, therefore, had surprised her. Refusing to reveal the whereabouts of the Valentine woman had been an unexpected act of insurrection and Sky was not prepared to tolerate it. Before this evening was over, Sky was determined that Wendy would tell her where Jo was.

She eased the tip of her finger into Wendy's sex and drew a small circle against the velvety inner wall. Using her finger and thumb, Sky teased the length of one silky pussy lip. The flesh was slick with excitement and Sky could not resist the urge to taste Wendy's musky, fragrant juice.

Beneath her, Wendy moaned with tortured excitement.

As Sky watched, Poppy moved from the side of the bed she had been resting against, walked round and nestled herself on Wendy's opposite side. Without a word to either of them, she began to nuzzle at Wendy's other breast. Watching the way her deft tongue licked against the erect nub of Wendy's nipple, Sky was touched by a fleeting pang of jealousy. She reached down to stroke Poppy's hair and her fingers caught a handful of lank tresses. With a casual tug of her wrist, she pulled Poppy away from Wendy's breast.

With the frightened look of a broken submissive, Poppy stared helplessly at Sky. Her meek expression made it clear that she was wondering what she had done to incur Sky's wrath.

'Leave her now,' Sky instructed coolly. 'Leave her and suck my tits.'

Nodding happily, Poppy placed her ripe lips round Sky's breast and began to suckle on her nipple.

Sky drew an excited breath, relishing the tingle of pleasure that sparked in her breast. Her fingers had been toying with the lips of Wendy's pussy and she saw that they were wet with the woman's cream. She licked the honey from her hands, before picking up one of the bulldog clips and brushing it gently against Wendy's sex.

Oblivious of what was caressing her, Wendy moaned happily.

Sky teased the clip open, surprised by the strong tension it required. She rolled her fingers against the slippery wetness, teasing the folds of her inner labia between finger and thumb. The thin length of warm flesh slipped from between her fingertips and Sky smiled to herself as she struggled to hold the skin firmly. Wendy was moaning beneath her, writhing gently from side to side as the thrill of Sky's intimate caress excited her. She held herself still as soon as Sky commanded but it was still difficult to grasp the delicate lips without the slick flesh sliding between her fingers.

Excited by the cruelty of what she was about to do, Sky took a moment to enjoy the pleasure of Poppy's mouth against her breast. The woman was no longer simply suckling at her breast: Sky could feel her becoming more adventurous, daring to tease the hardened nub of her nipple between gently biting teeth. The intensity of her enjoyment left Sky feeling hot and breathless.

Sliding the open clip over the pouting lips of Wendy's sex, Sky listened to the woman's sighs of pleasure growing beneath her. She teased the tip of her finger against Wendy's clitoris, extracting a groan of heartfelt elation. Having lured her into a false sense of security, Sky gently closed the clip.

Wendy's shriek was so shrill it could have shattered fine crystal. Every muscle in her body seemed to stiffen and a thousand pleas for Sky to stop tumbled over her lips. Her every breath was a snatched wail of distress.

Sky could feel the woman trying to sit up and move away from her. With deliberate calculation she lowered the lips of her sex over Wendy's face and held her against the bed. Wendy squirmed beneath her, still trying to escape in spite of the way she was being held. With a malicious grin twisting her lips, Sky lowered her mouth to Wendy's aching pussy and drew the tip of her tongue against the bead of her clitoris.

In a burst of spasmodic frenzy, Wendy bucked her hips up and down, rolling from side to side and almost pushing Sky from her position of dominance.

Determined to impose her will on the woman, Sky pushed herself hard on to Wendy's face, pinning her firmly against the bed.

'You're ready to tell me where she is, aren't you?' Sky muttered.

Between gasps for breath, she heard Wendy whisper her words of assent. The easy way that the woman had allowed herself to be dominated made Sky smile proudly. She drew the tip of her tongue against Wendy's clitoris for a second time, enjoying the contrary responses the action evoked. The clip was biting furiously hard against one lip of Wendy's inner labia and Sky could imagine that the pain was stark and severe. The sensations that fired from Wendy's sex were obviously more intense than she was prepared for. Each tentative flick of Sky's tongue evoked a nerve-shredding jolt of euphoria that had her writhing helplessly. Her cries were torn between screams for release and shrieks of elation.

Sky laughed softly to herself, enjoying the woman's discomfort more with each passing moment. She snapped her fingers at Poppy, gesturing for her to change breasts.

'You're ready to tell me where Jo Valentine is, but you haven't fulfilled your part of the bargain yet, have you?' Sky glanced down at Wendy, smiling into the expression of panicked confusion that strained her features. 'I'm only going to listen to you once you've made me come,' Sky explained, unable to stop the wicked smile from broaching her lips.

Knowing the woman beneath her was already at the outer limits of tolerable pain, Sky decided to add to her discomfort. She reached towards the bedside cabinet and retrieved a second bulldog clip. Making sure that Wendy could see what she was doing, Sky squeezed the clip slowly open.

Wendy shuddered. She buried her face against the intimate heat of Sky's sex and began to lick furiously at the pink folds. Her hands went to Sky's hips and she gripped tightly.

The urgency of her tongue, sliding eagerly over and into the warmth of her wet hole, left Sky shivering. Her fingers were trembling as she tried to guide the open bulldog clip over Wendy's other inner lip. Not knowing if her shivers were caused by the tongue between her legs or her own sadistic pleasure, Sky moved her trembling hand closer to Wendy's labia. With her other hand she teased the free lip of the woman's pussy between a wet finger and thumb.

The tongue that had been filling her sex was suddenly snatched away. Wendy pushed herself back on the bed, overcome by the wealth of stimulation that erupted between her legs. Sky tried to lower herself back over the woman's mouth but she rolled from side to side in such a feverish convulsion it was impossible to hold her. Determined to have the woman do her bidding, Sky placed the second clip around Wendy's sex and allowed it to close firmly against the delicate flesh.

Once again, Wendy shrieked. Her wordless protest came in a faltering stammer of distress that sent shivers racking her body. She stiffened on the bed, trembled violently, then collapsed, suddenly still and quiet.

With Poppy's mouth working its beautiful magic on her left nipple, Sky could not deny herself the mounting joy of her impending orgasm. With her face so close to the furious warmth of Wendy's sex, Sky could smell the delicious, sweet scent of her excitement. She could also see the way that the metal bit wickedly into the sensitive flesh.

Holding a clip in each hand, Sky pulled Wendy's labia wide open.

Beneath her, Wendy shuddered.

'Make me come,' Sky breathed softly. 'Then I'll take these off and let you talk.' As though she was making a gesture of goodwill, Sky flicked the tip of her tongue against Wendy's clitoris. With the clips pulling the flesh taut, her tongue was easily able to traverse the pulsing nub of her clitoris.

Wendy released a small gasp of pleasured pain and began to sob. Without needing to be told a second time, she placed her tongue over Sky's sex and began to pleasure the woman.

Sky groaned. She could feel the warm, deliberate wetness of Wendy's tongue as it stroked and licked the excited lips of her sex. The woman guided the tip against her clitoris then, before Sky could properly relish the experience, Wendy had slipped her tongue into her depths.

Shivering, Sky pushed herself against the squirming tongue, enjoying the delectable sensation of having it travel deep inside. The further down the tongue she squirmed, the greater her excitement became. The pressure of Wendy's lower lip rubbing at the thrusting nub of her clitoris sent her closer to the brink of orgasm than she had anticipated.

When she first fastened the clips on Wendy's pussy, Sky had imagined herself teasing the woman for hour upon hour. She had wanted to extract every last morsel of enjoyment from Wendy's misery before allowing her the privilege of administering an orgasm.

As Wendy deftly teased the lips of her sex, Sky could feel her plans changing. She braced herself for the impact of the climax, aware that it was going to be a strong one. The woman beneath her was holding tightly on to her hips, burying her face into the sodden furnace of Sky's hole. Her tongue slid against the heated lips of Sky's cleft then pushed into her again. Her lips kissed and stroked at the responsive flesh, evoking waves of delight that left both women panting with heartfelt urgency.

Wendy eased her tongue out and pushed the tip against the rim of Sky's arsehole.

With a groan of ecstasy, she pushed herself on to the intruding tongue, only vaguely wishing she could feel the penetration of something larger and more satisfying. The notion was swept from her mind as the first waves of pleasure struck. Her thoughts were lost in a spiralling frenzy of bliss and every hair on her body bristled. The climax was so great she could feel a spray of juice wetting her inner thighs and splashing on to Wendy's face.

Concentrating only on her own pleasure, Sky was barely aware that she was pulling on the bulldog clips. Wendy stiffened beneath her and Sky heard her agonised groan. The sound was distant and she drew no real pleasure from the woman's obvious discomfort. The strength of her own orgasm was more than enough for her. She found a moment to tickle the tip of her tongue against Wendy's clitoris, forcing her to relish the confusing sensations of delight and distress in the same kiss.

Then Sky was doing her best to ignore the woman. There was only one important person in this room, Sky reminded herself: the Black Widow. With that thought at the forefront of her mind, she rubbed herself on to the probing tongue at her anus and savoured the pleasure. When the last wave of euphoria finally began to recede, she brushed Poppy absently away from her breast and stared down at Wendy.

The woman was still forcing her tongue against the slippery wetness of Sky's holes and she had to be told twice before she stopped.

'Are you ready to tell me where I'll find Jo Valentine?' Sky asked.

With a heavy expression, Wendy nodded. Sky smiled, unable to contain the expression of self-satisfaction that sparkled in her eyes. She opened the clips fully before sliding them from Wendy's inner lips.

Wendy winced as the biting metal was removed from her.

Under other circumstances the sound of her discomfort would have been a spur to Sky's waning arousal. However, she was struck by a moment's sympathy when she saw the bruised lines that now marked the lips of Wendy's sex. Sky knew the marks would fade within the hour and the bruising would fade within a day but she still felt a pang of guilt as she saw the injury she had caused. The thought lasted only for an instant and was virtually forgotten before she could give it proper consideration. Her concern for Wendy was replaced by envy.

Wendy's aching cleft would be a haven of heightened sensitivity for the next day or two, giving her the chance to enjoy herself immensely. Thinking about this, Sky realised she had not been torturing the woman: she had been bestowing a benevolent gift on her. The realisation that she had just been charitable was whimsical enough to make her smile.

She eased her sex away from Wendy's mouth, shifted position on the bed and lay next to the woman.

Wendy stared at her with green eyes that were fearfully wide.

After commanding Poppy to serve drinks, Sky leant over Wendy and kissed her. The tips of her fingers went to the woman's breast, teasing the urgent thrust of her nipple and tracing circles against the areola. With each kiss she was able to taste the remnants of her climax on Wendy's face. The flavour rekindled the fading embers of her excitement and it took a deliberate effort for her to move her mouth away. Reminding herself that she had other matters to attend to beyond the salacious needs of her sexual appetite, Sky contented herself with stroking Wendy's stomach as she smiled down at her.

'Unless you want me to get the bulldog clips back,' Sky began, 'I'd suggest that you start telling me about Jo Valentine.' She took Wendy's nipple between her finger and thumb. Staring meaningfully into her face, she said, 'You wouldn't want me to punish you again, would you?'

With a frightened sob, Wendy shook her head and began to cry.

Sky could see her resistance wearing down, as though the emotions were visible in her tear-stained face. She had seen the same thing in the sauna, but this time the lesson seemed to have been properly learnt. There was no trace of defiance in the sultry green depths of Wendy's eyes. There was only an expression of sorrowful servility. It was exactly the way Sky wanted her to be.

Wendy nodded unhappily as if to confirm Sky's unspoken suspicions. 'Jo Valentine is the investigator that you're looking for,' she explained in a flat tone. 'She's been sent here by the other Mrs Meadows.' She graced Sky with a fearful expression.

When she spoke about Jo Valentine, Sky noticed a tinge of reluctance in her voice, as though she was unhappy divulging the information.

Her tone grew heavier and even more reluctant as she added, 'Right now, you'll find her in the east wing.'

Sky stared at Wendy's miserable face with a cruel smile. 'What's so special about the east wing?'

Wendy shook her head and turned away. 'Why don't you go and find out?'

Sky raised a suspicious eyebrow then let the outburst go. She could see that it had taken a lot for Wendy to betray the private investigator and Sky supposed she should have been grateful for that much of a concession. She realised Wendy was very frightened and might be too scared to tell her what she would find in the east wing. None of that excused her defiance, but it made it understandable, and because of that Sky let the challenge go unpunished. She took her drink from Poppy and sipped thoughtfully at the glass of fruit juice. 'So, Jo Valentine's in the east wing at this very moment.'

Wendy nodded, still unwilling to meet Sky's questioning eyes.

'Then I'll go and find her,' Sky decided. 'I think it's about time I spoke to this private investigator. Perhaps I'll also find what you've been hiding in the east wing?'

Accepting a glass of juice from Poppy, Wendy looked away. Her cheeks had darkened to a furious red blush and Sky longed to know what secret the woman was keeping.

Curiosity gnawed at her, but she resisted the temptation to force Wendy to talk. It would be far easier to go and investigate for herself. Admittedly, it was disconcerting that the woman whom she had just dominated was now defying her and would not even meet her gaze. Such insubordination could be dealt with later, she assured herself. It could be dealt with after she had investigated the mystery of the east wing.

A warning voice tried to insist that she should find out something more before she left Wendy, but curiosity had the better of her. The need to know what was hiding there seemed far more important than the need for caution, especially within the walls of a health farm that she now controlled. After all, Sky told herself confidently, surely there could not be anything so terrible waiting in the east wing.

Ten

Alone, and more than a little apprehensive, Jo took a tentative step towards the east wing, preparing to seek out the storeroom. Her heart thumped in her chest and she swallowed a nervous lump in her throat. Wrapping the robe tightly round herself for comfort, she moved bravely into the darkness. Warily, she moved towards a discreet corridor and squinted in the darkness, trying to discern lettering on one of the sterile white doors.

Her heart was beating faster than she wanted and her skin was chilled by a rash of gooseflesh. The key in her hand had been cold when it was initially pressed there. Now it felt hot and slick with her nervous sweat. As she willed her eyes to adjust to the gloom, she wondered what she should expect to find in the storeroom. She had been told she would find an answer there but people often said that to her and Jo had begun to realise that it was invariably an exaggeration. The place was a storeroom and she knew it was more likely she would find some brooms and a bottle of floor cleaner. Anything more than that and she supposed she should consider it a bonus.

Shivering with trepidation, she stroked her fingers over the dusty plaque of the last door in the corridor and realised this was the one she was looking for. She placed her hand against the knob and twisted it fully but it did not give. Feeling confident that she had the right room, Jo slid the key into the lock and began to twist it to one side. She tried to do this as quietly as she could, but was unable to mute the deafening click and shift of the tumblers as they obeyed the turn of the key. In the lightless corridor, the sound was like a thunderous wake-up call.

Jo held her breath and placed her hand on the door knob. She was about to twist it and push open the door when a small sound made her stop. She paused, straining to hear something identifiable behind the door. After a moment, she felt a nervous shiver tingle along her spine. She was certain that inside the storeroom she could hear the sound of someone breathing. It was a disturbing noise and the fear it evoked chilled her.

It had already been an unsettling evening, the only high point being the passion she had shared with Wendy. Tracing a wet tongue against her lips, Jo could still taste the tincture of pussy honey that lingered there. The flavour inspired a reflective smile as she remembered the intimacy she and Wendy had enjoyed. With her eyes closed, she was able to relive the moment when their naked bodies were finally entwined as they began to explore each other. The intimacy had been heady and the satisfaction intense.

It was only when they finished making love that Jo realised she was in Wendy's bedroom for a reason.

'It's time for you to follow me,' Wendy had said.

'I thought you wanted to talk.'

'There isn't the time to talk.' In the dim light of the bedroom, Wendy's face had been etched with a frown. 'And it isn't safe for you to be here. I'll have to show you.'

Outside the storeroom, with her hand resting on the door knob, Jo remembered the stealthy race along the health farm's darkened corridors towards the east wing. The memory of how close they had come to meeting the Black Widow still made her shiver.

Wendy had stopped close to the kitchen. She held Jo in the shadows and silenced her with a finger against her lips. Jo could smell the scent of her own pussy juice on Wendy's hand and the light, subtle fragrance increased the tingling wetness between her legs. The pulse within her humid cleft beat a fraction harder but she had done as Wendy said and remained silent.

The Black Widow had been standing in the kitchen doorway with her back to Jo and Wendy. Jo had not seen Sky Meadows previously but she recognised the woman on sight. The description that Allen and Wendy had given was flawless, from the stark styling of her blonde hair to the tight-fitting black lingerie she wore.

Jo had held her breath and struggled to get further into the concealing shadows. In the darkness it had been easy to hear what was going on.

'Sky? Is that you? Why don't you come in here and join us?' Beyond Allen's voice, Jo heard the giggle and pant of the breathless lovers who shared the kitchen with him.

'I'm trying to find Jo Valentine.' The Black Widow's voice was crisp and chilling. 'That woman and I have some business to attend to.'

In the shadows, Jo swallowed and said a prayer of thanks that the Black Widow had not managed to find her.

'Have you tried Wendy's room?' Allen suggested.

Wendy had released an angry sigh and muttered, 'Arsekisser.'

Jo was in heartfelt agreement with Wendy's curse.

'Why would she be there?' the Black Widow demanded.

There had been no audible reply to this question. Obviously angry, Sky stormed out of the kitchen and headed back towards the stairs.

With the key twisted fully in the storeroom door, Jo tried to stop her mind recounting the last few minutes. She still felt guilty for having left Wendy to deal with Sky, but the woman had insisted. The memory made her feel cowardly and manipulative even though she knew those were not her motivations. Despite Wendy's reassurances, Jo felt certain the woman had placed herself in an unenviable situation.

As soon as the Black Widow had stormed out of earshot, Wendy held Jo in her arms and whispered, 'You'll have to go on your own. I need to stop her from searching the entire building.'

'Will you be all right?' Jo had asked. 'She looks like she could be trouble.'

In the shadows, Wendy's smile had been barely visible. 'The Black Widow is trouble, but I think I know what I'm doing.' She had pressed a cold key into Jo's hand and told her it was for the storeroom. 'You'll need this.'

'What am I meant to be doing?'

Wendy's reply was infuriatingly enigmatic. 'You'll find out. I've got to get back to Sky. She won't rest until she's found one of us.'

'She's not likely to hurt you, is she?' Jo had asked.

Wendy shrugged by way of response. 'Perhaps. Maybe not. I don't know what she'll do and it doesn't matter anyway. The important thing is that you need to go to the east wing. You'll get all the answers you need from the storeroom.'

Now, listening to the sound of someone's muted breathing on the other side of the door, Jo wondered if that was true. Trying to quell the fearful hammering of her heartbeat, she willed herself to come to a quick decision. It was pitch black in the east-wing corridor and she could detect no telltale sliver of light beneath the storeroom door. That meant that, if there was someone in the storeroom, they were waiting in the dark. The thought was unnerving but it did not stop her. She could not deny being scared, but she was also intrigued. Preparing herself for whatever was waiting for her, Jo twisted the knob to one side and pushed the door open.

As she had thought, it was pitch black inside and she paused for a moment, trying to prepare herself for someone, or something, to lurch out at her. For an hour-long minute she waited just outside the door. She could no longer hear the breathing she had been listening to earlier. The nervous pounding of her own pulse beat like a drum at her temples. When she was almost convinced that nothing would reach out and grab her, Jo dared to reach a hand inside the room and tentatively scour the wall for a light switch. Her fingers fell on a small button and, without a moment's hesitancy, she threw it down.

Stark neon light spattered against the walls then buzzed into life as a constant bright bar along the ceiling. The room was suddenly filled with a brilliant whiteness that pained her dark-adjusted eyes. Jo blinked away the momentary sting and focused her gaze on the source of the breathing. She drew a startled breath, then stepped properly into the storeroom, closing the door behind herself without taking her gaze away from the man.

The walls were dungeon-like, bare and gloomy. The only things that adorned them were a set of manacles secured to one wall and a selection of whips, crops and canes mounted on another. Jo ignored all of these distractions. Her attention was riveted on the man.

He was sitting on a small wooden chair in the centre of the room. She saw that his ankles were tied to the chair's legs and his hands were secured behind him. Over his head he wore a tight-fitting leather mask. There was no space for eye-holes. From her place by the door, Jo could barely detect the two holes above his nostrils. The principal opening in the mask was a large circle over his mouth, pushed in slightly by a silencing ball gag. Intrigued, Jo stepped closer.

He was naked save for a pair of rubber shorts. Through the slit at the front, Jo noticed that his long pink length was standing proud. She smiled thoughtfully as she walked round the man, fascinated by his vulnerability. A frown crossed her brow when she remembered Wendy's reassurance that all would be revealed in the storeroom. There would be only one way to get any answers from this man, she thought, and that would involve taking off his gag.

With lurid images tumbling through her mind, she decided that removing his mask would have to be a last option. As she walked round him, she studied the long, eager length of hard pink flesh. He was huge, bigger than anyone she had ever seen before. She stared at his erection, unable to prevent a salacious smile from widening her lips.

Because its owner was bound and blindfold, his erection was hers, for her to do with as she wished. It was an exciting prospect. As all the possibilities of such a scenario occurred to her, she found it more and more difficult to deny the demanding pulse of her arousal.

There were a lot of questions spinning through her mind. She wanted to know who he was and how he had come to be secured like this. She also wanted to know who had tied him to the chair and why. She wanted to know a lot of things but, as the tingling urgency of her excitement increased, she realised that those answers could all wait for a little while.

Jo stepped out of the dressing-gown she had been wearing and stretched her naked body before him. She found it unbelievably arousing to stand bare in front of the man, realising that he could not see her or even know of her intentions. As she rolled the heel of her palm against her own bare breast, she was pleasantly startled by the prickle of pleasure that coursed from the tip. She stroked a finger against the lips of her sex, then dared to ease one into the warm haven of her pussy. Spurred on by the wealth of fire she found, Jo slid the finger out and smiled at the coating of dewy wetness she had left there. Putting the finger beneath the two tiny nostril holes in the mask, she watched the bound figure as he inhaled the sweet fragrance of her arousal.

His entire body stiffened as he detected the musky scent. His broad chest puffed out and his long hard cock grew more rigid, as though it was preparing itself for her. Once she had caught another glimpse of his stiffening length, Jo found herself unable to tear her gaze away from it. She guessed the cock was at least twelve inches long, with a massive girth that came close to being the thickness of her wrist.

As his excitement intensified, she watched his foreskin peel back. His cock stood tall and proud. The pale-pink flesh contrasted with the shiny black rubber of his shorts. With all of his foreskin rolled back, his broad, glistening dome was revealed to her. The eye of his cock was wet beneath a pearl of pre-come and Jo felt an irresistible urge to lick the bead of arousal away.

He shifted his head from side to side, his shoulders pulling forward as he struggled against his restraints.

Jo took a tentative step away from him before reminding herself that he was blindfolded and gagged. Her rational mind told her that he was trying to decide whether he was alone and suffering from the delusions of an overactive imagination or if he really had caught the fragrance of her pussy honey.

Encouraged and excited by his vulnerability, Jo wafted the tip of her finger beneath the nostrils of his mask again. For a second time she saw the man stiffen and watched his long, thick length twitch forcibly. He inhaled her fragrance in short, tentative bursts, releasing his breath in muffled groans.

Still fascinated by his huge cock, Jo knelt down in front of the man and traced a finger against the warm flesh. He groaned softly against his gag, unable to suppress the sound as she caressed him.

She knew that she should not really be trying to use him in this way, aware that he might have answers that could help with her case. At the back of her mind Jo knew she was wasting valuable time not pursuing this avenue of enquiry, but the heat between her legs was far more demanding than the nagging of her curiosity. Before she could waste more time on something as frivolous as thinking, she pushed her mouth over his length.

His cock was so big she had to stretch her lips to fit her mouth over him. That thought alone added to the heat burning in her loins. She had known a lot of men in her time and enjoyed most of them immensely. However, she did not think she had ever known one as large as this man. The thought of trying to accommodate this gargantuan cock in the warm, velvety haven of her pussy sent a shiver of anticipation coursing through her.

Sucking softly, she heard him groan. She glanced down between his legs and saw that his balls were a tight, pre-climactic sac. Tentatively, she traced a finger against them, stroking the wrinkled flesh of his scrotum through the thick swatch of dark hairs. His obvious appreciation only added to her enjoyment as she sucked on his swollen end. The debilitating taste of his pre-come filled her mouth. Her fingers traced the length of his cock as her mouth worked on the end and she tried not to think of his overwhelming size. Instead, she concentrated on teasing him with her mouth and her tongue. As soon as her jaw became uncomfortable stretching around him, she moved her lips away. Her tongue was coated with his sweet, salty flavour and she could feel the pulse of her urgent need beating more strongly as she savoured the taste.

Rather than trying to swallow him, which she knew she could never manage, Jo contented herself with licking and lapping at the thick solid shaft. Rolling the flat of her palm over the pulsing tip of his cock, she toyed with the idea of taking him between her legs. He was one hell of a size, she thought, unable to decide if that realisation inspired fear or arousal. Regardless of the feelings it aroused, she could not purge the image from her mind. She could picture herself straddling him, teasing the tip of his great organ against her tight, wet cleft, then slowly lowering herself on to him. The idea was vivid and overwhelming. Caught by the excitement of all the feelings it inspired, Jo traced her tongue against him for one last time. She stood up and took his length in both hands as she stood over him.

For a moment she was struck again by the question of who he was. It was a puzzle and she promised herself that, as soon as she had satisfied her appetite, she would deal with her curiosity. The identity of the man behind the mask was intriguing, but her urgency to find out more about him was nowhere near as demanding as her need to experience him. She was being taken over by the frantic pulse of her demanding appetite and Jo knew better than to ignore that feeling.

She tried to wrap her hand round him as she moved herself into the right position. The vast size of his cock made it an impossible task and her fingers could not encircle him properly. She had to use both hands to guide him against the lips of her sex. A tremor of nervous anticipation washed over her. She did not know if she would be able to satisfy herself on him, or even accommodate his vast girth between her legs, but she was determined to try.

He moaned as she rubbed the tip of his length against the wet folds of her pussy lips. Jo could see him struggling to get comfortable on his seat and she wondered if he wanted her to release him. It was only a passing thought, and one that she had no intention of acting upon. Perhaps he did want releasing, but there were things that she wanted and Jo was determined that her needs would be satisfied first. She drew a long, shuddering breath as she pushed the tip of his cock against herself. The purple head had hardly begun to enter her and already she could feel herself being stretched. The feelings of excitement and curiosity were now replaced by the threat of his entry.

The combination of fear and arousal was a powerful aphrodisiac and Jo was drawn by its irresistible call. Still holding him in both hands, she took a deep breath and braced herself for the wealth of protesting sensations that yearned to explode from her sex.

He groaned against the ball gag as she lowered herself on to him.

The sensation was incredible. Jo could feel her

inner walls being stretched wide open as she guided the huge length inside. The man beneath her was making soft, desperate sounds of protestation that she easily ignored. In all honesty she could barely hear his muffled words because of her own euphoric scream.

Her legs began to tremble as broad inescapable waves of pleasure washed over her. Reluctantly, she moved her hands from the fantastic girth of his cock and held his shoulders to steady herself. She wanted to slow down her acceptance of him. It was her intention to enjoy the millimetre-by-millimetre intrusion of his cock but her body was too weary with exhaustion and excitement. Her legs seemed to have forsaken the notion of muscle control and she could feel herself falling on to his cock with a furious speed that snatched the scream from her lips. Unconsciously, she found herself digging clawed fingers into the masked man's shoulders. She was aware that her hands and arms were trembling, but the sight of them came only through a misty haze of blissful delight.

Impaled on the pulsing length of his shaft, Jo released a trembling sigh. She dared to raise herself on him, revelling in the pleasure of his cock's slow, deliberate egress. Each subtle movement sent a sharp explosion of raw pleasure coursing through her, and Jo could feel herself speeding towards a cataclysmic orgasm. She tried to move herself further up his length, then stopped abruptly. His cock was such a vast size that she could feel it threatening to pull from her in a sudden rush. Common sense told her that if he did slip from inside her she would have difficulty forcing him back a second time. Frustrated by the closeness of her impending climax, she rolled her pelvis back and forth, pressing the base of his cock on to her clitoris. The feeling of his length brushing against her pearl sent electric shocks of pleasure sparkling through her pussy.

But still she wanted more.

She released her grip on his shoulders, silently chastising herself for leaving fingermarks on his bare flesh. Using one hand to tease the tip of her aching nipple, she rolled the hard nub between her thumb and index finger. It did occur to her that she could do something similar for the man beneath her, but she barely entertained the notion. His nipple was only a whisper away and she could have enhanced his enjoyment by placing her lips round the tiny bud of flesh, but Jo was far more concerned with her own satisfaction. She stole her other hand down to her sex lips and traced the tips of her fingers against his cock. He was slippery with the wetness of her juice and she rubbed their joined flesh lovingly. Her fingers touched her pussy lips, stretched to the limits by his massive cock, then ran against his hard, unyielding length. The opportunity to caress herself in such a way was disturbingly arousing and Jo did not hesitate to indulge herself.

She placed the tip of her index finger against the pulsing nub of her clitoris. The hard bead of pleasure was erect and, as soon as Jo touched it, her body erupted with an explosion of joy. Each nerve-ending seemed to sing a heart-warming song of gratitude. When his cock had entered her, Jo had been forced to scream with pleasure. Now she found herself beyond screaming. The intensity of the fire between her legs was so strong she could do nothing more than grunt her delight in bestial cries of elation.

Beneath her, he was making sounds of protest and Jo wondered if he was close to the point of his own climax. The cock between her legs was so large she could not detect any of the telltale twitching that she had felt in others. His solid length pulsed slightly but the throbbing reciprocation of her own flesh made it difficult to discern where his movement ended and her own began.

She found herself thinking about the pleasure of having him explode inside her. The thought was more than a little intimidating. She could feel a growing disquiet as she imagined his thick shaft twitching and convulsing deep within the inner recesses of her sex. Even that nervousness brought with it a dark anticipation.

She stroked her fingers harder against the pearl of her clitoris. The fingers at her nipple had been doing little to enhance her pleasure and she moved them down between her legs. Her hole was stretched wide open, the lips of her sex spread so fully that the hood of her clitoris was pulled taut. With eager fingers, she rubbed hard against the straining ball of pleasure.

Growling with satisfaction, Jo felt her inner muscles attempting to squeeze as the orgasm coursed through her. It was difficult to keep her hand moving as she tried to force her pleasure to a higher plateau. With grim determination, Jo rubbed the tip of her finger furiously, urging her body towards another blistering orgasm.

And then she felt him come.

The force of his climax was so powerful she screamed. His cock pulsed inside her and Jo felt as though she had been struck. The realisation that his climax had sparked off another orgasm was only distant. Her entire body was suddenly transported to a world of euphoria that her own fingers had not been able to inspire. She snatched her hands away from her sex, fearful of inducing any more pleasure.

His cock pulsed again.

This time Jo howled. She tried to slide herself away

from him but her legs refused to move. She could not lift herself up and had to endure the third and fourth pulses of his vast length as he shuddered his way through the last of his own orgasm. Each gigantic tremor of his rock-hard cock pressed painfully against her inner muscles. Jo squeezed her eyes tightly shut, forcing tears of pained enjoyment from the corners. It was only when she felt the trickle of his spent seed wetting her inner thighs that she dared to attempt moving away from him.

This time it was easier. Even flaccid, his cock was huge, but it was nowhere near as formidable as it had been during their lovemaking. Once she had finally pulled herself from him, Jo stared down at the spent organ with a fond smile on her lips. She could see that his flesh was glistening with the wetness of his spilt seed and the slick coating of her sex honey. The mingled juices shimmered beneath the neon light and the wet lustre was so appealing that Jo felt drawn to kneel down and experience the taste of him once again. It took a deliberate effort to stop herself. In her mind's eye she had already knelt down in front of him and traced her tongue against the intoxicating mixture of their combined fluids; already felt the stiffening of his length as he became hard again, allowing her to use him for a second time.

With a reluctant sigh, Jo stopped herself from travelling down this route. To try to distract the wandering of her salacious thoughts, she glanced idly around the storeroom. The first thing she had noticed on entering was a pair of manacles hanging from one wall. She could see that they were well worn and wondered how many hours this man had spent hanging from those metal cuffs. She had already come to the decision that he was not unhealthy. The strength and virility of his lovemaking had given testament to that fact, but she could also see that he was a long-time occupant of the storeroom.

Glancing at the adjoining wall, Jo tried to decide why the mixture of canes and crops was mounted there. She had studied the man's naked body as she fucked him and had not noticed any marks, cuts or scratches. Admittedly, she had not given him a thorough examination, but she felt sure she would have noticed the telltale signs of a recent whipping. There were a couple of marks that had most probably been caused by a long-ago chastisement but those were grazes that had faded to little more than a reddened memory.

Ruefully, Jo realised she was developing some expertise in this field.

It was a particularly wicked collection, Jo thought, studying the selection of implements. Tipped with a sharp sliver of silver, the cane looked exceptionally cruel. By the same token, she noticed that the flimsy ends of the cat-o'-nine-tails had each been knotted, adding to the brutality of the weapon. Stepping closer to the collection, she inhaled and caught the distant scent of vinegar. The acrid fragrance brought a smile of satisfaction to her lips. She had expected to smell as much, knowing that there were many masochists who soaked their crops and canes in vinegar. Actually detecting the scent made her feel as though she had accomplished something clever. A soft moan from the man made her turn and fix her gaze on his bound and helpless figure.

'I suppose that's enough fun for the moment,' Jo said with a reluctant smile. She took a last fond glance at the spent cock between his legs and stopped the lurid track of her thoughts. After snatching her dressing-gown from the floor, she fastened the cord then walked behind him. It only took a moment to unfasten the ball gag and as soon it was released she heard him whisper, 'Thank you.'

Jo could not decide if he was thanking her for the lovemaking they had shared, or simply for releasing his gag. Deciding that it was unimportant, she moved to the front of the chair and began to slide the mask from over his head.

'No,' he began. 'You shouldn't.'

'Don't interrupt me,' Jo told him firmly. 'Or I'll put the gag back on.'

He fell silent instantly.

Jo rolled the rubber mask slowly up his face, revealing a strong jaw, broad, sensuous lips and then an aquiline nose. Unable to resist the impulse, she pressed her mouth against his and enjoyed a kiss with the stranger. Her tongue explored the silky haven of his mouth and she could feel her pussy tingle as her body demanded more than just the simple stimulation of his tongue against hers.

Jo stopped the kiss when she felt her arousal intruding. She had already enjoyed herself enough this evening, she decided. Her entire body seemed to ache with the aftermath of the many orgasms that she had already endured. Wendy had done a good job of satisfying Jo's carnal demands before she entered the storeroom. Since discovering this man bound and ready for her, Jo had made a fairly good attempt at sating those appetites herself. While the notion of enduring another handful of orgasms was not that unappealing, Jo found herself exercising an uncharacteristic degree of restraint. She broke their kiss before it could develop into anything more intimate.

Slowly, she rolled the rubber mask further up his face. He had dark eyes that studied her with curiosity. She grinned down at him and was warmed by the smile he gave her in return. She found herself looking

233

at a modestly handsome man in his mid-thirties, with dark hair, dark eyes and a curious smile.

'Well,' Jo said, with a sigh of exasperation. 'I suppose I have a lot of questions, but the most important is, Who the fuck are you?'

'I'll tell you who he is,' a voice behind her said coolly.

Jo whirled round to see who had disturbed them. Standing in the doorway was the Black Widow. Still dressed in her black stockings, black basque and long black gloves, she looked more fearsome than ever. In one hand she was brandishing a cruel-looking cane, as evil and wicked as anything Jo had seen on the wall of the storeroom. Jo's eyes widened with nervous apprehension. She realised she had placed herself in a dangerous situation and she wondered just how bad things were.

'I'll tell you exactly who he is,' the Black Widow went on. She marched into the room, glaring at the man as she entered. 'His name is Malcolm Meadows and not only was he once my husband, but he has also been dead for the last two years.'

Jo stared from Malcolm to the Black Widow and swallowed nervously. Now she knew she was in trouble.

Eleven

'You lousy bastard,' Sky growled passionately.

Jo could see from Sky's frown that the woman was immensely angry. She was still trying to come to terms with the woman's revelations. The comment seemed to make no sense at all and Jo wanted to ask exactly what she meant. Staring at the fixed glare of annoyance on Sky's face, Jo decided not to ask for an explanation.

'You lousy fucking bastard,' Sky muttered, her outrage seeming to increase as she advanced slowly into the room.

Malcolm was staring at her, his features contorted by an expression of rising panic. He tried to exercise a conciliatory smile but the gesture fell flat on Sky's foul mood. Still tied to the chair, he attempted to shuffle backward, trying to get away from her as she bore down on him. 'It's been a long time, Sky,' he said quickly.

'It's been two years and a funeral,' Sky agreed. 'I'd call that a long time.'

Jo heard him swallow nervously. Standing on the sidelines and watching the action, she sympathised with his fear. If she had been in his position she would have been just as nervous. She knew she should intercede but a cowardly voice of caution told her to do nothing and Jo was quite happy to comply.

Neither of these two people was a paying client, she reminded herself. Therefore, there was no obvious financial benefit in risking her own skin.

'You're wearing the psycho-bitch costume,' he observed.

'It's more than a costume nowadays,' she said stiffly. 'It's a way of life.'

The comment seemed to go over his head and Jo wondered if he realised how much danger he was in. Judging by the trusting expression that split his lips, she doubted he knew how dangerous Sky had become. 'It looks good on you,' he said encouragingly. 'Better than I remember.'

Sky sniffed derisively. She was standing over Malcolm, glaring down at him with a boundless fury. 'Do you know the shit you've put me through?' she asked.

He stared up at her with wide-eyed innocence and shook his head. 'I never meant to hurt you,' he stammered. 'And I want to say now, honestly, you look fantastic, Sky. Better than I've ever seen you looking before –'

'What's that?' Sky broke in. She was speaking to Jo and pointing at the gag on the floor.

'He was wearing it when I found him,' Jo explained.

'He can wear it again,' Sky said angrily. 'Put it back on him.'

'But, Sky darling,' Malcolm began. 'You don't want to –'

She slapped her hand across the side of his face. The clap of flesh smacking flesh echoed around the storeroom like a pistol retort. Jo bit back a nervous cry when she heard the noise, startled by the sudden sound.

Malcolm glared unhappily. 'There was no need for that,' he whispered.

'There was every need for that,' Sky told him angrily. 'My life's been turned upside down and made into a misery. And it's all because of you. I'll be damned if I'm going to stand here and listen to you try and lie your way out of trouble again.'

'But I –' he broke in.

Sky slapped him again. This time his startled breath was lost beneath the sound of the blow. 'I don't want to hear it,' Sky hissed. She turned to Jo and pointed with the tip of the crop she was carrying. 'Didn't I just tell you to put the gag on him?'

Jo considered her options for a moment before realising she did not have any. She could have ignored Sky's command and simply walked out of the storeroom, but for her that was never an option. Admittedly neither of these two was a paying client, but they were an integral part of the case. Her curiosity had been piqued by the whole situation and she was loath to leave the room now. She felt close to the brink of discovery, sure that the conversation between Sky and Malcolm would help her resolve the current case. The temptation to stay and find out more was irresistible. Moving quickly, she retrieved the gag from the floor and fastened it in Malcolm's mouth.

Sky was exhaling in furious, bellowing gusts. She circled Malcolm and Jo, holding the cane behind her back as she moved. Every step she took emphasised the tension that bristled within her taut body. From the corner of her eye, Jo saw that the tip of the crop was quivering like a divining rod.

'I can't believe you let me suffer the way you did,' Sky hissed. She sliced the crop through the air, forcing the tip to whistle near Malcolm.

He flinched in his seat, as though he had anticipated being struck, making a sound against the

237

ball gag that was little more than a weak and ineffectual grunt. His eyes were wide and staring helplessly.

Jo took a step away from the couple, aware that this was now between Malcolm and the Black Widow.

'All the suffering you caused me,' Sky growled. 'I've spent two years thinking you were dead and I've spent all that time having to struggle for money because you –' She broke off and fixed him with an outraged expression. Her eyebrows were arched into a terrifying threat. 'You planned all of this deliberately, didn't you?'

He was shaking his head, trying desperately to make coherent sounds that might appease her.

Jo could see from the malevolent glimmer in Sky's eye that he was wasting his time, but she knew better than to tell him.

'You planned all of this to hurt me, didn't you?' Sky demanded. Malcolm was shaking his head from side to side in frank refusal of this suggestion but she ignored him. She raised the crop high above his head and brought it down with a vicious swipe. The tip caught him smartly on the balls.

Jo flinched as she empathised with Malcolm's suffering. She did not know what pain he had caused Sky, but she thought it would have to be something pretty drastic to merit this sort of punishment.

With a grunt of exasperation, Sky lunged at Malcolm for a second time. She caught his scrotum again, causing her former husband to howl with pained disbelief.

'How dare you treat me like that?' Sky bellowed. 'I was granting you the divorce you wanted. I was being the good obedient little wife and you just thought you'd walk over me some more . . .' Her voice trailed off as she stared at him.

238

Jo followed the line of her gaze and saw she was staring at Malcolm's cock. After she had fucked him, Jo had watched his cock shrivel down and fall flaccidly against his thigh. Now it was twitching back to life with a speed that was alarming.

'You're enjoying this, aren't you?' Sky demanded.

Malcolm did not bother to shake his head.

'How long has this sort of thing excited you?' she asked. Clearly knowing that she would not get a reply from him, Sky slapped the crop down against his inner thigh. A raised red line was left in its wake. 'You never even suggested we play games like this while we were married,' she muttered. 'And now I find you bound and gagged in a storeroom, getting your rocks off by having your balls beaten.' She shook her head slowly and made a small tutting sound at the back of her throat. 'What have you turned into, Malcolm?'

He stared up at her with a pitiable expression. His eyes were open so wide Jo could see he was trying to plead with her, but she could not decide if it was a plea for Sky to stop or continue.

With one slender hand, Sky reached her fingers round Malcolm's hard length and stroked his erection. There was a sly smile on her lips as she moved his foreskin back and forth over the swollen purple dome of his cock. She studied his massive shaft for a moment, seemingly lost in a world of fond recollections. Then she looked up and fixed her gaze on his eyes. 'How long is it since I did this for you?' she wondered aloud.

He shrugged, still regarding her with a healthy measure of apprehension.

'It's been a long time, hasn't it?' Sky said. 'It's been a very long time,' she reiterated. As she spoke, her hand continued to slide up and down his shaft with a quickening pace.

Jo watched, mesmerised by the scene. There was something exciting about the way the Black Widow wanked her husband, but Jo could sense more in the situation. Her attention was caught by the woman's delicate wrist sliding up and down over the mammoth cock. Jo tried to work out why Sky was now trying to please him. She did not think the woman had suddenly mellowed and she wanted to know her motivation.

'You like that, don't you?' Sky observed, smiling down at him.

Malcolm nodded, healthy caution colouring his gaze.

'I thought you would,' Sky told him. 'I've learnt how to please submissives like you since your funeral.' She continued to smile as she said, 'A little bit of pleasure is usually the best way to start. It helps to accentuate the intensity of what I do next.'

As though the words were her impetus, Sky pulled his foreskin down hard. Her hand gripped his cock tightly, sliding right down to the base.

From her vantage point, Jo could see the dome of his cock straining as his flesh was pulled uncomfortably taut. Malcolm made a struggling sound against his gag but it was as much of a protest as he could make. His arms and legs were secured against the chair and Jo suspected that, even if he could have moved, he would have remained sitting until Sky told him otherwise.

Sky lowered her mouth over the end of his cock and flicked the tip of her tongue against his glans. She was grinning up at him as she moved her lips close to the end of his length. One hand still held the base while the other teased the tip of the riding crop against his neck. Her enjoyment of her former husband's suffering was so obvious that Jo could have sensed it without looking at her.

'You really do like this, don't you?' Sky muttered, moving her head away from him. A pearl of pre-come glistened on her lower lip and she licked it up with a dart of her tongue. All the time she kept her gaze fixed on him. 'But I'll bet you like this a lot more,' she whispered. Taking a step away, she raised the riding crop high in the air and brought it sharply down. A thin red line appeared on his inner thigh where the blow had struck.

Before Jo had a chance to blink, Sky was delivering a second blow to Malcolm's other thigh. He grunted unhappily against his gag but the sound was as close as he could come to begging her to stop. Another red welt appeared on his pale flesh, burning so brightly it was painful to look at it.

Sky stared down at him with a merciless smile that brooked no pleas for leniency. 'This is how you've been getting your pleasure, isn't it?' she demanded. She was holding the crop like a pointer and levelling it between his eyes. When Malcolm made no reply, she slapped his legs twice more. 'Answer me for fuck's sake,' she snapped. 'Is this how you've been getting your rocks off ?'

His head was nodding up and down, as though it was pivoted on loose ball bearings.

'What a coincidence,' Sky growled. 'I've been getting my pleasure by doing something similar.' A cruel smile crossed her lips as she glared at him. 'There's an irony there that I can't quite put my finger on,' she told him. 'But I don't suppose that will matter for much longer. 'Before we're finished in here, one of us will have had enough of these sort of games, and I don't think it will be me.'

The fear in his eyes was so obvious Jo felt a finger of sympathy tapping her shoulder. The idea of intervening was not appealing but it nagged irritatingly. She was pulled from her thoughts by the sight of Sky staring at her. Jo frowned, wondering what she had done to evoke the woman's interest.

'What's that?' Sky asked, pointing just behind Jo.

Turning, Jo released a heavy sigh as she saw the thing that had caught Sky's attention. The woman was pointing at the silver-tipped cane. Somewhere far away, in the sanctuary of the main building, she could hear a distant knocking, but the sound seemed peripheral. The events that were taking place in the storeroom were far more important. Anxiously, she wished she could decide on the best course of action.

'Bring it here,' Sky snapped, clicking her fingers to give the command more urgency. She hurled her own crop to the floor and held out her hand expectantly. Staring down at Malcolm, she shook her head and graced him with a pitying expression. 'Darling,' she told him softly. 'After tonight, you'll wish that you never made me into the Black Widow.'

Wendy hurried down the stairs to answer the front door. Perhaps Sky Meadows had beaten her into submission and perhaps she would never be the same person again, but she still had an obligation to the guests at Elysian Fields. The way the front door was being pounded, Wendy knew that each one of those guests would soon be woken if she did not get there quickly.

She tried wrapping a gown round herself as she ran but the cord slipped through her hasty fingers and it was all she could manage to hold the seams over her naked body. Behind her, she heard the telltale footsteps of the Black Widow's other pet submissive and she turned to glare at the woman. 'Go back to the room, Poppy,' Wendy hissed. 'Sky won't be happy if you're not there when she gets back.'

Poppy stared back at her miserably. 'Let me come with you,' she begged.

There was something so pitiful in her beseeching expression that Wendy did not have the heart to bark the command a second time. She stood torn for a moment, wanting to answer the door and wanting to comfort and reassure Poppy before encouraging her back to Sky's bedroom.

The hammering began again and Wendy rolled her eyes. She stormed in the direction of the front door, trying not to care whether Poppy followed or not. The lateness of the hour and the lack of consideration that was being shown inspired an anger inside her that seemed to rankle with the submissive training that Sky had given. She knew that it was wrong to feel such emotions, but she was determined to vent her spleen on whomever she found standing at the front door.

After unfastening all three locks, she threw open the door and glared angrily out into the night.

'About bloody time,' Faye Meadows spat.

Wendy drew a shocked breath. For an instant she was struggling to find the right words. She watched a redhead walk through the door beside Faye and she caught the woman's curious gaze as she stared behind Wendy into the shadows of the hotel reception. Glancing in that direction, Wendy saw that Poppy had followed her. She realised it was the naked, mousy-haired submissive who had caught the woman's attention.

'This is not the greeting I was anticipating,' Faye said sharply. 'What's been going on here, Wendy? Where's John?'

Wendy shook her head. 'John left,' she stammered. 'His replacement has been –'

'Replacement?' Faye broke in. 'This is all news to

243

me. When did all this happen? And who's this replacement?' She paused, glancing into the shadows where the redhead was looking. 'And why is that woman standing naked and trying to hide behind the reception desk?'

'Come here, Poppy,' Wendy murmured.

'Poppy from the Knight Brothers,' Faye gasped. She studied the woman with an incredulous expression as Poppy stepped out of the shadows and moved closer to them.

Poppy seemed unembarrassed by her nudity and, although she did not hold herself with a confident or arrogant posture, there was something about her poise that showed she was not ashamed.

Faye's gaze was fixed on the woman's naked body, her salacious smile making her thoughts transparently obvious. 'I never thought you'd look so good naked,' Faye observed. She frowned slightly as she caught sight of a handful of bruises on Poppy's bare body. 'Who made those?'

'That's what I've been wanting to tell you,' Wendy began softly.

'The Black Widow made these marks,' Poppy whispered. To give emphasis to the marks she was referring to, she stroked the tips of her fingers against her bruised nipples. The subtle friction caused the buds to stand prouder as they all watched.

Faye frowned. 'Excuse me? The Black Widow?'

Wendy closed her eyes, wishing that Poppy would leave her to do the explaining. 'That's the nickname we have for –'

'Sky,' Poppy interrupted. 'Sky Meadows is the Black Widow.'

Faye's face was caught in a frown as dark as thunder. 'Sky Meadows is here?'

Wendy put a hand over her face, wishing she could be somewhere else.

'Where?' Faye demanded. 'Where is she?'

With her eyes closed, Wendy heard Poppy answer. Unperturbed by Faye's mounting anger, Poppy said that Sky was in the storeroom.

'The storeroom! The storeroom in the east wing?'

Wendy sensed the blow coming before it struck. Though the pain was not as harsh as the blows Sky administered, the failure it implied was far more agonising.

'The storeroom was supposed to be private,' Faye breathed angrily.

Wendy sniffed back a sob, wishing she could dare to look at the woman.

'Follow me, Sam,' Faye snapped. 'We have business to attend to.'

'Where are you going?' Wendy asked. Without realising she was doing it, she had reached up and grabbed hold of Faye's arm.

The woman glared down at her with a disparaging frown. 'I'm going to the storeroom,' she hissed. 'That is, I'm going there if you'll let go of my arm.'

Wendy shook her head. 'But you can't,' she implored her. The thought of what might happen if Faye and Sky came face to face was unthinkable. The two women were so powerfully dominant that Wendy could not picture the pair of them in the same room. Faye was in a thunderously foul mood and unfit to deal with anyone in a civil manner. If Sky had already made the inevitable discovery of the storeroom's secret, Wendy knew that her temper would be just as vitriolic. She did not dare think what sort of explosion would happen if the two women met.

Unable to stop her, she watched Faye shake herself

free. With purposeful strides, she was leading her red-haired companion towards the east wing.

Unhappily, Wendy followed.

Sky stroked the silver tip of the cane down Malcolm's chest. The razor-sharp end grazed his flesh, not quite breaking it but leaving a dark-red line in its wake. Jo watched the woman grin, as though she was proud of her handiwork.

'We have a lot of catching up to do,' Sky whispered. 'I've got to return a lot of suffering and unhappiness. The only consolation is that I'll get an awful lot of pleasure from doing it.' She knelt down in front of him and moved her mouth quickly over the end of his length.

Malcolm stiffened in his chair.

From her position by the wall, Jo could see Sky's lips stretching to accommodate him. As she watched, she saw the woman pressing her teeth against the swollen end of his shaft.

Malcolm groaned. He thrashed his head frenziedly as his body was treated to the subtle touch of Sky's tongue and the painful pressure of her biting. Soft sounds of distress ebbed from beneath the gag and he stared hopefully at Jo, as though she might be able to help him.

'Don't look at her,' Sky muttered, moving her lips away from his cock and guiding his face with one hand. 'Watch me while I do this,' she insisted. 'You wouldn't want to miss something if I took things too far, now would you?'

His attention was suddenly riveted to her.

Sky stood up and took a step away from him. She tested the silver-tipped cane through the air. It whistled harshly as it cut air and her smile broadened appreciatively.

Staring at the instrument, Jo tried not to think of the damage the silver tip could cause if it connected with naked flesh. The blow of an ordinary cane could be cruel and punishing. The bitter memory of canings she had received were enough to make her sympathise with Malcolm's predicament.

'Are you ready to start suffering, Malcolm?' Sky asked.

'I don't think that would be a wise idea,' Faye Meadows said firmly.

Jo watched the woman stride into the room, march directly up to Sky and snatch the cane from her hand.

Disarmed, Jo half-expected the Black Widow to back down, but that was not what happened. Instead, Sky slapped her open palm against Faye's cheek. The retort echoed in the confines of the storeroom. Her handprint was left on the woman's face when she moved her fingers away.

By way of retaliation, Faye raised the cane high and prepared to deliver a vicious blow.

'Wait!' Jo was surprised to hear Sam's voice. She turned to the doorway and saw her partner flanked by Wendy and Poppy. Hurrying into the room, Sam took the cane from Faye's hand and hurled it across the floor. 'I'm not going to stand by and watch you two beat one another senseless,' Sam told them both. 'There are things happening here that need to be resolved and this isn't the way to do it.'

Jo frowned. She noticed Sam was wearing a short skirt and beneath her raincoat she appeared to be topless. A hundred reasons occurred to Jo as to why Sam might be dressed like this, and she tried not to succumb to the flaring coals of jealousy that the images inspired.

Faye and Sky were glowering at one another with a passion so fierce it made the air between them crackle. 'I've already decided I'm going to punish him,' Sky whispered. 'I can do it just as well once I've taken care of this bitch.'

'You'll get hurt trying,' Faye retorted.

'If you two start fighting, I'm going to go and call the police. They can sort the pair of you out and you can finish the fight in a shared cell.'

For an agonising moment, the room was held in a frozen tableau. Faye towered over Sky, glowering threateningly. Sky met her gaze with venomous defiance, clearly prepared to meet any challenge the woman made. Strapped to the chair, almost lost in the shadow of the two women, Malcolm shifted his gaze from Faye to Sky.

Sam stared at the two women, her poker face showing no sign that her threat might have been an idle one.

Pragmatically, Jo wondered if Faye would still pay their fee if she was languishing in a prison cell. She decided this was definitely not the time to ask such a question.

Turning to Jo, Sam said, 'Can you get us all a drink, so we can sit down and discuss this rationally?' Her calm tone of voice seemed ludicrously out of place in the tense confines of the storeroom.

Jo shook her head. 'I've quit drinking,' she replied with a short smile. She was gratified to see Sam's lips purse into a frown of disapproval. 'But for this instance, I'll make an exception,' Jo said quickly. She reached into the pocket of her dressing-gown and pulled out her replenished hip flask. Without bothering to take a sip for herself, she handed the flask to Faye, who then passed it to Sam.

Sam took a brief drink and offered the flask to Sky.

'I'm not touching that,' the Black Widow growled. She glared at Faye and told Sam, 'She's been touching it.'

Sam pushed the flask into Sky's hand, her green eyes flashing angrily. 'You'll take a drink, you'll be civil, and you'll start discussing things properly.'

'Or else?' Sky ventured.

Sam's smile was terse. 'Or else, you'll do your talking with the police, and when they see the damage you've inflicted around here you'll have a lot more to worry about than some woman who stole your husband.'

'You're bluffing,' Sky growled.

'Try me,' Sam suggested. 'I can see what you've been up to just by looking at the bruises on these poor bastards.' She nodded her head towards Poppy and Wendy. 'The police could have you for assault and illegal imprisonment.' Behind her, Faye Meadows started to snigger and Sam whirled on her. 'And if I drop her in it, I'll drop you in it too. Insurance fraud is just as illegal.'

Jo raised her eyebrows, surprised by the control Sam was exercising. She did not know how Sam had managed to find out so much about the case and she still felt unclear on some points, but none of that mattered for the moment. She watched Faye and Sky studying one another with animosity and realised that Sam had cowed the pair of them.

The discussions took the rest of the night and Jo decided that calling them fraught was one hell of an understatement. The threat of violence was omnipresent and she had to physically intercede on two occasions to stop Faye and Sky from clawing at one another. However, she had to concede that Sam's negotiating skills were incredible and the fiery redhead eventually managed to get the two women talking in sentences that were not simply barbaric threats. Once Sam had explained the situation to the two women, and the options that they had left, the rest of the negotiation was a simple matter of getting them to reluctantly agree.

'So how soon did you have it figured out?' Jo asked, teasing the buttons open on Sam's raincoat. They were back in her room, making use of the oversized bed she had christened with Allen. Dawn was edging over the horizon and shards of pale sunlight were creeping into the bedroom through the flimsy curtains. She was weary. Her eyes felt dry and desperate to sleep but Sam's nearness had worked its usual magical spell on her. 'Come on,' Jo encouraged, catching a glimpse of bare flesh as she released another button. 'Tell me when you first had it figured out.'

Lying back on the bed, Sam laughed as Jo undressed her. 'I had it figured out from day one,' she said arrogantly. 'As soon as I heard the name "Elysian Fields", I knew what was happening.'

Jo suppressed the rising irritation that Sam's arrogance inspired. She thought she had heard the murmur of an untruth in the back of Sam's words but she ignored the temptation to challenge her. Jo was desperate to enjoy the sight of Sam's nudity and the thought of having an argument first did not appeal to her. When she had first heard the name of the health farm, she had assumed that Elysian was a shade of green. It was a thought she was not going to share with Sam. However, she was caught between showing her ignorance and giving in to the needs of her curiosity. Eventually, as she pulled the raincoat from Sam's shoulders, her inquisitiveness won over.

'So what does "Elysian Fields" mean? I can see you're bursting to show off all the benefits of your finishing-school education.' She managed to say the words without giving away the true depth of her arousal. Sam's bare chest was always an exhilarating sight. The enticing mounds of her breasts invariably inflamed the embers of Jo's passion. The dark-red circles of her areolae were lightly wrinkled, but Jo knew the flesh would smooth out beneath the caress of her fingertip. Testing the theory, she watched Sam's nipple stiffen.

At the same moment, Sam caught a breath of excitement. She made herself comfortable on the bed as she was touched, teasing a hand inside Jo's robe. Her fingers went to the smooth flesh of Jo's sides, then worked their way up to the gently yielding contours of her breasts.

Simultaneously, the women sighed. 'Sky had the original idea for this place,' Sam explained. 'But Malcolm stole it from her and also stole all the money they had, just before he disappeared in his supposedly fatal accident.'

Jo was pressing warm kisses against the soft flesh of Sam's neck. Her lips brushed against the sensitive skin in a series of delicate kisses that sent shivers running though the redhead's body. Jo could feel the gentle tremor of Sam's mounting excitement and she realised the quickening pulse of her own arousal was marking the same tempo. Her need to touch and hold Sam was a burning fever. 'I'd gleaned that Malcolm wasn't dead,' Jo remarked dryly, working the words around a kiss on Sam's shoulder. 'But –'

'But Malcolm wasn't dead,' Sam went on, ignoring the interruption. She was pretending to be unmoved by the kisses that Jo was delivering. Her laboured breathing inflected her words with a huskiness that gave away her true feelings. 'Faye found herself engaged to a man who was pretending to be dead. He was doing it to cheat Sky and defraud an insurance company. Faye's a fairly law-abiding sort, so she wasn't best pleased.'

Moving her lips lower, Jo made a sound that was meant to indicate agreement. She traced her tongue down to the rise of Sam's small breast, allowing it to move close to the swell of her nipple. Knowing that Sam was enjoying her ministrations, Jo deliberately moved her mouth away and fixed her with a curious smile. 'So Faye had nothing to do with the insurance fraud?'

Sam was obviously disappointed that Jo had stopped kissing her but she hid her annoyance well. After exercising an uneasy smile, she explained, 'Faye didn't want to but she had no other option. Malcolm had bequeathed his estate and the insurance money to her, cutting Sky completely out of his will. But in order to get those benefits his death had to look realistic and Faye had to go along with the insurance claim. She's not really Mrs Meadows, by the way. She just adopted that name after the reading of the will.'

Jo nodded. 'You'll pardon me for saying this, but I think she could have been feeding you some bullshit there. Faye doesn't look like the sort who would just "go along" with plans that she's not a hundred per cent behind.'

Sam shook her head and sat up on the bed. 'She didn't want to go along with the plans but once Malcolm had started it all she was left with the choice of either going along with it or turning him in to the police. She went for the easiest option, but she made Malcolm suffer for it.'

Thinking of the man's imprisonment in the storeroom, Jo smiled to herself. It was definitely a suitable punishment. It also occurred to her that there was some advantage in knowing where there was a man, with such a huge cock, bound and gagged and waiting to be used. A lascivious smile crossed her lips as one or two possible ideas sprang to mind.

'What are you smiling at?' Sam asked.

Jo pushed Sam back on the bed without replying. She realised the insurance fraud was now immaterial. Faye and Sky had promised they would not pursue the claim any further and their assurances had seemed sincere. She tugged Sam's skirt away with an effortless flick of her wrist. Then paused as another thought occurred to her. A frown crossed her brow. 'None of that explains why this place is called Elysian Fields.'

'Oh yes! I was saying, wasn't I? It's part of Greek mythology.'

Jo frowned, not bothering to hide her ignorance.

'Elysian Fields was the dwelling place of the blessed after death,' Sam told her.

Jo took a moment to think about this, smiling at the thought that she had missed such an obvious clue. She was secretly pleased that she had never revealed her ignorance in thinking that "Elysian" was a shade of green and made a mental note not to tell Sam about that misconception. Staring down at her, Jo found her thoughts about the case were suddenly lacking in importance. Naked, Sam looked as gorgeous as ever. Jo found her gaze drawn to the shaved lips of Sam's pussy and her eyes widened with excitement. Unable to stop herself, she traced a slow finger against the silky-smooth flesh.

Sam trembled on the bed.

'When did you do this?' Jo asked, drawing her finger against the shaved lips.

There was a note of arousal colouring Sam's words when she replied. 'I'll tell you all about it when we prepare our report.'

Jo shook her head, moving her lips close to the warmth of Sam's sex. She could smell the musky fragrance of the redhead's excitement. The shaved lips glistened with the slick wetness of her arousal. As the tip of her finger brushed against Sam's sex, Jo was thrilled by a bristling charge of electricity. 'There won't be a report,' Jo told her. 'Faye was trying to defraud an insurance company and, while she's promised to drop the claim, you and I are still accessories to that crime by our knowledge of it. I don't want any record of our being involved and I'm happy to make this case one of those that the tax man doesn't know about.'

'That's not very legal,' Sam whispered, her words made breathless by Jo's inquisitive finger.

'Defrauding an insurance company isn't very legal either,' Jo replied. 'And, from what you told me before, I doubt your work as a lap dancer conformed to all the local by-laws,' she added meaningfully. 'But I can overlook those matters if you can overlook the others.'

'Do I have a choice?' Sam asked.

Jo moved her lips over Sam's sex and prepared to stroke her tongue against the velvety slickness. 'Not really,' she said, inhaling the sweet florid fragrance of Sam's arousal. 'You have no choice at all.'

Sam sighed. 'Then in that case, I'll simply lie here all pliant and obedient.'

Tasting the sweet flavour of Sam's sex, Jo smiled to herself. Having Sam lie beneath her, all pliant and obedient, was all that she had ever wanted.

In the storeroom, Sky linked her arm in Faye's and graced her with a soft smile. The two women were standing side by side, watching as Poppy and Wendy finished securing Malcolm into the birthing-stool. He had protested, grunted and threatened but in the end he had seen that his struggles were futile.

The shorts had been stripped from him and he sat

naked in the stool. His wrists and ankles were secured and his vulnerable body was on display for the pair of them to admire.

'You had this specially made?' Faye asked. After the discussions with Sam and Sky she had changed out of the business suit she had been wearing. Following Sky's lead, she now stood boldly in black stockings and stilettos, a black basque and long black gloves. Her dark-blonde hair was tied up, away from her face, reinforcing the impression of austerity given by her attire. In one hand, she held the silver-tipped riding crop that had been mounted on the wall.

Sky nodded, trying not to admire the woman's body as she spoke to her. 'This birthing-stool was part of my plan. I thought it would be quite an effective tool in helping me to get my own way here. I suppose it was in a way.'

'I can see how it would be helpful,' Faye remarked. She took a step closer to Malcolm and stroked one gloved hand up his leg. The leather-coated tips of her fingers skirted close to his balls, then she moved her hand away. 'He's quite helpless in this, isn't he?'

The ball gag had opened Malcolm's mouth into a wide O of silent protest that they both ignored. He stared from Faye to Sky then back to Faye. His apprehension was so total it would have been amusing under other circumstances.

'He's *totally* helpless,' Sky corrected absently. She moved to Malcolm's other side and stroked her fingers up his leg. As Faye had done, she allowed her fingertips to trail tantalisingly close to his balls. His huge cock was rigid and begging to be touched. His nervous gaze kept shifting from Faye to herself and she found his obvious fear exciting. 'Do you think we can live with the arrangements that Sam suggested?' Sky asked thoughtfully.

Faye shrugged. 'We can only try,' she replied. 'We can't do any more than that.' Her conciliatory tone and easy manner suggested that she was genuinely willing to give the arrangement some commitment.

Sky nodded. She slid her hand round Malcolm's length, caressing his thick shaft. He sighed quietly and fixed her with beseeching eyes.

'Do you think that Poppy will be all right handling our affairs?' Faye asked.

Sky turned to stare at the solicitor. After she and Wendy had finished securing Malcolm to the birthing-stool, she had moved back to her position in the corner of the room. She knelt on the floor, completely naked, staring down at her bare knees. Her manner was so servile and submissive that Sky knew she would have no problem with Poppy ever again. 'Poppy will do everything we ask her to do,' Sky declared confidently. 'She's already given me a couple of ideas about the compensation claims that I can serve against the Knight brothers. If what she says is true, I could be a very wealthy woman soon. I'm sure she'll handle everything perfectly and I might even consider paying her.'

Faye grunted dry laughter. She placed her hand over Sky's as it caressed Malcolm's cock. Together, the two women slid their hands slowly up and down his rigid length.

For a moment Sky was mesmerised by the sight of his length being teased by their hands. His foreskin was pulled tight by the strength of his erection, but as they moved their hands up and down the soft pink flesh was pushed and pulled back and forth over the swollen end of his shaft. It had been so long since she had seen him and his cock that Sky felt a moment's disquiet. His cruel deception, and the suffering it had caused, had been malicious. While she realised she still loved him, there was a shift in the perspective of her feelings. She just wished she could put her finger on the thing that was troubling her.

'You really want to punish him, don't you?' Faye whispered.

Malcolm looked up, startled.

Sky studied Faye with an incredulous smile, unable to believe that the woman had managed to touch on the exact thought that she had been entertaining. She nodded excitedly and said, 'Yes. I do. I really think he deserves to be punished, don't you?'

Faye's smile was positively chilling. The ice in her eyes sparkled with malicious venom. 'I think he deserves that and a damned sight more.' She stroked her hand up his cock and smiled down at him. 'And I think I know the best way.'

With a quizzical smile, Sky glanced at Faye. She watched the woman lift the silver-tipped riding crop she had been holding.

Malcolm made a pleading sound against the ball gag. He struggled against his restraints, but it was futile. As Malcolm watched, Faye threw the riding crop to the floor. It landed with a clatter but the sound was lost beneath the heavy sigh of relief he released. Beads of sweat were coating his forehead and upper lip.

'You're not going to beat him?' Sky asked.

Faye shook her head. 'There are far better ways to punish Malcolm,' she assured her. Moving around the birthing-stool, she pressed her body close to Sky's and touched the tips of her fingers against the swell of her breast.

Sky drew a startled breath but remained where she had been standing. She smiled up into the cerulean blue of the woman's eyes, astonished by the unexpected intimacy of her touch.

With a grin, Faye moved her mouth closer to Sky's. Her lips were a ripe red pout, so succulent they begged to be tasted. Unable to resist, Sky kissed her. She felt Faye's tongue slide into her mouth; felt excited by each inquisitive caress that explored her body. She was aware of her own curious fingers only when she heard Faye snatch a sharp breath. Sky glanced down and saw she had placed her fingers over the woman's nipple. The thrusting nub was clearly visible through the tight satin fabric of her basque. When she glanced up, she saw that Faye was smiling at her.

'This is going to be the ultimate torture for Malcolm,' Faye assured her. 'He's having to watch the pair of us enjoying one another, and he can't participate.' Her laugh was truly malicious, made sweeter to Sky's ears because it mocked Malcolm's suffering. 'The poor bastard will go insane watching us indulging ourselves while he's tied to that birthing-stool.'

The idea was so wicked that Sky could not stop herself from grinning in response. She kissed Faye again, allowing the gesture to seal their new partnership. Her roving hands began to explore the woman's body and she was treated to the thrill of having her own flesh caressed. As they kissed, she heard Malcolm making small sounds of protest. The exclamations were so pitiful they were inspiring.

Perhaps this was not how she had wanted to run Elysian Fields, Sky thought, but that did not seem to matter right now. They still had to pretend that Malcolm was dead, even though they were going to stop pursuing the insurance claim. They had agreed to organise a new identity for Malcolm at a later date, but Sky had already decided that it would be a much later date. It occurred to her that if they were going to continue with the charade of his death, she could continue to rule as the Black Widow. The thought made her smile as she kissed Faye and listened to Malcolm's helpless whimpering.